THE CANDID LIFE OF MEENA DAVE

NAMRATA PATEL

LAKE UNION
PUBLISHING

Published by Lake Union Publishing, Seattle

www.apub.com

Amazon, the Amazon logo, and Lake Union Publishing are trademarks of Amazon.com, Inc., or its affiliates.

ISBN-13: 9781542039079
ISBN-10: 154203907X

Cover design and illustration by Kimberly Glyder

Printed in the United States of America

THE
CANDID
LIFE
OF
MEENA
DAVE

For my parents, Arvind and Pushpa, and my sister, Amy.

AUTHOR'S NOTE

The immigrant experience lies on a continuum from those who immigrated recently to those who arrived hundreds of years ago. Yet often, in America, we think of historical immigration as western European to the exclusion of others who came to the US in smaller numbers.

My perception of Indian immigration was shaped by what I lived, not what I learned about in school. It wasn't until graduate school that I discovered stories of those who came generations before me, particularly in academic spaces.

I learned that there were Indians in America as early as 1790, when captains who worked for the East India Company brought them to the eastern United States as their servants. There have been other pockets here and there of a few hundred Indians who came seeking opportunity, including the Sikhs in the 1900s. A few years ago I came across an academic paper by Ross Bassett, who catalogued every Indian graduate from MIT from its founding to the year 2000. In *MIT-Trained Swadeshis: MIT and Indian Nationalism, 1880–1947*, he writes about the hundred Indian men who came to Boston to study at MIT for the singular purpose of rebuilding India postcolonization. They were, for the most part, from elite families; some were followers of Gandhi; and they influenced the technological future of independent India.

I thought about how little I knew about Indian immigration, how few stories show Indians in America beyond the first or second generation. I live in Boston. I walk along the same paths that they might have. Yet I never knew this part of my cultural history. I imagined how lonely it might have been for them to be so far away and in an unfamiliar place. Yet they came in groups, possibly finding their own community. I wanted to examine those themes along with what third-generation assimilation could look like. How would an individualistic culture affect a fundamentally collective one?

I wrote *The Candid Life of Meena Dave* not only to give an example of Indian American history but also to touch on what it could mean to build community in isolation. That I wrote this during the recent pandemic allowed me to explore these themes as an individual and as part of a shared experience.

Identity is something most of us examine at some point in our lives. It is universal to feel comfortable or uncomfortable in our bodies, our skins, our commonness, and our otherness.

It is Meena's story; however, I believe it resonates with all of us who found ourselves untethered and discovered our anchors.

CHAPTER ONE

Meena Dave was tired, and not just from thirty-six hours of travel. She'd expected a trinket, a ring of some sort, when she'd learned about an inheritance. It should have been easy, a quick stop in Boston on her way to New York from Auckland.

"If you had responded to our initial inquiries."

Meena heard judgment in the husky voice of the woman who sat on the other side of the large mahogany desk. The tall woman in the black, fitted pantsuit belonged in this corner office with oversize windows.

"I was in New Zealand," Meena said. *And Tasmania, Tokyo, and Nova Scotia before that.* She sat taller to fight the weight of fatigue in her body. Besides, most of her communication happened via email or text. She didn't check her actual mail for months at a time.

"As I mentioned," Sandhya Shah continued, "you've wasted half of the allotted one year, but at least you've managed to make it within the window."

Meena reread the paperwork. "Are you sure you have the right person? I didn't know Neha Patel." Another reason she hadn't prioritized this when she'd picked up her mail from her Manhattan PO box three months earlier on her way from Portugal to the Pacific.

"We've verified your identity, and we don't make careless mistakes at Menon and Shah."

Meena glanced at the index card in her hand. It was like the ones she'd made herself in high school when studying for the SAT. This had a single word and its definition.

engineer (noun)
1 a.: a designer or builder of engines
b.: a person who is trained in or follows as a profession a branch of engineering
c.: a person who carries through an enterprise by skillful or artful contrivance
engineer (verb)
2 a.: to contrive or plan out usually with more or less subtle skill and craft
b.: to guide the course of

"And what is this?" Meena held it up to the lawyer.

"It was part of the packet to be turned over to you along with the keys." Sandhya tapped a manicured nail on the stack in front of Meena. "As soon as you sign the paperwork, you can take possession."

Meena skimmed the few paragraphs she could understand and glossed over the legalese.

"To review the terms . . ."

"I have to wait out the full year—well, six months now—before I can sell it," Meena cut off the lawyer.

"And it can only be sold to one of the other four owners of the building," Sandhya said. "No outside buyers."

Meena resisted the urge to take her long hair out of its messy bun and braid the edges. A habit her mom had never approved of. Hannah Dave, the only mother who counted. She stared out the large windows. The sky was thick with clouds. *Leaf-diving sky,* her dad had called it. They'd go out in the backyard and rake the fallen leaves into heaping piles. Then Meena would take a running start and jump in, belly-first. This was why she'd avoided the state of Massachusetts since she'd left it right after high school. Too many memories.

"What if I don't want it?" Not that Meena was reckless. An apartment in the historic area of Back Bay wasn't something she could turn down when she supported herself as a freelance photojournalist.

"Do you not?" The lawyer knew Meena's hesitation was a bluff.

Meena resisted the urge to sigh. "I don't actually have to live there." Her life wasn't suited to permanence. "I have a flight out in a few hours."

Sandhya looked at Meena as if none of this was her problem. "The keys are in this envelope along with the building passcode. The utilities, including Wi-Fi, have been paid for until April, then you can decide what you want to do next."

Meena picked up the pen. "Needs must." She murmured her mother's favorite phrase and signed where the plastic tabs indicated.

Sandhya gathered the papers, gave Meena the duplicates, and stood to signal the end of the meeting.

"What if no one in the building offers to buy?"

"Then you keep it until they do," Sandhya said. "The apartment is in a condominium, so you will be responsible for maintenance, utilities, and expenses even if you don't live there."

Meena shoved her copies of the paperwork into a large yellow envelope along with the keys and the index card and nodded to the lawyer before lifting her heavy backpack onto one shoulder. She walked out of the building into the bustling area of Downtown Crossing and headed toward Boston Common. While the city was familiar from childhood school trips, she still needed the map on her phone to guide her to the address.

It was barely ten in the morning, and Back Bay was about a twenty-minute walk. She would check it out, assess the condition of the place, and figure out her next steps. If she couldn't do anything with it for six months, she'd let it sit. Staying here wasn't an option. She was in between assignments, which meant scheduling editor meetings in New York to line up more gigs. More importantly, this state was her past, and Meena didn't look back. Ever.

She didn't know Neha Patel, but people didn't leave strangers gifts this large. There was a connection here, and she'd be foolish not to consider the likeliest reason for the apartment falling into her hands. Hannah Dave had been Meena's mother in every sense but the biological. This inheritance, the weight of it, with specific conditions, felt as if someone were easing their guilt in the afterlife.

~~~

She was close, maybe a block or two away, when chaos in the form of a tiny puppy upended it all. One minute she was staring at her phone, envelope in hand. The next she was tangled up in a loose leash, and she lost her balance thanks to her heavy backpack and fell to her knees. She winced as she heard her phone hit the concrete. Then the little monster got a hold of her envelope and shook it around in its mouth hard enough for the keys to pop out. Which distracted the fur ball enough to replace the envelope with the key ring as its new chew toy. She reached for it as a brisk gust of October wind sent the envelope flying away from her.

She raced over and stopped the rolling paper with one booted foot, slid it toward her, and lunged left for the leash to keep the puppy from running off with her keys. She teetered in an unnatural warrior pose. "Oh no you don't."

The fur ball tilted its head as if curious about her awkward position with one foot on the envelope and her other leg and arm stretched out to keep the dog in place.

"Wally, stop," a man shouted as he ran toward Meena and the pup. He eyed her awkward stance. "Impressive."

"Yoga."

"Namaste."

"That's not OK." People often assumed her identity simply because of her brown skin.

"I'm Indian," he said, grinning. "I'm allowed."

Meena handed him the leash and picked up the papers. She found her phone and begged, "Don't be dead."

"Talking to inanimate objects could be a sign of injury," he said. "Are you sure you're not hurt?"

Meena let out a frustrated breath. "Doctor?"

"Special effects engineer." He grinned as he picked up the puppy. "What do you have here, Wally?"

"My keys."

He tugged them from between Wally's teeth and stared at them. Meena noticed curiosity on his face. She reached over and took them from him, then wiped them down on her cargo jacket.

"Do you need directions?"

"I'm fine." She'd been on her own since she was sixteen. Help wasn't necessary.

"On behalf of Wally," he said, "I apologize. I let go for one second and he ran off. He's a work in progress. I hope."

There was frustration mixed with adoration in his voice as he put the puppy down on the ground but kept a firm grasp on the leash.

Meena didn't want to return his smile but had to admit that he was effortlessly friendly. An inch or two taller than her five-foot-eight height, he was dressed for fall in an REI parka over jeans. His black hair ruffled in the breeze. Meena would bet he used his dimples to charm himself into and out of whatever he wanted.

Wally ran around her and tangled up his leash in between her legs. Meena lost her balance and grabbed the man's shoulder. He wrapped his free hand around her and held her steady. "Wally, stop. Heel. Sit." With his hand still holding her, he unclipped the leash and grabbed the puppy up in his other arm. "We need to work on manners."

Meena let go and stepped back. "Good luck." She turned away.

"Wait," the man called out to her. "If you're going somewhere nearby, we can walk with you. I live in this neighborhood."

"I don't know you," Meena said.

"Sam Vora," he offered.

Meena shook her phone. The screen was black, likely a permanent condition. Still, she remembered the map, and she wasn't directionally challenged. The apartment was one street over. "I'm good."

"According to the art of conversation, when one person introduces themselves, it's usually an invitation for the other to do the same," Sam said.

Meena gave him a slight smile. "Take care, Sam Vora."

She picked up her backpack and headed in the opposite direction from the man and his dog.

CHAPTER TWO

The white stone façade of Ten Marlborough Street shimmered in the midmorning sun. The three-story building on a historic street was elegant and understated, clean and well kept. The Back Bay area of Boston was a hub for tourists, old Bostonians, college students, and shoppers. It was expansive and quaint, bracketed by Fenway, the famed baseball stadium, on one end and the Public Garden and Boston Common on the other. Within it were charming, tree-lined streets where tourists flocked for iconic pictures.

On either side of number ten were Victorian redbrick buildings so snug, there wasn't an inch of space between them. Two tall, dense hedges separated the yard from the sidewalk, and the stone walkway to the building was absent of autumn debris. The path divided the yard in half, the yard itself landscaped in perfect symmetry, with lush flower beds and stone planters that teemed with maroon, orange, and yellow flowers. The white stone steps with black iron railings held a pumpkin symmetrically on either end of each stair. The double doors, framed by iron lanterns on either side, were austere in their cool black lacquer sheen, more intimidating than inviting. The gold-colored doorknobs were attached to wide rectangular plates of the same metal. An ornate keyhole lay beneath the knob on the right-hand door. The gold number plate stood next to the gold mail slot on the left-hand door. No dust or handprints to be seen.

It was rare for Meena to be awestruck by a building, but her hand shook as she reached the knob. There was something unwelcoming about the pristine, tall doors.

Meena pushed aside her nerves. There was nothing to fear. The apartment in this building was hers only in the technical sense. She pulled the keys from her jacket pocket. The large one, with faint puppy teeth marks, had sharp edges and a long metal bar attached to a full loop at the end. There was an *E* etched into the bar. The key looked as if it would fit the keyhole in front of her. The others were the usual kind, likely for the inside doors. A sticky note tucked into the envelope indicated the four-digit alarm code. Old-world elegance with new-world practicality. Meena spotted the gold entry box to the right and slid the cover upward to reveal the keypad. She typed in the sequence and heard a faint snick.

As she turned the knob on the door on the right, Meena noticed the letter *E* etched into the gold plate that surrounded it. She pushed through and stepped into the quiet hallway. The small space was brightly lit by the high chandelier overhead. Its crystals twinkled in the light from the bulb in the middle. The scents of sage and cedar were incongruous after the cool starkness of the exterior facade, as if warmth were reserved only for those inside.

The door to her right was ajar, a fall wreath made of pine cones and berries attached below the gold knocker. Unit 1. Opposite was number 2. A matching wreath adorned the door. Meena frowned. She placed her backpack on the ground and pulled out the packet from the lawyer to confirm this was the correct apartment. She glanced at the wreath. Maybe the people from across the hall had put up the decoration.

She'd been told that this unit was unoccupied, waiting for her. She slid a key into the lock, anticipating it might not be the right one. But it went right in. She turned the knob and tried pushing the door open only to realize that she'd locked it instead. The place had been left unlocked. Puzzled, Meena turned the key again to unlock the door and gingerly nudged it open inch by inch. She stood at the threshold bewildered by the scene in front of her. The place was fully furnished, complete with unopened mail on the small table next to the door, as if someone still lived there.

She took a few steps into the apartment. It was clean, though cluttered with an overwhelming amount of stuff. The throw pillows on the sofa were fluffed and arranged on each end. Books, lamps, ottomans, and chairs were packed tightly in the large living area. Dozens of knick-knacks covered every surface. It was bright and cheerful, even with the dark wall-to-wall built-in shelving.

Color exploded in the room. A pair of deep-blue reading chairs sat on either side of the fireplace. A bright-yellow sofa, large enough to fit three, marked the edge of the open living area. A dark coffee table sat in front of it. A stack of books was on one corner and a set of antique coasters on another. Meena moved farther into the apartment. Half-used candles perched in massive iron holders. The gray rug was thick under her feet. Books filled every shelf built into the walls. It was as if the apartment were in an old library, minus the dust. Sunny-yellow paint covered the walls of the small bathroom and kitchen. The place seemed to be frozen in time. A snapshot. Even the air was slightly pungent from the leftover scent of cleaning supplies.

It was as if Neha had gone out to run an errand and never returned. This wasn't the home of someone who had known she was going to die. Meena wandered into the enormous bedroom. The bed was covered with a bright-pink comforter and deep-coral pillows. *You never know the last time you'll sleep in your own bed.* Meena felt sympathy for the woman who had lived here. Neha must have loved this place. She must have lived here a long time to accumulate so many things. Oddly, there were no photos. No wedding pictures in silver frames or family photos on the fireplace mantel. The apartment was absent of anything personal. Only art, abstract and kitsch, hung on the few walls that had no shelves.

"Who are you?"

Meena turned at the sharp voice by the front door. A woman in a red silk shirt and black pants stood with her arms crossed.

"Meena. And you are?"

"The caretaker of this building," the woman said. "What are you doing here?"

Meena held up the keys. "I'm the new owner."

"That's not possible. This is Neha's apartment."

Meena heard the shakiness in the woman's voice and softened her face to appear more approachable. A tactic she'd honed well in reassuring uneasy subjects. "She left it to me. I have the paperwork."

The woman straightened her shoulders. "I see. And you are moving in?"

No. The reaction was knee jerk. She didn't live anywhere. Meena had a base in London—a small room in her college friend Zoe's flat where she kept her things—and a PO box in Manhattan for mail. "I'm still figuring that out."

"Well, do it soon," the woman ordered. "This is a place that's meant to be lived in, not sit empty."

Meena gave her a wide smile. Maybe this woman would want to buy it. It was too soon for that, but if the option was there, it would make things less complicated. "I didn't get your name."

"Sabina."

"Nice to meet you."

The woman nodded and left. Meena headed to the door and locked it.

She grabbed her laptop from her backpack, looked around at the overwhelming number of things that were now hers to deal with, and sighed. If only it had been a portable heirloom like a Tongan woven mat or even a clichéd locket with a photo.

Except Meena didn't live with if-onlys. A few months of therapy in her teens had taught her that things happen, circumstances change. An undetected rusty gas pipe can blow up a house as a couple eat breakfast. In an instant, their teenage daughter becomes an orphan. There's nothing to do but accept it and move forward. She logged on to change her flight. New York City would have to wait a week while she figured out what to do about Neha and this place.

~☙~

Meena woke and blinked to adjust her eyes in the dark. It took her a few seconds to get her bearings. Streetlight streamed through the front windows. Meena rose from the sofa. She'd slept in her jacket and boots, her laptop still open on the coffee table next to her. She was used to waking up in strange places at odd times. According to the length of her assignment, her body clock was quick to adjust to wherever she was.

She glanced at her watch, a silver Timex she'd bought in a street market in Kathmandu a few years back. It still worked. Six. She'd slept most of the day. She rolled her neck. Caffeine. In the kitchen she spotted a box of Lipton tea bags, then found mugs. None of them matched. Each looked as if it had been picked up from a yard sale. The one she took out was in the shape of a basketball. While the water heated in the microwave, she riffled through the box of Lipton. The first packet she grabbed was empty, yet still sealed. Meena opened it and unfolded the paper to reveal a note.

The handwriting was familiar, the same small, precise penmanship as on the index card.

Never trust a person who is too lazy to brew tea. The only use for generic tea bags is to reduce puffiness around the eyes. If you drink this stuff, I do not want to know you.

"How narrow-minded of you, tea." Meena spoke aloud to no one as she shuffled through the box and found another packet that had a bag in it. As she steeped it in the hot water, Meena reread the note. What an odd person. It had to be Neha, she deduced. It was quirky enough to fit the woman who'd lived in this apartment, a woman who had mismatched mugs in odd shapes, a sugar jar in the form of a frog with the top of its head serving as the lid.

With tea in hand, she went back to the living room and added the sleeve with the note to the envelope holding the index card. She grabbed the quilt from the back of the sofa and gathered it over her lap. It was soft, and she could feel the unevenness of the stitching. Someone had made this, not with a machine but with a needle and thread. Perhaps Neha had been a quilter, a crafter. Maybe it had been a gift to her from someone.

The chill in the air was comfortable. The quiet settled around her. No street sounds of cars or people. It didn't even feel as if she were in a major city. For a few minutes she could breathe, appreciate that in this moment she wasn't chasing a story, preparing, traveling, or shooting. She was simply here, in this quiet house. Gifted to her by a stranger.

Likely from her past.

Meena reached for her phone, then remembered it was broken. She'd have to take care of it in the morning. She woke her computer and opened the video chat to call Zoe, her only constant in life since they'd met as roommates at George Washington University their freshman year. It was a little after eleven o'clock on a Friday night in London, which meant Zoe was either out or just getting home.

"Where are you?"

That was how Zoe always answered Meena's calls.

"Boston," Meena said.

"Assignment?"

Meena saw Zoe's face through the screen. Her makeup was still perfect, winged eyeliner and deep-red lipstick. Zoe knew exactly how to enhance the beauty of her Mediterranean genes.

"No." Meena chewed on her lip. "Personal."

"Well, I hope it's a vacation," Zoe said. "You haven't had a proper break since last Christmas—oh, wait, I mean the Christmas before that, since you missed last year because you were chasing reindeer in Lapland."

"And this is a not-so-subtle reminder that you still haven't forgiven me for missing your annual pre-Christmas dinner."

"And that you will not miss it this year," Zoe said. "How long are you there?"

"Not sure. It was only supposed to be for a few hours, but things got a little complicated."

"You met a man? Is that why you're cuddled on a garish yellow sofa?"

Meena laughed. Zoe loved romance. "No."

"Are you going to tell me?"

"Someone left me an apartment in their will."

"Wow, really?" Zoe's pencil-thin eyebrows shot up. "Who?"

"A woman I never knew. I don't even know how she found me. It's a great location and the building is nice. The place is fully furnished, clean, and lived in."

"And there was no explanation?"

Just a vague index card. "No."

"How did she die?" Zoe asked.

"No idea," Meena said. "I asked the lawyer, but she was the buttoned-up type. It was mostly *Sign here, here, and here.* She wouldn't even tell me anything about Neha. Like, *Here's what you need to know, let us make sure you are who you are, and there's the exit.*"

"Sounds like an episode of *The Living and the Dead*," Zoe said.

"You watch too much television."

"You don't watch enough. What's the place like?"

Meena stared at the light fixture on the ceiling. "It's old. Not run-down, but historic, with crown molding, and the ceiling light fixture has a plaster carving surrounding it. It's library shabby chic mixed with country kitsch."

"Sounds fantastic."

"There are no photos of her."

"I know it's not something you talk about, ever," Zoe said. "But could she be . . . connected to your biological family?" Zoe was the only person in Meena's life who knew she had been adopted as a baby.

"It would make sense," Meena agreed. "My dad always told me that mine was a private, closed adoption. They didn't know anything about the mother, not even her ethnicity or where she lived." The past was best left there. Occasionally she'd toyed with the idea of getting a genetic test to know her biological history, just so she'd have a point of reference. She traveled the world but didn't know where she belonged. She hadn't taken that step. She'd had loving parents. She didn't want to betray the people who had chosen her. She didn't need to search for something if finding it could take away from the family she'd once had.

"I get that you don't want to know . . ." Zoe gentled her voice.

"I had two incredible parents," Meena explained. "We were a perfect family."

"Right," Zoe said. "What are you going to do?"

"I'm taking a week to sort it out. It's going to be a while before I can sell."

"You can sublet it."

For the first time that day, Meena had a plan. "You're absolutely right. I can rent it out until someone wants to buy it." And if no one in the building made an offer, she'd have an additional source of income. "It's the perfect solution."

"You're welcome," Zoe said. "Now I'm off to bed. Pre-Christmas dinner. Write it down in your diary."

"It's already in there." Meena tapped her head. It was a running joke that Meena didn't use her planner. She had an online calendar that managed her life. The physical ones Zoe gifted her every year sat unused.

Meena got up from the couch and walked around the room thoughtfully. Her parents had never talked about the adoption. When Meena was old enough to notice that she didn't at all resemble them, with their fair skin and light hair, she'd asked the obvious question. They'd told Meena that she'd been a blessing from God and that blood did not make family, love did, and there was plenty between them. Later, when Meena wanted to know more, both Hannah and Jameson Dave had hesitated to discuss how she'd come to them. Eventually Meena had accepted that it didn't matter. Her questions only caused them pain, so she stopped asking. It was enough to know she was the only child of middle-class parents. She had been baptized into the Catholic Church. Their community was hers.

When she was on assignment in places with other brown-skinned people, she tried to see if she could sense a familiarity, if she could fit among them. But the only place that had ever felt like home was the predominantly white hippie enclave of Northampton.

Hannah and Jameson Dave had taken her in. Loved her. And for sixteen years she'd been given the gift of family. That was more than some others got. She'd made peace with it. The past was behind her. The present was where she had control, and she preferred to stay in it. When they died, she'd stopped thinking about it altogether. She didn't want to taint their love by looking for anything beyond the family they'd been to each other.

Meena let out a long breath and allowed herself to process the truth that had been at the back of her mind all day. Neha had left her this place for a reason. Meena had to figure out if she wanted to know what that was.

CHAPTER THREE

Meena grabbed her wallet and keys and headed out. It was a brisk morning, and she was starving. As soon as she opened the door, a familiar black-and-white fur ball raced through her legs and into her apartment.

Meena's eyes narrowed as she chased him to the other side of the sofa. "I know you." At the sound of her voice, he charged for her. She held out her hand. "Stop." The puppy slid along the hardwood floor and came to a clumsy halt. His chin flopped over her boots.

"I believe we've met?" She squatted and held out her hand for a sniff. When he nudged her, she gave him a little rub. He turned his small head to invite more scratches.

She laughed at his pleasure. His fur was soft, and she felt the warmth of his body as he rolled over and exposed his tummy.

"Wally."

Meena looked up. "Seems like he keeps running away from you."

Sam came into the apartment. "More like he wants belly rubs."

Wally popped up, ran to his owner, and chewed on the hem of Sam's jeans.

Sam reached down and tugged his pants out of Wally's grip. "It's you. Yoga-in-the-street person."

"You don't seem surprised to see me." Meena tilted her head.

"The key Wally was chewing on is pretty distinctive."

Meena remembered the engraved *E* on the bar of the large old-timey key. "What are you doing here, Sam Vora?"

"I live across the hall."

"Nice wreath skills." Meena pointed to the door.

Sam looked toward it. "Oh, that's not me. It's the aunties. Tanvi does the decorating. Are you moving in?"

Meena stood. "More like staying here, temporarily."

"Why?"

"You're very suspicious."

"I'm making friendly conversation." Sam grinned. "It's the aunties you need to worry about. They're going to have a lot of questions."

Meena wondered if he was referring to the woman she'd met the day before.

"You travel light," Sam said.

"In a way." Her luggage was in a storage locker near the airport because she hadn't wanted to tote it to her meeting with the lawyer.

He rubbed Wally's fur as he tugged the lace of his sneaker out of the dog's mouth. Sam had an easygoing way about him, as if he were used to wandering up to strangers and making small talk. His hair was still messy, and he'd swapped the parka for a black sweater. His dark eyes were wide and open, framed by sharp eyebrows. He had all the markers of attractiveness, including high cheekbones. He was soft with sharp edges. Meena found herself wondering what he would be like in bed. She turned away. This wasn't the time or place for a distraction, even if it had been a while. Eight months? Argentina and a professional polo player.

Her stomach growled, reminding her she had more immediate needs. "I appreciate the visit, but I'm on my way out."

At the sound of her voice, Wally pepped up and zoomed back and forth between them.

"If you're looking for breakfast options, head to Boylston Street, a few blocks away from the river," he said. "There's also a little café on the corner of Commonwealth and Mass Ave."

"Thanks." Meena watched as he tugged Wally and headed for the door. He looked unburdened, his expression so sincere that Meena itched for her camera. She wanted to see him through the lens, capture his eyes, see what was behind them. Intelligence and kindness were obvious, but what else? It was hard to tell without learning more, looking deeper.

"Any tips on where to get a new phone?" She surprised herself with the question. She never asked for help with something she could do herself.

"The Apple Store on Boylston across from the Prudential Center is your best bet," Sam said. "There's a little fix-your-phone place on Newbury too."

"I think it's done for." It had served her well for the last four years, and while she wasn't looking forward to the expense of a new unlocked phone, it was a work necessity.

"It was Wally's fault." Sam bent down to give the pup a pat. "We can replace it if you'd like."

She laughed. "It was mine for juggling phone, papers, and a backpack and not paying attention."

"Sam, what are you . . . ?" A woman with long black hair stuck her head into the apartment. "What is going on? Who are you?"

Meena straightened from where she'd been leaning against the back of the sofa.

Wally bounced up and ran to the newest person in the room.

"Tanvi auntie," Sam said. "This is . . . I don't know your name."

Meena almost laughed at the surprise on his face. "Meena Dave."

"Dave?" the woman said. "You're pronouncing it wrong. Not in the Indian way."

"Indian?"

Tanvi looked surprised. "Aren't you? Oh, are you Pakistani or Bangladeshi?"

Meena stayed quiet.

"What's your ethnicity?"

A question Meena had never been able to answer.

"Tanvi auntie," Sam said. "You can't ask that."

"I didn't say, *What are you?* or *Where are you from?*" Tanvi defended herself. "It is a fair question."

"I grew up in Northampton," Meena explained. "And have an American passport."

"But where are your parents from? What are you doing in Neha's apartment?"

Meena gave them a friendly smile. "I'm happy to chat later, but I'm on my way out."

"I was going to teach Wally a few tricks in the backyard. Why don't you come with us, Tanvi auntie?" Sam picked up the pup. "We can catch up with Meena later."

As they walked out of her unit, Meena heard Tanvi say, "Sabina is going to lose her shit."

~❦~

A few hours later, she was sated thanks to a sausage, egg, and cheese from the café Sam had mentioned. She'd even showered to freshen up, though she didn't have a change of clothes because she had yet to pick up her suitcase. Luckily, her A-cups required little support. As a teenager she'd been shapeless and skinny. Dresses had hung off her, jeans had needed to be slouchy to fake that there was a slight butt somewhere.

She'd filled out a little in the hips, but there were no curves, only sharp angles. At least she didn't have to worry about not being asked to the freshman dance anymore. Meena got dressed in the same tank, sweater, and jeans she'd been wearing for three days, sniffed her armpits, and hoped the shower had helped.

She went into Neha's bedroom to look in the large vanity mirror while she fixed her long black hair. The room had another fireplace in the shared wall between it and the living room. This one was decorative, with a giant bouquet of pink and white silk carnations in an orange bronze vase in the center. It matched the cheery bedroom. To her left, wide white french doors opened to a small veranda overlooking a fenced-in garden. The bedding, in pink and purples, popped with color. The white vanity had fairy lights around the mirror. It seemed like a young girl's bedroom, not that of a woman in her midsixties. A small trinket box sat on the vanity, and Meena flipped it open to find an index card.

I am a lexicographer. A mouthful of a word, one that doesn't quite roll off the tongue. Not like chef, cop, maid, judge. *I write dictionaries. I keep a record of our ever-evolving language. I like knowing that what I document, what I write, can be read long after I'm gone. I have no children. Only words I spend my life defining.*

Meena recognized the handwriting, the same as on the tea bag packet and index card. She sat on the edge of the bed and looked around, wondering if there were more notes.

For a few minutes, she allowed herself to acknowledge her fatigue. Usually something like hidden notes popping up would tickle her curiosity. She loved puzzles of all kinds. Right now, though, in this place, it felt too heavy a lift. Mostly because Meena hadn't been searching for this; it had found her, stopped her in her tracks as she was living her life.

She reined in her thoughts. Everything was temporary. She'd learned that from a Buddhist monk in Burma. She'd adopted it as her mantra. When her mind wandered to what had once been, she'd rein it back to the present. For now, she was here, and she had things to do.

Meena added the note to the others she'd collected. She grabbed her shoes, her wallet, and her broken phone. It was going to be an afternoon of errands. As she went to get her jacket from one of the blue chairs, she brushed up against a book on the fireplace mantel and it fell.

Shakespeare's *Love's Labour's Lost*. A sliver of white paper peeked out from inside. Meena opened the book and tugged out the note card.

My husband left three days ago. I haven't gone to look for him. In fact, I wish him well. We did not suit, married only because we had both given in to societal convention. He was constantly seeking happiness. An elusive, subjective, situational concept.

He's a regular sort of person. I use the present tense because I do not believe he's dead.

I suppose I could start at the beginning, but to what end? That's a fun sentence. I could parse it out. It should not make sense, yet it does because the English language is fluid and alive.

Meena flipped over the note card.

Beginning—a noun and an adjective. As a noun, the point at which something begins. You need more, especially if you do not know the word begin. *The first part—a rudimentary stage or an early period. It can be an adjective as well—just starting out. Being first.*

I imagine it took us months to define this word, annotate it, dissect it in different ways, stare at it until it no longer made sense, became a mere jumble of letters in a certain order.

Meena sat on the couch, reread the note, then glanced around the room. What a curious woman Neha had been. She rubbed the prickles on her arm. The room was chilly, but it was the haunting words of the note that unnerved her.

It wasn't signed. But as with the others, Meena sensed it had been written by Neha. The handwriting was the same. A very exact penmanship with the words small and precise. She wrote in straight lines even on the unlined paper. The opposite of her chaotic apartment. The stranger had found a way to communicate from beyond the grave. Curiosity crashed like a giant wave over Meena. She needed to know more.

She flipped open her laptop and logged in. She typed "Neha Patel" in the search bar. Close to twenty-four million results. She narrowed the search down to Boston and added the street address. Finally a match. An obituary without a photo. *What is with this woman and not having photos?* It was a short mention of her death in the *Boston Globe*.

Neha A. Patel, 65, of Boston, Massachusetts, passed away on April 24 from natural causes. She is survived by her parents, Ambalalbhai Dhirubhai Patel and Chanchalben Ambalalbhai Patel. Harvard graduate. Editor, Merriam-Webster.

That was all. No mention of a husband, even though the note said she'd had one. Meena dug around a little more but couldn't find anything more than cursory information. She wondered if *Love's Labour's Lost* was a hint or just a convenient place for Neha to hide her note.

Meena added the card to the envelope with the others. As the sun rose higher, the living room filled with light and color, and she turned over the things she knew, searched for threads and meaning.

Surprised by a knock at the door, Meena answered. Three women barreled in without invitation.

CHAPTER FOUR

"Can I help you?" Meena asked.

She recognized two of the three women. They were about the same age, possibly in their fifties, though their skin was flawless in differing shades of brown. Each carried something in her hand: a container, a bouquet of flowers, or a thermos.

The woman she didn't recognize was in jeans and a sweatshirt with a Boston University logo. Her short hair was layered at the top. The one with the flower arrangement was Tanvi from this morning. She still wore a long velvet dress with several necklaces draped around her neck, but her hair was now in a big bun with a coil of beads holding it together. The one with the thermos was the first woman she'd met, Sabina. Today she was in a long green silk shirt with leggings. She wore her hair in a braid that lay over her right shoulder. She had a small red dot on her forehead between her sharply arched eyebrows.

"Ay, why are you wearing shoes in the house?" Sabina asked. "Where are your slippers?"

"Again . . . can I help you?"

"No," Tanvi cut her off. "We're here to welcome you with chai and parathas. And fresh flowers, which will make you feel more at home." She placed the big arrangement on the console table next to the door.

"Thank you"—Meena hesitated—"but I'm on my way out."

"To go where?" the woman with the container asked.

Meena pursed her lips. She wasn't used to answering to anyone. "The airport."

"Leaving already?" Sabina asked.

"Only to get my suitcase."

"Why did you leave it there?" the woman with the container said.

Meena sighed and closed the door behind her. They were settling in at the dining table by the front windows, and Meena realized they weren't going to budge until she answered their questions.

"Take off your shoes and sit." Tanvi waved her over. "Food and tea will give you energy for your errands."

Meena knew that in many Asian cultures, shoes in the house were a no-no. She complied and joined them at the table.

"Chai and chitchat," Tanvi said. "That's how things are in the Engineer's House."

"Who?"

"This house," Sabina said with obvious pride. "It has been called the Engineer's House for almost one hundred years, named by the original residents who lived here while they studied at MIT."

Meena thought back to the index card that had come with the deed to the house. That must be what it referred to.

"This is Uma." Tanvi pointed to the woman in the BU sweatshirt. "She brought parathas because they're her specialty."

"Savory and full of flavor." Uma glared at Tanvi while speaking.

"She's also very opinionated. Thinks my cooking is bland. But my husband has high blood pressure," Tanvi said.

"That's salt, but what about all the missing spices?" Uma asked.

"Heartburn."

Uma rolled her eyes and shook her head.

"Sabina brought chai." Tanvi walked toward the kitchen. "She's the boss of this building."

"The caretaker," Sabina clarified. "I'm responsible for the building and its families."

"She will interrogate you and is the guilty-until-proven-innocent type," Tanvi called out.

"That's not true," Sabina said.

"Once, when we were teenagers"—Uma lit a candle on the corner table next to the window—"she told me I had lost her favorite winter hat because she had lent it to me. I told her for weeks I had returned it. But she didn't believe me. Then one day, she found it under her bed when she was cleaning."

"I apologized," Sabina muttered. "You never let that go."

Meena listened to their chatter as they brought over plates and mugs from Neha's kitchen. She took a seat and looked through the window. It was a sunny day. A few people walked past, and a couple took photos of the street. She spotted Wally running around on the small plot of grass in the front yard, sniffing the sturdy red flowers so meticulously planted against the hedgerow. Meena caught Sam's eyes. He put his finger up to his lips, the universal sign for *Don't tell anyone I'm here.* She nodded and turned her attention to the women, who were busying themselves as if they often came into this apartment to take it over.

Though she wasn't that hungry, Meena wanted to try the flatbread Uma served her. It was like a tortilla, but smaller and green, with sesame seeds in it.

"What's this?"

"Spinach paratha." Uma rolled one up, dipped it in her chai, and took a bite. "Have you never tried?"

"I don't think so," Meena said.

"This is a Gujarati specialty," Tanvi clarified. "Warm parathas with mango pickle and hot chai. Comfort food."

Meena ripped the bread with both hands.

"No. Like this. Watch." Sabina pressed the thumb of her right hand into the paratha, then used her index and middle finger to rip a piece of it off. Once she had a sizable piece in her hand, she used it to scoop up a little of the mango pickle before gracefully gliding it into her mouth.

"I don't think I can do that." The movements of the fingers seemed acrobatic.

"Try." Sabina nudged the plate closer to Meena.

Meena gave it a go and managed to tear off a large chunk. Spice, salt, and heat exploded in her mouth. It was delicious and comforting. When she ate Indian, it was usually butter chicken or tikka masala, though curry chips in London were a hangover favorite. This was very different from what was served in restaurants. "It's delicious."

"You must not be Indian," Sabina said. "You have the look, but . . ."

"Let's remember our Do No Harm Club." Tanvi tapped Sabina's arm. "We apologize, Meena. It's just that everyone in the Engineer's House is of Indian descent, and we assumed you were too. But of course, you are the one who would know best."

"Thank you," Meena said. "What's a Do No Harm Club?"

"It started because whenever we read books or watched movies," Tanvi explained, "Uma would always point out problems. So we started a club where we learn about inclusivity and belonging."

"What is your family background?" Sabina asked.

Meena preferred to ask the questions, not answer them. "I grew up in Northampton."

"Huh," Uma said.

Meena changed the topic back to them. "Do you all live in the building?"

"Yes. I'm above you." Uma pointed to the ceiling.

"I'm across the hall from Uma," Tanvi added. "And Sabina has the top floor."

"What do you do?" Sabina asked.

"I'm a photojournalist."

"Fun." Tanvi clapped her hands. "Do you have an Instagram?"

"Yes." It was part of her work now. Most photographers had some social media presence. Meena wasn't the best at posting, and it was never about her or her life, only her work.

Tanvi pulled out her phone. "Is it under Meena Dave?"

Meena snapped up. Tanvi had pronounced her last name "duh-veh." "Dave," Meena corrected. Not that hard to pronounce. A very common name, and while it wasn't short for David, it was that easy.

"Duh-veh," Uma said. "That's the Gujarati version. That's why we thought you might be Indian and that you were likely using an American version of your name."

"I've only ever known it pronounced as Dave," Meena said.

"You should ask your parents," Uma advised. "They could have changed it a few generations ago to fit in."

Meena's chest tightened at the casual mention of her parents as if they were still alive.

"It's an Irish name. At one time the name was Gaelic, and when my father's family came over, it got changed, was shortened." It was what her father had told her when she'd asked about their family history. She'd wanted so very much to be a part of something more than just the three of them.

"Is your ethnic background from your mother's or your father's side?" Sabina asked.

"Yes." Meena didn't know for sure, but her brown skin had to come from at least one of her birth parents. It was a fifty-fifty shot.

"And how did you know Neha?" Sabina asked.

"I didn't," Meena said. "I'm here because she left me this apartment."

"I spoke to Neha's lawyer yesterday," Sabina said. "She did not tell me anything except to confirm your name."

"You checked up on me?"

"I had to verify," Sabina said. "It's my duty."

Maybe *they* knew why Neha had left the place to Meena. "Neha must have told you who I was, why she left this to me."

Sabina's back stiffened. "No. I tried to discuss her plans with her, but she always changed the topic. When she died, we were only told what pertained to us."

"She left us little mementos," Tanvi added.

"No mention of what she planned to do with this place," Sabina said.

So Meena wouldn't find out much from these three. Disappointed, she sipped the hot chai. It needed sugar, and she reached for it. Sabina took the jar and spooned two teaspoons into Meena's mug and stirred. Meena nodded her thanks.

"We took care of this apartment." Uma wiped her hands on a paper napkin. "We didn't know what else to do."

"And do you plan to stay?" Sabina asked. "Live here?"

No. "I'm still figuring things out." And now, with the notes, she wanted to know more.

"Neha never mentioned your name," Tanvi remarked, "and we knew her our entire lives."

"Then again, Neha wasn't, uh, what's a nonoffensive way to say *all there?*" Uma said. "She did what she wanted and rarely cared about any rules."

"She can't ignore all of them." Sabina made a tiny pile of paratha crumbs on her plate. "There is a strict entailment process in this building."

"And Neha found a way around it. She did whatever she wanted," Uma said. "Like the time she hired a contractor. Took out the second bedroom, made this into a giant open-plan living room, dining area, and then added built-ins on most of the walls for her books. She didn't ask any of our permission. Then she gave away all of the furniture one day to total strangers."

"Is that what you think happened?" Meena asked. "On a whim she came across one of my stories, found my name, and left me this place?"

It was unlikely, but Meena wanted to know how much the aunties knew.

"No," Sabina said. "I do not think you are random. And you don't think that either."

"I've never heard her name or knew of her until yesterday." Meena finished her chai.

Sabina gave her a look, searched for something. "While you're here, if you need anything, ask. We help each other in this building."

Meena smiled and stood. "Thank you for the chai and paratha." She tripped over the pronunciation. She was conversationally versed in only a few languages; Gujarati wasn't one of them. "I can clean up after I get back and return your containers."

"Don't be silly." Tanvi shooed her off. "The kitchen will be spotless by the time you get back. And knock on Sam's door. He can drive you to pick up your bags."

"It's OK," Meena said. "I'm good."

She paused at the door. They didn't seem to be in a rush. Uma added more tea to her cup as they chatted away. That this wasn't their apartment didn't seem to faze them. Meena didn't know what to do, so she grabbed the keys and her laptop and camera bag. She didn't want to be loaded up, but her backpack contained thousands of dollars' worth of equipment. Her life was in this bag. And, she realized, she had no idea who these women were.

CHAPTER FIVE

Two days later, Meena wandered out to the veranda off Neha's bedroom. It was a crisp day, and she wrapped her long gray sweater around her and took a deep breath. The air had a hint of burning wood and pine. When she was a child, fall had been her favorite season, even if it meant the end of summer and back to school. She used to mark the day the cord of wood would be delivered for winter and excitedly watch as it was stacked in the backyard. It had been her job to get as many logs as she could carry and bring them in so her father could light the fireplace. Jameson Dave had been methodical in the building and maintaining of fire. Meena would sit and watch the flames for hours, loving how the blue, yellow, and orange colors morphed.

At the sound of voices, she peered down into the garden. Sabina, Uma, and Tanvi were in discussion as if they were plotting out a football play. They were armed with rakes, gardening gloves, and large paper bags and dressed in leggings and oversize sweatshirts. Meena watched as they worked in different areas of the garden. Uma was by the rose vines that wrapped around a trellis along the back wooden fence. She pinched off the dried petals that had once been red and snipped off twigs with small shears. Tanvi cleared the area around the small iron table with four chairs. A matching bench in the same teal tone was off to one side under an arbor of small trees. The lush branches were starting to change their color as they hung down toward the ground. Sabina raked the leaves scattered around the stone pathway.

It was a pretty garden, well tended. Meena went back into the living room and grabbed her camera. She wanted a look around, and her camera helped her see better. The three seemed to have a rhythm about them, and Meena snapped to see if she could unearth the beats of their friendship.

Their voices carried as they offered one another commentary and instructions. While they mainly spoke in another language, there was enough English that Meena could make out the context. As she snapped away, she could see their fondness for each other.

"Meena," Uma shouted at her. "Why are you taking our picture?"

"Oh, sorry, it's something I do." She released the camera, placed it on a little table on the patio.

"We haven't seen you in a couple of days. How are you?" Tanvi asked.

"I'm good," Meena said.

"Are you managing to eat?" Sabina asked.

"Takeout."

"I am making a big lasagna today," Sabina stated. "I will drop some off."

"Thank you."

Meena looked through her shots as she went back in. It was nice to simply shoot, not on assignment, but for herself—to feed her creativity and curiosity. She'd been going from gig to gig for so long, she couldn't remember the last time she'd picked up her camera just because. She rolled her neck and shoulders. This week was helping her shake off some of the wear she'd put on her bones this past decade.

She shuffled through the notebooks on Neha's desk. Maybe there would be another note. She pulled open the drawer and riffled around. In the back she felt something stiff and tugged it out. A card in an envelope. It was sealed with red wax, with **NP** imprinted in the center. She opened it and pulled out the card.

history (noun)
1: a branch of knowledge that records and explains past events
2 a.: events that form the subject matter of history
b.: events of the past
c.: one that is finished or done
heritage (noun)
1: something transmitted by or acquired from a predecessor

Meena scanned the words. Neha had been a dictionary editor, so the definition could be for her work. Except Meena's gut told her it could also be a message. These words didn't seem to be random choices or the product of a stream of consciousness. She put the note back in the envelope and placed it with the others. Each added something, as with a series of clues. Meena wondered if they were for her.

CHAPTER SIX

The mid-October day was warm and sunny as Meena walked toward Back Bay from Kenmore Square. Her meeting with a broker had gone better than expected, and Clifton Warney was confident the place would be rented within a week of being on the market. He was eager to see it, but Meena needed a few days to clear out some of Neha's things.

As she crossed to the center path of Commonwealth Avenue, the street grew quieter. The large tree-lined mall was bursting with autumn colors. Leaves in shades of amber, gold, and brown clung desperately to the drying branches, delaying their inevitable fall to the ground. She navigated around tourists who stopped to take photos of various statues. The Boston Women's Memorial seemed to be the most popular, with mothers and daughters posing next to the three bronze sculptures.

It was something her father would have done, made Meena and Hannah stand there as he took endless shots with his 35 millimeter. He'd loved his camera, had shown Meena how to use it when she'd been a curious eight-year-old. She'd received her very own for her fifteenth birthday. She'd had it for a little over a year before the explosion took it, along with all their family photographs. Meena rubbed her knuckles against her chest to ease the tightening.

Heritage. She didn't have one. Not in the genetic sense. She was who her parents had raised her to be. Sunday Mass, PB&Js in her brown-bag lunch. Books where the parents looked like hers, but she didn't resemble the children. She wouldn't let it be important. She'd been loved. That was the only thing that mattered.

You and I, Meena, are dreamers, her father would say.

And I'm here to make sure you can do, her mother would add. *Dreams do not put food on the table.*

Meena pushed away the memory to focus on the practical things like getting the apartment ready for renters. She also wanted to pull apart the significance of the note card she'd found that morning, this one in the bottom of a trinket box.

The women of this building are in charge, the husbands super-fluous. The husbands married into the history of EH but did not have the same care or responsibilities. The running and keeping of EH is for the women directly descended from the original engineers.

Meena let her thoughts percolate as she walked away from Commonwealth Avenue and onto Newbury Street. Just a block over, the street changed significantly, shoppers laden with bags browsing the lunch menus of the numerous cafés along their way. The shop windows showcased mannequins in sportswear, evening gowns, and everything in between. Each low-rise building was neatly packed, snug against the next, with stores on the top two floors, a restaurant in the basement.

Meena rarely shopped. She didn't need anything more than a few pairs of jeans, versatile yoga pants, T-shirts, sweaters, a multipurpose black dress for formal things or business meetings, and a coat. A pair of sneakers and her sturdy boots got her through most of the terrain she covered. If she needed something different, she got it from wherever she was, like a headscarf in a Muslim country or all-weather gloves in Kyiv. She would sell things back or give them away as she went.

Most of what she owned was what she needed for work. Two cameras, favorite Canon lenses, the Canon fixed 35 millimeter and fixed 50 millimeter, along with her laptop and charger, camera batteries, memory cards, off-camera flash cord, and various cables and external hard drives, and the other pieces of equipment she had to buy when an assignment called for it.

Meena paused in front of Sephora. Her one indulgence was makeup. She had a small pouch of lipsticks, liners, mascara, and moisturizers. She always had gloss in her jacket pocket. It made her feel better, brighter, when she had a pop of color on her lips.

Her mother had been the same. Hannah Dave had never left her bedroom without being fully made up. From the soft waves of her auburn hair to the dab of Chanel No. 5 behind her ears, she was always ready for company.

It's the sign of a woman who takes care of herself. For Hannah, the time she spent getting ready was only for herself, an hour to focus on the external parts of her, from moist skin to brushed eyebrows. The scent of Pond's Cold Cream put Meena right back into that bedroom.

The wind whipped her loose hair into her face, and she brushed it away as she headed back toward the Engineer's House. Meena's mind wandered back to Neha. Without photos or anything more on the internet, Meena had spent a bit of time imagining what Neha looked like. She pictured a stout woman with frizzy hair. There hadn't been any makeup in the apartment, only a serviceable moisturizer, soap, and a two-in-one shampoo/conditioner. She could have been tall based on the length of the pants in the closet, and broad shouldered.

A cursory search of the apartment gave only a few clues to the woman. Colorful sweaters in her closet, plain pants and skirts. The pantry full of canned and boxed goods, the fridge bare, though one of the aunties had likely cleaned it out. Furniture packed so closely it left little open space, but the apartment wasn't cluttered or messy.

"Wally, wait."

Meena braced as the puppy came barreling toward her, shifting her weight to both feet. She squatted as the dog threw himself into her. Excited and happy. She gave him rubs, scratches, and coos. "Hi, Wally. Hi."

She glanced up as Sam stood over them. "Why is it that he's always trying to escape?"

"Because I'm the one that tells him no, makes him get off the couch, stops him from chewing on things that aren't his toys."

"Aww." Meena scratched him. "But he's such a good boy."

"For other people," Sam said. "It's a con."

"I don't believe that for a second." She stood as Wally became distracted by a squirrel in a tree and began to yip at it.

"You're not going to be able to catch the squirrel, Wallster." Sam bent down and clipped the leash onto Wally's harness.

"Why was he loose?" Meena asked.

"Because he saw you and ran out of the yard," Sam muttered.

"Ah."

She warmed at the idea that the puppy had wanted to see her. She'd always wanted a dog when she was young, had even asked Santa for one. But her lifestyle could never allow her to have a dog. She didn't even have consistent *people* in her life. Just Zoe, whom she saw twice a year. She knew people, of course. She had a professional network, past mentors, local contacts. She socialized with them when she saw them, but they didn't really know her.

"Were you coming or going?"

"Meandering," Meena said. "It's a beautiful day."

"We were doing some training on the word *stay*." Sam jiggled the leash. "Weren't we, Wally?"

"I don't think it took."

Sam shook his head. "Want to join us for a little walk around the block? He can't go for long, but I'm hoping he'll fall asleep after this so I can get work done."

"What are you working on?"

"A television show right now," Sam said. "It's fun, and the showrunner and directors have given me the freedom to be creative. I'm working on a multidimensional monster that's the entry point for different galaxies. Wally, come."

Meena laughed as the dog completely ignored Sam.

"Wally," Meena said.

The dog looked up and trotted over to her.

"It's because you're the new, shiny person," Sam pointed out. "But I have treats."

They walked a bit and turned the corner, heading away from Newbury toward Beacon Street. Beyond it was Storrow Drive and then the Charles River. It was quiet in the mostly residential area. Thursday afternoon meant the professionals who lived here were working.

"Did Wally get as excited when he saw Neha?" Meena asked.

Sam tugged the leash and walked a little bit. "No. They never met. Wally wasn't even born when she died. He's only ten weeks, and I got him two weeks ago. That's why he loves and ignores me interchangeably."

"Oh," Meena said. "I don't know much about dogs."

"This one is a baby," Sam explained. "But he'll grow to be about seventy pounds."

"I hope he understands your commands by then."

"We're signing up for puppy school once he's fully vaccinated."

They walked to the end of the block and turned right, toward Marlborough Street. The Public Garden was to their left.

"Wally was a gift from Neha." Sam smiled. "She left me a dog in her will. Ever since I was a little kid, I wanted a dog, but my parents would tell me it wasn't allowed. Sabina's family are the original caretakers, and she's the current one. She's not a fan of chaos or mess, so the homeowners' agreements have a lot of clauses."

"And you're all OK with it?"

"For the most part."

"Even Neha?" From the notes, Meena got the sense that Neha had had strong opinions and wouldn't have been so easily led.

"She was a challenge to Sabina auntie, most of the time indirectly. Like the pet policy. Neha left a puppy for me in her will. Made it so Sabina couldn't say no. I know she's not a fan of me having a dog, but she hasn't outright told me he wasn't welcome. So we let a few things ride."

Meena was starting to understand him. "You don't pick battles; you just outlast them."

He gave her a small grin. Dimples indented his cheeks. Then he tripped over the leash. Meena held in her laugh and helped him untangle himself.

"What was Neha like?" Meena asked.

"Extraordinary in an unexpected way," Sam disclosed. "She was so smart that sometimes her brain needed release, so she'd have these spurts of unpredictability. Once, when I was in college, she came to my dorm at MIT and asked me to drive her to Vermont. She had a very specific craving for Ben & Jerry's and wanted to go to their factory. I told her there's a Ben & Jerry's shop right down Newbury, but she didn't want that. We drove three hours in the middle of February for ice cream."

Sam grinned, and Meena squelched the spark of attraction. It surprised her. For Meena, attraction meant a one-night stand, and it wasn't a good idea to get involved with someone she would run into over and over again.

"Neha seemed like a good person," she said.

"She had her moments." Sam glanced away. "She was also petty. Case in point: Wally. Neha wanted me to have a dog because she had a soft spot for me, and she wanted to stick it to Sabina one more time."

"The two of you were good friends."

"In a way. She'd grown up with my mom. My parents lived in my place before me. They're now in Germany with my brother and his family. I came back from LA to live here. I grew up with her as Neha auntie, but in the last few years, we were friends. She liked people who did things for her that she didn't want to do herself."

"Did she live alone?" Meena wondered if Sam knew Neha's husband or why he had left.

"She didn't have use for a lot of people," Sam said. "Not even me, unless it was on her terms. She had her limits as to how much time she spent away from her work and her books."

"She has a massive collection."

He nodded and focused his attention on Wally. Sam gently tugged away a fallen branch that was three times the dog's size.

Meena sensed Sam was done talking about Neha. "You bought the apartment from your parents?"

There was hesitation in Sam's voice. "No. It became mine. The apartments in the Engineer's House are entailed, meaning they can't be sold on the market. The eldest child inherits the unit when they turn twenty-five."

"But the other women, the aunties, they still live in their units."

"It's a technicality. It's up to the kids as to when they want to take it over."

"Not a firm rule."

"Are you making conversation or interviewing me?"

Meena smiled. "Habit. I ask a lot of questions."

"You'll fit right in with the aunties," Sam said. "Wally, no." He tugged a crumpled napkin out of Wally's mouth.

"Did Neha have any siblings or children?"

Sam glanced at her and then looked away. "No."

Meena pushed a little more. "Do you think Neha left the apartment to me on a whim? Or by accident?"

Sam kept quiet and focused on teaching Wally how to walk on a leash.

Meena sensed he was holding back and tried again. "If the apartments are entailed . . ."

"She didn't have anyone to pass it on to," Sam said. "Her parents are in Africa, and she had no other family."

He sounded so definitive, it made Meena question her assumptions about her ties to Neha. If she and Neha weren't biologically connected, why would Neha leave her actual home to Meena? A sliver of something snagged her mind. *Petty.* Was Meena ammo? Like a dog that wasn't allowed but had been gifted posthumously?

As they turned right and approached their building, Wally did loops around her, and Meena became entangled with his leash. Sam caught her with one arm to steady her. For a few seconds embarrassment, comfort, and attraction swirled around her. She glanced into his dark-brown eyes. There was gentle humor in them that made her feel as if she knew him much better than she did. Meena disentangled herself from the leash.

"When is puppy school?" she asked.

"Not soon enough," Sam said. "We need to learn a lot of things, don't we, beast?"

Meena increased her pace to distract herself from the weird tingles on her arm where Sam had held her steady. As they came up to the front steps, Tanvi called out to them. "There you two are. Have you been out for a walk? Isn't fall romantic?"

CHAPTER SEVEN

Tanvi held conical candleholders, and Uma stepped out the front doors with more.

"Here, Auntie. Meena, can you hold Wally's leash for a second?" Sam thrust the loop of the leash into her hand as he ran up the stairs to take the items from the aunties and place them on each step, next to the pumpkins.

"Thank you, Sameer." Sabina stepped out with a box. "We looked for you, but you were out."

"Wally needed a walk," Sam said.

At the sound of his name, Wally barked and tried to climb up on the step to nibble on a pumpkin. "No." Meena gently tugged him back, his harness straining with his effort to get to the others. She knelt and scratched under his chin until he sat down on the cold path.

"We knocked on your door too, Meena." Tanvi pointed to the two of them. "I didn't realize you were together."

"We aren't, weren't," Meena explained.

Tanvi and Uma raised their eyebrows while Sabina dragged out a bin full of decorations.

"It's just that we met. Ran into each other. I was walking and he was walking." Meena shut her mouth. It was unusual for her to be tongue-tied or awkward, but these women seemed to imply and assume there was something between her and Sam, and it made her wary.

"Don't be so shy about it, there is nothing wrong with a shared walk," Tanvi said. "More people should do it. Especially on a beautiful day like today. I love the colors and the crunch of leaves under my feet. They say spring is the perfect time for lovers. I disagree. There is something about prewinter coziness that makes you want to cuddle up with someone."

Refusing to pick up what Tanvi was putting down, Meena gave Wally extra belly rubs. Sam stayed silent too and busied himself with the box of decorations.

"Ay, poet," Uma said. "Less prattle, more spiders."

Tanvi sighed and grabbed a few decorations.

"Sam"—Uma held up glittery ceramic ghosts—"can you hang these up next to the doors? I don't have your height."

Sam hooked them to the iron lanterns on either side of the front doors.

The pup was getting tired and flopped his chin on Meena's feet. She sat on the ground, shuddered with the shock of the cold concrete, and stroked Wally as his little black eyes slowly closed in sleep. She'd never taken care of anyone or anything this small, and Sam had entrusted her with this tiny little fur ball. She smiled; it was nice being asked to help. Especially with such an easy and pleasurable task. Meena pulled him into her lap. He nipped a bit before settling down.

"I can take him inside," Sam said.

"He's fine." Meena stroked Wally's soft fur.

"Meena, you and Sam are in charge of hot cider and small paper cups," Sabina stated. "I'm assigning you a shared task since you're still new."

"Make sure the cups are made with recycled paper," Uma added.

Meena looked at Sam for an explanation.

"For Halloween." Sam gestured toward the houses on either side of the building. "This street gets a lot of kid traffic from all over the city. The buildings up and down this block are known for decorations and lots of candy."

"Every year we have a theme at the Engineer's House," Sabina said. "We spend the evening outside from six p.m. to eight p.m. handing out treats and hot drinks to kids and parents."

The building and garden began to transform into something she could only describe with the term *upscale terror*, if there was such a thing. There were no down-to-earth cotton spiderwebs or ghosts made from sheets. The decorations looked expensive, made of glass, not plastic, with ribbons, not streamers. Sam strung orange and white fairy lights on the trees. Sabina wrapped purple ones around the railings. Tanvi added tall silk witch hats to the tops of the hedges that served as a fence to the garden on either side of the center path. Uma hung a violet-and-black wreath with small ceramic skulls on one of the doors.

Meena wished she had her camera with her. Instead she pulled out her phone and snapped pictures as they worked. There was a cadence to the way they moved together, chattering, checking in with each other about height and alignment. There were casual touches, a hand on Tanvi's back as Uma passed by, a pat on Sam's shoulder from Sabina. They smiled and laughed. Uma jumped out in front of Sam with a loud "Boo," and Sam overdramatized his fear.

"If I knew I was going to be in a photo"—Tanvi preened—"I would have done my hair."

"You look fabulous, and this looks fun. Is it OK if I take a few pictures?" Meena should have asked before taking photos, but the urge to document the scene had made her impulsive.

"I don't mind," Tanvi offered. "I'm happy to be a model. I have natural beauty."

"When is your next salon appointment," Uma said, "to dye your hair back to its original color?"

Tanvi stuck her tongue out at Uma, and Meena captured the image.

"I want to see." Tanvi came over.

Meena held out the phone.

"These are incredible." Tanvi slid her fingers to look at more. "There is so much in each one. It's art."

Her heart swelled with pride. "Thank you."

"You could print these," Tanvi said. "Publish them."

These were casual, just fun shots of people going about their day. Maybe there was something here, about the three of them, this building.

"We looked you up," Uma said. "Your Instagram is terrific. You've been all over the world. I want to bring some of your stories into one of my classes at BU, especially your work around climate change and ecotourism."

"Thank you."

"You're a photographer?" Sam asked.

It made her happy to know that he hadn't researched her. She liked their easiness, that they were getting to know each other naturally. She preferred discovery to information dumps.

"Photojournalist." Uma poked him. "You should see her work, Sam."

Meena knew what would happen next. Questions about where she'd been, what she'd done, where she was going. She took Wally off her lap, stood, then picked him back up again. "I think he needs a proper nap. I can take him inside with me."

"Just go into my place, the door's unlocked," Sam instructed. "His crate is in the living room. Lock it so he stays put."

"OK." It felt weird to just walk into his place, but it would shift the attention away from her.

"Don't forget about the cups," Uma reminded Meena. "Sam will get the hot cider. Sabina has a silver urn for it."

Meena nodded as she headed up the steps. "This all looks great."

"It won't be the same," Tanvi said, "without Neha."

Meena stopped. "Did she help you with the decorating?"

Tanvi laughed. "No. She liked to play a living ghost by sitting at her window, and when kids came up, she would slowly move her face closer and closer. With her white makeup, red lips, and a long black wig, she loved to scare all the kids."

Tanvi's eyes glistened, and her voice trembled as she recounted the memory. Everyone stopped midactivity. Sabina squeezed Tanvi's hand to comfort her.

"I'm sorry for your loss." It was a rote statement, one Meena heard each time someone found out about her own loss. Meena didn't know what to say, but she felt for them. These women cared about Neha and missed her.

Tanvi composed herself. "Well, now you're here. And you'll get the cups."

Meena nodded. "I'll make sure they're recycled." Meena left them and dropped off a snoozing Wally in his crate before crossing the hall. She barely took in Sam's living room; it felt too intrusive. Back in the apartment, Meena went to the windows. She could imagine a woman sitting in a chair playing dead.

She dropped her keys at the small console table and noticed a book. It was tiny, pocket size. *Einstein's Dreams*. The mustard-and-black cover was muted and simple. She picked it up, thumbed through it. She came across two folded pieces of thin, smooth stationery with a Victorian design. She unfolded the note and saw Neha's handwriting.

I work in beige. My office desk clear except for what enables me to do my work—pens, pencils, highlighters, index cards, paper clips, etc. The quiet is quite deafening at times, perfect for the solitary work of determining a word's definition, parts of speech, and roots.

My work is my life, and my passion is to do it well, to continually improve. This week I'm learning Icelandic. I'm fascinated by the construction of their words. Gluggaveður. *The last five letters can be inferred to refer to weather. It is an old root. The literal translation, however, is "window weather." I was delighted by the discovery.*

Meena could relate. The quiet was deafening, and more so right now. As with Neha, Meena's work was her life. But lately she'd had the sense that it wasn't enough. The excitement of a new place, the discovery of a new story, documenting a moment in time, it challenged her and fueled her. Still, in the last few years, there had also been a growing sense of emptiness. If she was honest with herself, she was missing something, though she didn't know what.

All she did know was that for this one week, she'd put everything on hold so she could stay in Boston, sort through Neha's things, and move on. But she was beginning to feel a pull, the need to know more, especially to see where these notes would lead.

CHAPTER EIGHT

There was nothing casual about Clifton Warney. Even the faint pin-stripes on his black three-piece suit matched his pink silk tie.

"This is magnificent." Clifton stood in the space separating the dining area and the living room. "Once you get rid of everything, you'll have people lining up to live here. Location alone will get you a great price, though it is only one bedroom, and that does limit the type of clients. It is great for a young couple."

"Everything?" Meena had hoped to keep the furnishings for now. She didn't have time for a wholesale clean-out and honestly didn't even know where to start. "I've organized a bit, but I don't have a lot of time. I'm due in New York on Tuesday."

"That leaves you this weekend." Clifton pulled out his phone. "I can recommend a company to come pack it all up and store it."

Which would mean additional cost. "You said something about possibly starting the lease in January?" She would have to do a full-year lease, which would mean not selling until the following year's end.

"Yes," Clifton said. "September, which you just missed, and January are two big times for the rental market turnover. Which means you need to get this place cleared out as soon as possible so I can market it in November and get someone signed before the end-of-year holidays."

Meena mentally ran through her calendar. She had planned to be in New York until mid-November. She'd pitched a story to *Gramophone* to cover the Festival Bach Montreal in early December before heading to London. She could come back for a week at the beginning of November depending on how her editor meetings panned out. "What if it's cleared out by mid-November?"

Clifton pursed his lips and tapped his finger against his chin. "Let me see what's available and how competitive the market is for this area. We're not talking college students here, which would be easy, though international graduate students might be able to swing four thousand dollars per month."

Meena laughed. "Are you serious?"

"If you clear it out and give the floors a quick polish, then yes, we can get that for this location."

"What if I were to sell it?"

Clifton narrowed his eyes. "You'd have to get it appraised, but ballpark, if you updated the kitchen, freshened up the paint, I'd say about two and a half to three million dollars. Now, if you put in a little elbow grease, you can get more, if you take out the built-ins."

Meena braced herself against the back of the sofa. This was life-changing money. She needed to think, process. She knew the apartment was big and had assumed it was worth some money, but not this much. "I . . . OK. Let me think things through. I'm heading to New York in two days. Can we touch base early next week? I'll have a better idea about when I can come back and clear this place out."

He nodded. "If you are considering selling, this type of unit doesn't come on the market that often."

She also didn't know if she had to use a broker since she could only sell to owners in this building. "I guess I have a lot to think about."

As she showed him out, Uma was on her way down the stairs.

"Who was that?"

Getting right to the point, this one. "Where are you off to?"

"Office hours," Uma muttered. "Students will be lining up to get as much information as they can for the midterms. Did you have company?"

"Oh, uh, no." Meena shook her head. "He's helping me with something."

"What sort of something?" Uma asked.

Meena wasn't ready to get into it. "Just apartment stuff."

"Hmmm. Did you clear it with Sabina?"

"Why?"

Uma sighed. "I don't have time right now, but she's in charge, and if you're doing anything with the place like renovating, you'll need her permission."

Meena made fists with her hands, squeezed, then released to handle the rising frustration as Uma opened the front door and headed out. The short woman was huddled in a brown jacket, a bulky shoulder bag tapping against her thigh as she rushed down the outside steps. Meena closed the front door before heading back into her apartment.

She gave in, reached up, and released the bun. Her long, thick hair fell around her. She picked out a few strands along her right shoulder and began to wrap them around each other. It was a bad habit, as the miniature braids created hard-to-untangle knots. She'd done it as a kid whenever she was studying something complicated like chemistry or when she was nervous or needed to think. Whenever her mom would catch Meena doing this, she would gently take Meena's hands from her hair and give her something else to hold, like a glass of water or a pencil.

But Hannah wasn't here, hadn't been for a long time, and sometimes Meena needed to give in. The furniture, books, lamps, boxes, trinkets, paintings, vases, candles seemed as if they were closing in on her. There was only enough space to stand and navigate through the clutter. She didn't have time for this. She had a flight booked for Sunday afternoon, and a day and a half wasn't enough to make even the smallest difference.

She leaned against the fireplace mantel and stared at the piles of books on the desk against the back windows. Then there were the notes. There had to be more than the few she'd found. Little missives from the dead with possible clues to Meena's own history. If she shoved everything in boxes, she might not find them all.

Meena let go of her hair. The question wasn't about renting or selling or even getting back to her life. What she needed to figure out was if she wanted to know anything more than that she and Neha were connected in some way. It should be enough. It was in the past, which could never be changed.

And yet.

CHAPTER NINE

Taken down by a ceramic hedgehog. Throughout her career, Meena Dave had aimed her lens at charging bulls in Barcelona. She'd hoisted herself up to the summit of Denali, followed a group of extreme kayakers in Costa Rica. From the Mawlid al-Nabi in Cairo to the disappearing glaciers on Kilimanjaro, from Tasmania to Transylvania, she'd survived with minor scratches.

A week in this apartment and she'd forgotten to take care. The searing pain through her wrist was a reminder to never let her guard down, but the sliver of paper she'd spotted on the bright-green figurine on the very top of the bookcase had tempted her. She was agile enough, or so she thought, to climb up the built-in shelves with toes and fingertips. She hadn't counted on her foot slipping as she grabbed the tail.

"Meena, are you OK?" Sam knocked on the door. "I heard a crash. Your door's locked."

The pain in her wrist morphed into a throbbing ache. Meena lay in the scant floor space between the blue chair and the built-ins. Green ceramic pieces lay around her. "I'm fine."

"I have a spare key," Sam said. "Hang on."

Of course he did. She'd noticed that Sam usually kept his door ajar, and the aunties only gave a short knock before going into his place.

Meena folded her left wrist against her body. Her skin bruised as it swelled. Pain radiated from the tips of her fingers to the top of her shoulder. Still she lay and stared at the ceiling. The crystal chandelier was too modern, too elegant for this room.

Son of a biscuit. Meena sat up and clutched her wrist. She had a flight in four hours. She needed ice and some aspirin. She looked around at the shattered pieces, careful not to add cuts to her other hand as she plucked out the piece of paper, her original goal. Using the floor to assist her, she unrolled it and hoped to see the familiar and precise penmanship.

Hedgehogs share an ancestry with shrews. Not the Shakespeare version, but the mammal. I've never seen one outside of pictures. Their spines are prickly but not poisonous. They roll up into themselves when faced with the unknown. I can relate.

Well, this note was unhelpful and clearly not worth the damage she'd done to her wrist.

"Meena, I'm coming in." Sam saw her on the far side of the room. "Oh no, what happened?"

"Hedgehog."

"Did you hit your head?"

Meena tucked the note into the back pocket of her jeans. "No, tried to reach for something and slipped."

"Let's take a look." Sam squatted down.

"I'm fine."

"Your hand looks like it's swelling up," he said.

"I can see that." She sighed and tried to stand, placing her good hand on the floor for balance. She attempted different positions, unable to find support to get to her feet. Meena shifted again, a groan escaping as pain jostled her arm. She sat in frustration. "I just need an ice pack of some kind."

"You need to go to the ER," Sam advised. "It could be broken."

"Don't have time." Meena placed her good hand on a chair and hoisted herself up. "I have a flight in a few hours."

Sam stood with her. He was in gray sweatpants and a black long-sleeved jersey with an image of a robot from *WALL-E* on it. "Let me drive you to get it checked out first. Tufts ER is close."

Meena didn't want to add this to her growing list of things.

"I'll figure it out," she said.

He stepped back, gave her space. She could see concern in his dark-brown eyes. At the same time, she appreciated that he didn't press her.

"I can call a Lyft." Meena reached for her phone.

"If you prefer."

What would it be like to just accept help? Meena wasn't wired that way. Not for personal things. Professionally she relied on a network of other photojournalists, editors, guides, assistants, and local experts. That was in service to her career. When it came to herself, she managed things on her own. Sam was nice, but she didn't want to be a burden. She'd been taking care of herself for a long time.

She did let him help her gather her things before she went out to wait for the car. He looked worried, so she gave him a big smile to hide the pain. "I'll be back in a few. I'm sure it's just a sprain."

⁂

"Your X-rays show a Colles fracture," Dr. Yan said. "It's common when you fall on an outstretched hand. It's isolated in the distal radial metaphyseal region with a dorsal angulation."

"I don't know what any of that means." Her back against the medical table, Meena cupped her wrist and held it against her chest.

"See this?" Dr. Yan turned her tablet to show Meena the scan. "That little crack in your wrist is the primary injury."

Her first broken bone of any kind. She knew the swelling was going to be bad but had held out hope for a severe sprain. "What happens now?"

"We'll do a closed reduction to manipulate the bones in place and then fit you for a cast from the top of your hand to your elbow."

"How long is this going to take?" Time was speeding by. She'd already waited for X-rays. "I have a flight in two hours."

"That's not going to be possible," Dr. Yan stated.

She rested her head against the back of the exam table and closed her eyes. She didn't want to reschedule again. She'd had everything arranged. A packing company, recommended by Clifton, was scheduled for the middle of the week to take everything to storage. Cleaners toward the end of the week, then the place would be listed. She had planned to do everything, including rental agreements, remotely.

She'd made peace. Decided that it was best to deal with this in a matter-of-fact way. It was enough to know that Neha had left the apartment to her. The notes were a nice distraction, that was all. Meena didn't want it to mean anything more. She had a life, a career. Those were her priorities.

Then she'd seen the piece of paper sticking out of the hedgehog's mouth.

The throbbing eased as the local anesthetic took effect. Her wrist and hand were still puffy, as if someone had blown air into a latex glove. Dark bruises ran up her arm and above the elbow, and she couldn't move her fingers. "Can I work my camera?" Even if she relied solely on autofocus, the trick would be holding it and working it while also juggling the many other pieces of gear she might need while shooting an assignment—even an assignment that typically wouldn't have been physically demanding.

"Likely not for the next few days because of the pain. Once the soreness eases, you should be OK since you're right-handed," Dr. Yan said. "I don't recommend flying around right now. Once we release you, go home. Rest for a few days, then see how you feel."

A few hours later, as her flight was likely landing at LaGuardia, Meena entered the apartment, pain pills in hand.

The door had been left unlocked, and the first thing Meena noticed was that the ceramic fragments had been cleaned up. Likely Sam. She sat on the couch and stretched her legs out with her feet on the coffee table. She'd wanted to leave, get back to her regularly scheduled life. But she'd still reached for another note.

CHAPTER TEN

"Chutes and ladders!" Meena was thirty-four years old and still couldn't curse because she was afraid of disappointing her mother.

She'd wanted a cup of tea, but because she only had one hand, she'd knocked the hot water over as she ripped open the tea bag packet with her teeth. Though she'd dropped the ceramic mug to the floor, it stayed intact. The handle wasn't so lucky, now in fragments.

She sat back against the stainless-steel fridge and cradled her arm. It had been three days since she'd broken her wrist. She'd slept for most of it, occasionally woken up by Sam knocking on her door with an ice pack or one auntie or another bringing her food. There had been a foggy conversation with Sabina that she needed to follow up on about canceling the packers and cleaners. It was fine; it would even save her some money to do everything herself. Once she could manage the pain. Everything hurt—her arm, her shoulder, and her back from sleeping on the couch. But she couldn't sleep in Neha's bed. It was better to keep the distance, stay on the sofa to remember that this was temporary. She leaned her head back. The hair she couldn't put up got caught in something, and she yanked it out. Now her scalp hurt.

She swallowed the rising tears.

Your life is full, Meena. There's no reason to cry. Her father used to say that whenever Meena was upset.

She never let herself feel sorry for her circumstances when, in the grand scheme of things, she was able bodied, unencumbered by chronic illness, and able to support herself. This was an inconvenience, that was all. Yet. Just once, she wanted to wallow.

According to Dr. Yan, her wrist needed eight weeks before the cast was removed. She would have to deal with it. She'd sent messages to all the editors she'd had meetings with to ask to reschedule one more time. This time she wasn't rushing it. She'd wait until mid-November, take the time to clear the place out, list it for rental, and then rebook her flight to New York.

Deciding to forgo tea, Meena grabbed her camera bag and laid out her equipment on the coffee table. Fidgeting with her gear helped calm her mind, distracted her from wandering thoughts. She dropped her 70–200-millimeter zoom lens and let out a little screech. It cost more than a couple of months of rent. She picked up the lens, gingerly examined it from all angles, and gave a small thanks that it seemed OK. The only way she'd know for sure was by attaching it and shooting.

She laid the lens down and smoothed her fingers over it to assess it for unseen damage. She'd used it in Africa for a story on elephant conservation. Picking up the camera, Meena decided to attach a flash. It popped out and hit the corner of the table.

"Peanut shells." Meena caught the flash and put it next to the 70–200. If there was damage, she didn't want to know. Frustration rose even as she tried to squelch it. This cast was her enemy. So was being confined in this apartment. The walks in the neighborhood around the building were no longer interesting. Enough of the pretty streets and ornate doors. The piles of multicolored leaves were drying up. The city air was suffocating. She wanted to be in Pakistan at the K2 base camp or on the Trans-Siberian Railway. She wanted her arm free from restriction.

The knock on her door added to the agony. She wasn't in the mood for food or ice. She didn't want anyone to see her with her hair wild, her face unwashed, still in her tank top and yoga pants.

Meena answered the door. "Sam."

"You look disappointed," Sam said. "Expecting someone else?"

Meena shook her head. "Is there something you need?"

"What happened?" He pointed to her tank top.

"Water stain."

Then he pointed to her hair. "And?"

She ran her hand over the giant frizzy nest. She knew it was a mess and didn't need him to point it out.

"Well, you see." She held up the arm with the thick dark-blue cast. "I have to deal with this, which makes it tough to deal with this." She pointed to her hair. "It's not as if I'm enjoying the tangles or the fact that I have to constantly shove it back because it's always in my way. And this?" She pointed to her shirt. "All I wanted is a cup of tea, but this thick piece of plaster knocked it over." She walked away from the door. Sam followed. "And this tank is on the third wear because the nearest laundromat is four blocks away and the idea of dragging my clothes there is a little too much right now. Any more comments about how I look?"

She flopped down on the sofa, her face warm from letting loose on an undeserving Sam. She just needed to show people she was calm and capable. She rarely let anyone see what she was feeling. She wasn't someone who whined at the smallest setback.

Sam wandered around the living room. "Is this all the stuff you use for work?"

"Yeah," Meena said, appreciating that he hadn't acknowledged her outburst. "A few lenses, a couple of strobes, camera bodies, batteries, and a few other things."

"My equipment wouldn't fit in a backpack," Sam said. "It's tough to design full-scale, in-depth special effects for movies without multiple large monitors."

"How's the gateway-to-the-galaxies monster coming along?"

"You remembered." Sam grinned.

"I have a good memory."

"I eat almonds."

"Huh?"

"I tend to forget stuff I don't need to know. Uma told me I should eat almonds to improve my memory. Five per day."

"And you do it."

"Yup," Sam said. "Like vitamins."

"You're nice," she said.

He laughed. "Not really. It's an easy thing to do, and I like them."

He had a gentle way about him, never in a rush, never bossy. He reminded her of Malcolm, a man she'd photographed on the northernmost inhabited island in Scotland. He'd been building a house for over a decade. He'd told Meena that he wasn't concerned with finishing the project, it was about the build itself.

Meena itched to pick up her camera and take pictures of Sam as he sat on the other side of the sofa. His face held no tension. He hadn't even mentioned why he'd knocked on her door.

"Can I show you something?" he asked.

Meena nodded.

"Come with me."

He led her toward the small hallway dividing the bedroom and bathroom. He pressed against what Meena had assumed was a decorative wall and slid it open to reveal a closet.

Meena groaned. Inside was a shiny stainless-steel stacked washer and dryer. On the door was a small shelf holding detergent and fabric softener.

"Now you can wash this tank that's on its third wear," Sam said. "It might be for the best."

She laughed. "Are you saying I smell?"

"Not you. But the shirt, yeah."

She appreciated his honesty. "You're right. Thank you for showing me."

They walked past her mostly packed suitcase on their way to the living room. "Guess you'll have to stay for a bit."

She laughed as she curled up on the couch. "It was supposed to be a few hours that turned into a few days to now a few weeks."

"It's good," Sam said. "You can explore. Get to know everyone in the building."

That wasn't on her to-do list. "The aunties knock on my door twice a day with lunch and dinner." They would try to stay, have conversations, but Meena used the crutch of her aching wrist to thank them and get them to leave.

"It's how it works in this building. We take care of each other."

She heard the warmth in his voice.

"If Neha was too distracted by her work," Sam continued, "Sabina would come and clean, mop the floors, dust, and all that. Uma kept her pantry stocked. Tanvi did the grocery shopping for her. Neha couldn't be bothered with the details of life. Her brain needed to be full of things she didn't know. She didn't make space for things like laundry."

"Funny." Meena noticed the gleam in his dark-brown eyes.

"I try. Neha and I were friends. She wasn't like my mom or the aunties. She was . . . well, at times erratic. She could go weeks without wanting to be around people. Then she'd have this burst of energy and she'd want to do everything." Sam paced the living room, picking up a small toy dinosaur on a table only to put it back down. "Every May, Neha would pick a Saturday. All of us would meet in the hall at nine a.m. sharp. The aunties, their husbands, the kids. The whole building was required for the annual tradition of walking the Freedom Trail. She'd wear her brightest shirt and pepper us with facts at every landmark."

Meena picked at the edge of her cast. She'd had something like that with her parents. Four Sundays in February. An annual arts festival in their town. The three of them would plan out which venues to go to each Sunday. They'd end the day with dinner in a restaurant, which was always a treat.

"Speaking of," Sam said, and he sighed heavily. "I'm here on behalf of the aunties."

"Uh-oh."

Sam sat next to her on the sofa. "Don't blame the messenger, though in this I'm hoping you'll agree for selfish reasons." He took a deep breath. "They would like you to stop locking your door."

Meena frowned. "What? Why?"

"The only door that's locked in this building is the main one. With security alarms and everything. During the day, except for when you absolutely need privacy, we all keep our doors unlocked. It's a way to live like a family."

As a person who always preferred the safety of bolts and door chains, Meena wasn't on board.

"Also, our two units have the only access to the back garden," Sam said. "The aunties come and go there, and since you moved in, they've been using my apartment. Tanvi gets distracted by Wally, Uma always wants to chat about my work. Sabina begins to clean up after me. So please. For my sake?"

She hated to disappoint him. "I can't. I don't live like that. Locks are safety, something I don't take for granted. And I haven't met their husbands. I'm not sure I like the idea of strangers walking in and out of my apartment."

"I get that," Sam said. "You work in unfamiliar places most of the time. You don't have to worry about that here. This is a safe building. The only downside is lack of privacy. For what it's worth, the aunties are way more formidable than their husbands. The uncles hang out on the roof garden—their domain, as they like to say. You don't have to worry about them coming in here. At least think about it."

She gave him a small nod. "Where is Wally?"

"In his crate," Sam said. "He's in a time-out because he prefers chewing on the leg of my dining table instead of the dozen or so toys all over the apartment."

"Poor puppy."

"Yeah, you get to say that because he's not the one staring you dead in the face as he bites into the couch after you've said no three times," Sam said. There was so much love in Sam's voice as he talked about Wally's antics.

"Would you like to have dinner?" he asked, suddenly.

The non sequitur jarred her. "I don't do that."

"Eat in the evenings?"

"I mean date." He was attractive and nice, and she was tempted. She wanted to, not just for the sex, but to sit across a table from him, flirt, laugh. She wanted to hear more of his deep voice, stare at his sheepish smile. That was why she needed to keep her distance. She didn't need or want more friends, and her life wasn't suited to relationships.

"OK." Sam leaned against the back of the sofa. "I only ask because you've been cooped up in this place for a while. It might be good to go out."

Meena's face burned at her mistake. "I'm sorry. I shouldn't have assumed."

"It's fine," Sam said. "I mean, you're beautiful and I'm not repulsive. We're both single."

"We don't have to talk about it."

"But I want to." Sam gave her a quick wink. "In great depth. Tell me more about why you don't date."

She laughed and her taut muscles relaxed. It surprised Meena how quickly he could put her at ease. "I *have* been craving something that isn't Chinese or pizza."

He stood. "Perfect. There's a place not too far from here. A local favorite. It's got a big menu and a great beer list."

"Sounds good. Dinner, not a date," she clarified.

"Dinner," Sam said. "I'll leave it to you to pick the day. That should give you enough time to do laundry."

"I do not smell."

Sam pinched his nose with his thumb and index finger as he left her apartment.

Automatically Meena locked the door behind him. She stood at the closed door for a while. What would it be like to trust people enough to leave the door to your home unlocked? That was for people who were cared for, had family. Meena took care of herself. She tapped the wooden door and backed away. She didn't touch the lock. She couldn't do it.

CHAPTER ELEVEN

It took a week to get accustomed to the cast, but Meena hadn't made a dent in clearing out the place. She'd managed to pack up the small trinkets that were all over the apartment. Dust catchers in odd shapes and all types of materials. She'd taken her time going through the pieces and seeing if they contained any hidden clues.

She'd found only two. One was a small pink napkin with the chorus of Madonna's "Like a Virgin," the other a grocery store receipt, the back of which held a short quote from *The Scarlet Letter*: "She had not known the weight, until she felt the freedom." Meena had added them to her small collection.

She closed the second box she'd filled and looked around. There were still more things on tables and mantels. It would take a miracle to clear this place out in the next three weeks. She was grateful for the knock at the door, a much-needed distraction from poking around in Neha's life.

"Sabina," Meena answered the door.

Sabina walked in as if it were her right. Dressed in dark pants and a flowing white silk shirt, the woman looked elegant next to Meena in a dusty T-shirt and jeans.

"How are you feeling?" Sabina asked. "What are you doing?"

"Clearing some of these things out."

"Are you sure you're not overdoing it?"

Meena shook her head. Sabina wasn't as friendly as Tanvi or as direct as Uma. She came off as cold.

"I'm managing fine," Meena said.

"Here, sit." Sabina led her to the kitchen table. "Have you eaten?"

Leftover Chinese for breakfast. "Yes."

Sabina began to clear off the takeout containers and wipe down the table.

"You don't have to do that," Meena said.

"You need help. And I'm not injured."

Meena couldn't figure the woman out. On one hand she was distant, almost aloof, and on the other she'd brought Meena food, added sugar to Meena's chai, and wiped down the kitchen counters.

"I spoke with Clifton Warney," Sabina said.

Meena sat up. "How do you know about him?"

"The day after you hurt yourself, we came to help you. You were out of it and mumbled about a few things you had planned to do. I took care of it."

Meena couldn't imagine handing off anything on her list to anyone, not even in a foggy state. "I don't remember."

Sabina brought over two glasses of water and put one in front of Meena. "I asked you about your intentions to rent this apartment out, and you told me things were already in motion. I saw Clifton's business card on the console table by the door and called him. Then I took care of the rest."

"That wasn't your place," Meena argued.

"I did it to save you the trouble," Sabina said. "The units in this building are all owner occupied. It's always been that way and is written very clearly in the building agreement."

"I looked through the paperwork from the lawyers. There was no mention of any kind of rule."

"I can review that paperwork if you'd like," Sabina offered. "It is very clear in the bylaws of the homeowners' agreement, which supersedes anything in the will."

Meena drank her water. She needed to think, and look for this document Sabina had mentioned.

"You don't know much about owning an apartment in a condominium building, do you?" Sabina asked.

Meena shook her head. "It's not my area of expertise."

"Then let me help," Sabina said. "I know your job is to travel everywhere, and having to manage this place from all over the world is not very efficient."

It was true, and in a way it was a bit of a relief if she didn't have the option to rent it out. She hadn't wanted to be a landlord. And she couldn't sell it just yet. But she also wasn't going to hand over everything to Sabina. "I'd like to look through this agreement."

"Of course." Sabina retreated. "I'll email it to you."

Meena rattled off her address, and Sabina typed it in her phone.

"How are you settling in?" Sabina asked.

"I'm used to navigating new places," Meena said. "It doesn't take me long to get situated."

"That's a great skill." Sabina stood and washed out her water glass. "I've traveled a bit myself, but I'm very susceptible to jet lag."

"Some time zones are easier than others."

"Oh, before I forget . . ." Sabina tapped a finger to her chin. "What about your utilities? I was surprised to not get any bills these last few months, and yet everything seems to be in order."

"Yes," Meena said. "It was taken care of by the attorneys until I was able to get here."

"I see."

Sabina's eyes didn't give anything away, but Meena could tell that she didn't like not knowing what was happening. It would be easy to fill Sabina in on the terms, make her an ally of sorts. She held off. She wanted to know more. Not just about Neha but also about Sabina. Meena could tell when someone was angling for information, and Sabina wanted to know something. Meena wasn't sure what that was.

CHAPTER TWELVE

The moaning was her cue. Meena fussed with her hair in the oval mirror next to the front door. The gilded frame added structure to the glass. The distressed sepia-toned console table under it matched in style.

She pursed her lips to set the pink gloss as another moan pealed out from the hall. It was alternately soft and loud. Meena blew away the loose hair that brushed her forehead. This was the best she'd been able to do. The pumpkin-colored beret she'd picked up at the local market tilted to the right, and with a slight shake of her head, it slid off. She gave up and gathered all her hair with the fingers on her casted hand and bound it in a hair tie with her right hand. It was messy, but in an acceptable way.

The moaning reached a crescendo.

"I feel you, robotic ghost," Meena mumbled. She brushed on mascara, then rose on her toes to see as much of her black-clad reflection as possible. She looked like a beatnik from the sixties. She gave one more wistful glance at the beret, shrugged, and accepted that this was the best she could hope for tonight.

It was showtime. She slung her camera on her shoulder, grabbed the package of two hundred small paper cups (recycled), and headed out the door. She ran into Wally in the hall and went to her knees to give him rubs as he jumped around her. She was as excited to see him as he was to play with her.

"Hi!" Meena gave him scratches around his ears. "Oh, I know. I missed you too. It's been a whole six hours since you ran into my apartment and chewed on the strap of my camera bag."

His yips were getting deeper. He was growing up.

"What are you supposed to be?" Meena assessed the dog's costume. He was wrapped in a light-gray blanket with his legs sticking out. A thick fabric cone was wrapped around his neck, and above his ear was a green ball stuck to the inside of the cone.

Wally tilted his head as if puzzled by her curiosity.

"Hey."

She glanced up as Sam closed the door behind him. Meena caught her jaw before it fell. He was in a tuxedo, and his usually messy hair was slicked back. He was clean shaven and smelled like soap and musk. She wanted to rub under his chin instead of Wally's. Meena stood back up. "Hi."

"Mime without a face?" Sam asked.

Meena, confused by his question, tilted her head the same way Wally had.

"Your costume," Sam said.

"A cat without a tail, ears, or whiskers."

"When the aunties ask, say deconstructed mime, or you'll be forced into one of their old outfits," Sam advised. "You definitely do not want that."

"Thanks for the tip," Meena said. "Why so fancy, Sam?"

He picked up Wally, then held out his hand to her as if to shake. "Vora. Sam Vora." His face was serious.

She frowned and shook his hand. It was warm, and she held on a second longer than she should have. "I don't understand."

"Double oh seven," he said. "And Wally is my martini. Shaken, not stirred. One olive."

"Ah, OK."

"You do know what I'm talking about, right?"

"You're James Bond," Meena guessed.

"Exactly," Sam said. "Not impressed?"

"Very fancy."

"I know I'm not Daniel Craig." Sam sighed. "But I think I can pull off Bond. Maybe if I tried for a British accent."

Meena tapped her finger to her chin. "Let's hear it."

"Sounds a bit old-fashioned, doesn't it?" Sam said in an exaggerated British accent. "I mean, pistols at dawn."

"Oh no. No. Don't do that." Meena shook her head.

"It's not that bad, but you have to admit, that's a classic line," Sam said. "*The Man with the Golden Gun*?"

Meena raised her eyebrows.

"What's *your* favorite Bond movie?" Sam asked. "Please don't say *Die Another Day*."

"I haven't seen any of them." Meena laughed at Sam's shocked face. "I'm not a movie person."

His face fell, his shoulders drooped. "That is possibly the saddest thing you could say to me." Wally barked. "My dog agrees."

They both turned as they heard footfalls from above.

"Sam, Meena," Tanvi called out. "Open the door, we're ready."

Meena silently asked Sam to translate.

"Let's get outside." Sam ushered her down the steps. "The aunties make an entrance, or in this case an exit."

He clipped a leash to Wally and handed it to Meena. She followed him out to the front stoop and watched as Sam opened both sides of the front doors. It was the first time she'd seen the space's full width. It made the building seem more welcoming. Meena took Wally down to the path. From where she stood, the Engineer's House was warm yet mighty. The decorations, the lights, the smoke that mimicked fog, all of it gave the house an aura of grandness. She glanced around as the neighbors from other buildings came forward on the sidewalk.

Sam yelled up, "Ready." Then he jogged down to stand with Meena and Wally.

One by one they descended the inside stairwell. Meena lifted the camera to her face to frame and take the photos. It was getting easier, as she rested the body of the camera on the cast and relied a lot more on her dominant hand to keep the camera in place, focus, and click.

Uma stepped out first. She wore a large, dark-brown rectangular box. It was glossy and covered her from neck to knees. Her face stuck out from a cutout at the top. Her arms and legs were clad in dark-brown fitted sleeves and tights. Her shoes were chunky and matched the rest of her. She stood to one side on the front stoop. Then Sabina came through. In the same costume but in all white. She stopped next to Uma. Then Tanvi floated down. The same but in pink. The three drew their arms down straight and moved to stand together so the edges of their boxes touched.

Sam laughed next to her, and the neighbors joined him in applause.

Meena leaned over and whispered, "I don't get it."

"Neapolitan ice cream," Sam said.

Meena saw it and laughed.

"It's candy time." Tanvi held up her cauldron filled with treats.

The kids rushed past them to get their treats. Sam gave her a wave to prod her to the cider station he'd set up at the bottom of the steps. They went to work, pouring warm cider from the silver urn into paper cups for kids and their parents as they came and left with their goodies. Uma handed out full-size HERSHEY'S Bars. Sabina added little boxes of NILLA Wafers. Tanvi dropped in satchels full of strawberry STARBURSTs.

Meena took more photos. She waved a casual hello to the aunties' husbands. She'd seen them in passing, and they'd waved, but she hadn't formally met them. They weren't in costume as they stood in the front yard and mingled with neighbors.

Through her lens, Meena saw the women chat with the kids as they handed out treats. They were in their element. They owned the stoop with their commanding presence. There was a bond among them in the way they stood together, as if they'd done this time and time again. And where had Neha fit in? Alongside them, adjacent, or in opposition? What Meena had learned of Neha so far didn't seem to fit here.

She changed her focus to the miniature superheroes, animals, princesses, ballerinas, zombies, and athletes accompanied by a mix of costumed and noncostumed adults.

Before she outgrew trick-or-treating, Meena had gone around the neighborhood with her mom. Her favorite year was when she'd dressed as Wonder Woman, with her mom as Hippolyta. Her dad had stayed behind to hand out candy at their house. She'd held her mother's hand as they went from door to door. Meena pushed back the memory. She forced herself to focus, as usual, on the images in her lens.

⚘

The urn was empty, the path strewn with ribbons and bows from costume malfunctions. The lively street was now muted as people on surrounding stoops began their cleanup efforts.

The uncles headed inside after bidding everyone good night. The aunties, their costumes discarded, sat wrapped in thick sweaters on the steps and munched on leftover candy and cookies. Meena was next to Sam on the stairs below with Wally sleeping between them. She stroked his fur as he snoozed. He'd had a blast running around the kids as far as the leash would allow. And he'd scored quite a few belly rubs and dog treats.

"Do you always wear a group costume?" Meena asked.

"Since we were little girls," Tanvi said. "We've been condiments, Charlie's Angels . . ."

"The Sanderson sisters from *Hocus Pocus* was fun." Uma popped a cookie in her mouth.

"One year we were Amar, Akbar, and Anthony." Sabina unwrapped a piece of candy.

"I don't know who they are." Meena scratched at the edge of the cast.

Sam shook his head. "She doesn't watch movies."

"That's classic Bollywood," Sabina said.

Tanvi patted Sabina's shoulder. "We should have a movie night."

"I'll bring my DVD of *Goldfinger*," Sam offered.

"No," both Sabina and Uma were quick to reply.

Sam objected. "She's never seen any Bond movies."

Meena frowned. "That doesn't sound like a movie I want to watch."

He gave her an exaggerated hurt look. His bow tie had come loose and hung around his neck. A few curls were winning against whatever product he'd used to slick back his hair. Meena held up her camera. She wanted to capture him like this. Elegance undone.

In profile, he was accessibly handsome. She snapped a few pictures. There were crinkles on the side of his eye as if he laughed and smiled readily. He had a small dimple on the side of his chin. A faint scar next to it. He stared at her. Through the lens. And for a moment, she couldn't look away. She saw the depth in his eyes. There was an abyss within him, if one was willing to search for it.

Uncomfortable, she lowered her camera.

"Sorry," Meena said.

His eyes cleared to cover the depth. "I don't mind modeling for you." The uncomplicated casualness came over his face. "Vora. Sam Vora."

"Your accent needs work, darling." Tanvi spoke in a perfect upper-class British accent.

The aunties laughed.

To break the link between her and Sam, Meena stood and aimed her camera at the aunties. "I want to capture the aftermath." Wally looked up to assure himself that everyone was still there, then flopped his head back down and closed his eyes.

"How did you decide who would be what flavor?" Meena asked.

"We figured it out during our planning meeting," Tanvi said. "Sometimes it's easy and we naturally fall into it. Like of course I'm Curly, Uma is Moe, and Sabina is Larry. It was like that this time."

"Because my personality is dark." Uma made an exaggerated frown.

"According to this one"—Sabina pointed to Uma—"the world is a terrible place, and we have to spend every waking hour making sure we remember."

Uma nudged Tanvi's shoulder. "And try to change it."

"Sabina is very obviously vanilla," Tanvi said.

"Boring," Uma added. "Pristine. Clean. Pure."

Meena captured Sabina's eye roll.

"And Tanvi is tart and sweet." Sabina tossed a piece of candy at Tanvi.

"More tart than sweet," added Uma.

Tanvi fluffed her big updo, which was wrapped in a sparkly chain of glittering glass strawberries.

"I did have more fun than these two in high school," Tanvi said. "Multiple boyfriends until I met my husband in college."

"Pi, right?" Meena recalled the person she'd met earlier. "I chatted with him earlier."

"Yes, Piyush, but Pi for short because he's a math professor and thinks it is funny," Tanvi said. "I humor him because that's the secret to a successful marriage."

"Jiten uncle is married to Sabina auntie." Sam stroked Wally's tired head.

Meena jumped in: "The investment banker."

"And Vin, the lawyer"—Uma popped a cookie in her mouth—"is mine."

"Yes," Meena said. "He was telling me that your daughter is in law school."

"When our children were young," Sabina explained, "our Halloweens were elaborate. All our holidays were. Each one an event."

There was a wistfulness in Sabina's voice. She missed the past.

"I'm fine with it." Uma wiped crumbs off her chest. "Less work. And I'm tired."

"We should clean up." Sam stood. "I'll grab the urn and wash it out."

The aunties stood and picked up their discarded costumes. Wally became aware of the fuss and jumped up.

"I can walk him," Meena said.

"Thank you." Sam gave her a small smile. "That would be great."

Meena led Wally to the end of the path away from the building. The pup sniffed along the ground, weaving from side to side as Meena held on to the leash with her uncased hand. She'd had fun tonight. The occupants of the Engineer's House were interesting and generous with their friendship. She hadn't spent this kind of time with the same people in a while, getting to know them just because they were neighbors.

Wally tugged on the leash to get her to turn around.

"Too tired for a walk?"

Wally tugged again.

"OK, let's go."

As she approached number ten, the building loomed large. The windows were dark, signaling the end of the festivities. The front porch was clear even as the decorations remained. She headed up the front steps. The door had been left ajar. For her. A warmth settled over her. The people inside had thought of her, knew she would be back, and had left the light on for her in the form of a slightly open door. It had been a long time since she'd been expected home.

CHAPTER THIRTEEN

Meena's mother used to say there were two people you could never lie to: God and yourself. Yet over time Meena had honed the traits of denial, avoidance, and evasion when it came to thinking about who she was and where she'd come from. But with the four new pastel-pink Post-it Notes in her hand, Neha's precise handwriting covering almost every millimeter of each one, Meena had no choice. She had to confront the past.

All she'd wanted to do was replace the tissue box under the ceramic fish-head cover. One handed, she'd lifted it off the empty container, and there they were. At first Meena was giddy with excitement. She'd come to love these little missives from Neha.

1. *Boston winter is incomparable. At first, it's like a painting of snow-covered branches. Quiet hovers over the city. Then the scenery changes from bright white to black and sooty. I'm watching two college students dig out a car on the street, their faces red from exertion.*

2. *I hope you've found my little hiding spaces. I found it fun to figure out where to keep these notes. Not too obvious because I couldn't risk Sabina stumbling on them when she cleaned. It's what she will do when I die. Likely with glee. She doesn't*

like me. The feeling is mutual. She doesn't know this, but she won't get this apartment when I'm gone.

3. *I am not a nice person. When you were born, I promised you a life away from here, from me. I don't always keep my promises. Things don't always go according to plan.*

4. *Meena (proper noun)*
   Origin: Sanskrit
   fish
   wife of Shiva

Meena sat in the tall blue armchair next to the fireplace and shuffled the notes with one hand. She took out the others, reviewed them again. So. There it was. The confirmation of what Meena had suspected all along, that Neha was her birth mother. Her mind raced. Her hands shook as she looked at the notes again. Her chest tightened, and Meena breathed through the constriction. She needed to think, not feel. She needed to use her journalist brain, not her orphan brain.

A knock on her door startled her, and Meena stood quickly. The cast made it difficult, but she quickly stuffed everything into her backpack, ran a hand over her face, and took a calming breath before answering.

"If you would leave the door unlocked"—Uma walked inside—"it wouldn't take you so long to get to the door."

"We aren't thieves," Tanvi explained. "We are your neighbors. You don't have to protect anything."

"Except myself." Her voice was curt.

Sabina raised an eyebrow.

Meena adjusted her tone. "It's how I feel safe."

Tanvi walked over to her and cupped her cheek. "You aren't in danger here. We look out for one another. Care for each other."

Meena almost leaned into her gentle affection. It took strength to force herself to step back. She hadn't experienced tenderness in a long time, and she couldn't think about the way Hannah Dave used to cup her cheek the same way.

"Come here, Meena," Sabina said. "Sit at the table. I'm tired of your messy hair. I'm going to braid it so it stays out of your way."

"It's also good to sleep with your hair bound," Tanvi said. "You lose less of it. I put oil in mine at night. That's why it's so healthy and strong. Unlike Uma here."

"I prefer mine short." Uma rubbed the bare back of her neck. "Less fuss."

"How you present your hair," Sabina lectured, "tells the world how well you take care of yourself."

"Or it tells the world that your priority is your vanity," Uma argued. "Where is your brush?"

"My hair is fine," Meena said.

Tanvi laughed. "You do not have aunties in your life, do you?"

"I don't understand."

"When an auntie says she will fix your hair," Tanvi said, "she's not doing you a favor or being nice. She's giving you an order."

Meena shrugged. This wasn't a battle she was going to pick. And not that she would ever admit it, but she did want her hair braided and out of the way. Meena went to her suitcase on the living room floor, took out her travel bag, and handed it to Sabina.

"Sit," Sabina said.

Sabina stood behind her and brushed out and braided her hair, while Tanvi poured chai from a thermos. Sabina wasn't gentle about it, but it felt good to have someone do this one small task for her. And it allowed Meena time to quiet the emotions threatening to escape. She wasn't ready to admit her assumption about the notes, much less talk about it. "Thank you."

"You're welcome." Sabina cleaned out the brush and threw the excess hair in the kitchen bin before washing her hands and joining them at the table.

"You have such a lovely face," Uma said. "With your hair pulled back, your eyes really stand out. Wide and dark. There is a bit of amber in the dark brown. Very striking."

"I will take you to my eyebrow salon." Tanvi clapped her hands. "Just a cleanup—they're so thick. A finely shaped brow can make up for so many beauty flaws."

Meena touched her brow. "What flaws?"

Tanvi laughed. "You don't have any. Yet."

"I will text you the name of my eye cream." Uma reached for her phone. "You're too young for those tiny wrinkles."

"I haven't really been able to . . ."

"And your lips are dry," Sabina said. "Vaseline before bed. Every night."

Had they picked Neha apart like this? Did Meena resemble Neha? Curiosity chafed at her.

"I was wondering why there are no photos in the apartment." Meena picked up the cup Tanvi had put in front of her and let the aroma of chai warm her. She rested her casted arm on the tabletop and crossed her legs in the chair, tucked her bare feet into the nooks of her bent knees.

"Neha wasn't a fan of memories." Tanvi slid a full bowl in front of Meena.

"Upma." Sabina served the rest of them before sitting down in front of her own setting. "It's South Indian. Makes for a hearty breakfast." Sabina added two sugars to Meena's chai.

"It's my specialty," Uma bragged. "My family is from the North, but this is my favorite."

"You all must have photos of her," Meena said.

Tanvi took her seat. "I'm sure we have some. I'll look through some old albums and find a few for you."

"Why the curiosity?" Sabina asked. "You said you didn't know her or why she left this apartment to you."

"I am a journalist," Meena reminded them.

"Unlike this model here"—Uma pointed to Tanvi—"Neha did not like to have her photo taken. Not even during Diwali or Halloween. She avoided the camera."

"Was she shy?"

Uma laughed. "More just being contrary."

Meena let the topic drop and scooped up a spoonful from her bowl. It had a texture like grits and contained finely diced carrots, peas, and onions. Crunchy yellow lentils broke up the mushy texture. Flavors exploded in her mouth. She could normally handle heat, but she hadn't been expecting the bite from the green chilis to hit the back of her throat first thing. She coughed and took a sip of hot chai.

"It isn't very spicy." Uma took another bite.

A lie. "I grew up on meat and potatoes," Meena said.

"No seasoning?" Sabina asked.

Meena held the cup of chai with both hands, taking in the warmth. "Salt, mustard, black pepper, occasionally garlic, and lots of herbs my mom grew in the garden."

"But what about cumin and turmeric? Cloves, asafetida. There are hundreds of spices that meld in a million different ways to flavor food," Uma said. "Didn't your mother cook?"

"It wasn't a priority for her." Meena defended her mom: "She was a botanist. Her career came first."

"That makes sense," Uma agreed. "I don't cook if I can avoid it."

Meena was glad the aunties hadn't picked up on the past tense when she mentioned her mother.

"The trick is to marry someone who can," Tanvi said. "My husband is very good in the kitchen. *And* the bedroom."

Meena almost choked on her tea. "Congratulations."

"Don't encourage her," Sabina said.

Tanvi winked at Meena. "Human sexuality is perfectly fine to discuss, even in mixed company. Or I should say especially in mixed company."

Meena liked Tanvi. There was always a smile on her round face, and she dressed artistically, always wearing long velvet dresses and her hair adorned with chains, pins, and ribbons. Her eyes were lined, with a flare on the outer edges. Meena wondered if Neha's patchwork style had ever clashed with Tanvi's aesthetic, or if Neha had ever sat there with the three of them as they discussed food and sex.

"Speaking of," Tanvi teased. "What do you think of our Sam?"

Meena put her cup down. "He's nice."

"Meh," Tanvi grumbled. "Potato chips are nice. What do you think of him as a man? A single, handsome man?"

Meena ate a little more, in small bites to manage the heat level. "I didn't notice."

"You are a bad liar," Tanvi observed. "Your eyes look away and your nose twitches."

Mena dropped her spoon. Her mom used to say the same thing. A wave of longing washed over her. She breathed through it and picked up the mug.

Tanvi sighed and rested her elbow on the table. The dozen or so bracelets she wore on her wrist clinked with the movement. "Sam needs company, and I can tell that he likes you."

Meena kept her voice casual. "As a person. Besides, he likes everybody."

"Not so," Sabina muttered.

Meena glanced at her, but Sabina didn't repeat her words.

"I'm sure he has friends," Meena said.

"Yes. Dinus, Ava, and Luis." Uma counted them out on her hand. "But he's all work all the time. He needs a girlfriend, a woman. Sam is the type who will do well with a wife. He's good husband material."

"We've trained him well," Tanvi added. "In all the things. Well, not *all* the things. But I'm sure he's gained experience in that area as well."

Meena wasn't prone to blushing, but her face warmed at the idea of Sam's level of sexual experience. Alas. Sam wasn't one-night-stand material.

"It would be good for him to settle down," Sabina stated. "Maybe with a nice Indian woman. It isn't that way anymore in our culture, though it used to be."

"We are always evolving," Uma said. "For the better."

"There is something to be said for shared culture, language, and tradition," Sabina argued.

Meena sipped her chai to swallow the lump in her throat. She'd been telling herself it was OK to not know her cultural identity. Her parents, their culture, had been enough. But her connection with Neha wasn't only biological; heritage and legacy came with knowing.

"And all those can be taught," Uma quipped. "My daughter's girlfriend is Ecuadorian. They swap recipes and cook for each other. They celebrate her holiday traditions and ours."

"Sameer's family would prefer that he stayed within our culture," Sabina said. "The Voras have always been more conservative. His grandfather was a staunch Hindu who made his expectations known to his children and grandchildren."

"His grandfather is dead," Uma barked. "Besides, expectations aren't the same as rules. He's his own man."

"Sam's younger brother is married to a British Gujarati woman." Tanvi turned to Meena. "They just had their third child. Sadly, Sam hasn't met his niece. Maybe never will."

"Why?"

"He's estranged from his family," Uma added. "So much for following tradition."

Meena caught the glance Uma sent Sabina. They were speaking about things Meena had no context for, and she genuinely wanted to know.

"His family lives in Europe?"

"Munich," Tanvi said. "The parents went to live with his younger brother's family."

"What about you?" Sabina asked. "You said your mother was a botanist. Is she retired?"

"She died." These women were sharp and remembered everything. Meena needed to be more on guard, especially while she was feeling raw. "So did my father." Meena didn't wait for the question that had been coming. Headed it off to close off the topic.

Tanvi reached over and patted Meena's hand. She had to close her eyes against another kind gesture.

"It was a long time ago," Meena specified. "I was sixteen."

"Oh no." Tanvi patted her hand. "Did you stay with other family?"

Meena channeled the script she used on the rare occasion that this topic came up. "It was an accident. They were great parents. I had an amazing childhood, and I have a good life."

"You've been on your own," Sabina said.

"I'm good at it."

"That doesn't mean you aren't lonely," Uma said.

"No matter." Tanvi squeezed her hand. "Now you have us. And Sam."

"Stop your matchmaking," Uma chided. "This is a sensitive moment."

Meena jumped at the change in topic. "He did ask me to have dinner."

"When?" Tanvi asked. "Where? Oh, we need to go shopping. I've seen you in the same jeans and sweaters, and you have to add a little more color into your wardrobe."

Like Neha.

"My clothes are fine." Meena straightened the hem of her gray T-shirt with her free hand. "I can't have too much, or it won't fit in my suitcase. Besides, Sam and I don't have firm plans."

"It's a start." Uma grinned. "My husband asked me to dinner after our graduate-level economics class, and a year later we were married."

Meena leaned away from the table. "Uh, that's not . . ."

"Don't scare her," Sabina said.

"I'll design the wedding invitations." Tanvi patted the cast twice.

Horror came over Meena's face. She finished off the chai in her mug and stood.

"Sit back down." Tanvi reached for Meena. "I was joking with you."

"I need a shower." Meena walked away from them.

She needed to escape. Not just the room and the aunties, but this apartment, this city, the state of Massachusetts.

When she came out of the bathroom, the aunties had thankfully left. She locked the front door. She had to do, not think. Her chest would not loosen, she couldn't take a deep enough breath. Panic, pain, and discomfort clogged her throat. She had parents, she reminded herself. She wouldn't let Neha mean anything. She knew one more thing about herself than she had yesterday. That was all. In the meantime, she had emails to check. Meetings to schedule.

Then she saw it. A lifeline in the form of a message from *Condé Nast Traveler*. She was needed far away from here.

CHAPTER FOURTEEN

Meena was in Slippbarinn, Reykjavík's first cocktail bar. The three blond men in her viewfinder laughed as they flexed and performed for the camera. She laughed at their antics. They were enjoying themselves. She took a few more photos of a bartender mixing drinks behind a sturdy bar made of wooden slats. The cocktail shelves behind him glowed red, green, and white. A few days on assignment and she'd managed well with the cast; instead of letting it frustrate her, she had adapted and adjusted to make it work.

The crowd was sparse, likely because it was just past 5:00 p.m. local time, even though the sky outside was deep black. This was her third establishment of the day for the quick story on bar culture in Reykjavík. She'd first gone to Pablo Discobar, an upscale place for expats and people who could afford expensive cocktails, then to Kaldi Bar, a beer experience. Slippbarinn was her last stop of the day. The exhaustion she'd thought she'd left behind weighed her down. The assignment felt like a means to an end. She didn't feel her usual spark of interest, her joy at finding the right shot to convey the message.

Meena turned her camera back to the laughing faces of the three guys and snapped a few more shots of the brightly lit place. They'd already signed the photo releases so they could be part of the story. Iceland bars didn't have a lot of rules, and on weekend nights they stayed open until 4:30 a.m. It was just the kind of assignment she needed right now: quick, not a lot of prep, and distracting. She'd been here for three days so far, and she'd barely thought about the Engineer's House.

Or at least she'd tried not to think about it.

Got a quick assignment. Off to Iceland.

She'd left a note taped to her front door, just under the new cornucopia wreath that Sabina had swapped for the Halloween one. She'd left the apartment unlocked and taken a late-night flight. From Reykjavík she'd go straight to Manhattan and get those editor meetings back on the calendar. Then Christmas in London, then on to the next assignment.

She'd deal with the apartment in April.

She took the strap off her neck to roll the stiffness out.

A blond with big curls and glasses approached her and took a seat on a square wooden barstool. He was cute in a boyish way, like Sam, though they looked nothing alike. This one was in his late twenties and built for battering down opponents in a sporting arena, with thick thighs and a broad chest. She watched the flex of his forearm as he raised a pint to his lips.

He winked at her. "I'm Odkell."

She gave him a friendly smile. An evening's distraction was just what she needed to put the last month in the rearview. This was how she lived her life. Fun nights that ended with her knowing that there was little chance of seeing the other person again.

"Meena."

"Pretty name," Odkell said. "I like the look of you."

"I'm not certain about the look of you."

He laughed in a baritone. "I find that vodka helps."

"That's not a strong selling point." She was done taking photos for the night and ordered a martini from the bartender.

He shifted to face her. "My face is not enough? You demand more. Fine. I play football. Not for the national team, but I know a few of the players. This is a small island."

"I'm not a sports person."

He took her hands in his. "I'm a, um, *klár*." He tapped his head.

"Smart?"

"Yes." He smiled wide, showing off his crooked teeth. "You know Icelandic?"

"No, only a few words, phrases I picked up while preparing for this trip." Another word came to Meena, from Neha's notes. "Window weather."

"*Gluggaveður,*" Odkell translated. "It's a very common phrase. The tourists like it. Where did you hear it?"

She paused. "I read it somewhere." *In a note written to me by a woman who is probably my birth mother.*

He rubbed the palm of her hand with his fingers. "What happened to your arm?"

"A silly injury." She took her hand from his.

"I see I have lost my chance before I tried. Want to get drunk instead?" Odkell raised his glass. "I promise I am safe."

Meena laughed. "I'm not a big drinker."

"Ah, in Iceland it is our national pastime." Odkell finished off his drink. "I will teach you."

Meena watched as he held up two fingers and ordered Reyka vodka. She'd have a drink or two, but she wasn't going to get drunk with him. Though her instincts told her she would be safe, it wasn't her style. She was responsible for herself, and she didn't take that responsibility lightly. She laughed and raised her vodka. "*Skol.*"

He tapped his glass to hers and shot it in two gulps. "How long will you stay?"

"I leave tomorrow," Meena said.

"Back home?"

The word shot through her. A sharp memory of the front door being left ajar for her on Halloween night made her body tense. Her heart ached from that small gesture by people she had gotten to know. People who had been kind to her even when Meena hadn't been receptive.

"Did I say something wrong?"

"No." Meena shook her head. "Just a memory."

He gave her a broad grin. "You haven't lived if you are not trying to forget."

She gave him a soft smile.

"My grandfather says it," Odkell said. "It's our family motto. We believe in making mistakes and having regrets. As long as it hurts no one."

"But it's OK if you hurt yourself?"

He shrugged. "Why not? It is your experience. If you die, it is a good way to go."

"You're not afraid?"

"Of pain? No. I am a good healer," Odkell answered. "I have scars as my memories. To fear is to torture yourself." Odkell put his hand on hers and squeezed. "Drink more. I can see that sadness is coming for you. I will tell you a joke and make it go away." He took her hand in both of his. "What do you do if you get lost in an Icelandic forest?"

Her forehead bunched up.

"Stand up."

She tilted her head.

"Because we have very short trees." He laughed at his own joke.

Meena patted his hands. "You can add *hilarious* to your list of considerations."

"I will," Odkell said. "It was lovely to meet you, Meena. And don't be afraid, *já*? You will survive it."

"Or there's always Reyka."

He lifted another full glass and drank deep. She patted his shoulder, grabbed her backpack, and walked out into the dark, frigid night. Luckily her hotel was only a few minutes' walk. The icy air filled her chest. It was clean, pure. There was no scent of chimney smoke, no tall Victorian buildings. Meena looked up at the night sky. It seemed closer here. She raised her gloved hand to it to trace the stars. The counselor at the foster residence used to tell her that he believed people became stardust when they left the earth. She'd silently fought against his new-age philosophy. Even though Hannah and Jameson Dave lived in the arty town of Northampton, they were too pragmatic for crystals and Reiki.

The stars twinkled above her. Meena stood in the middle of the quiet street and searched. Whether it was because of the vodka, the crisp chill, or something else, she let the memories in. There on a street with a very long name, the love she'd had for her parents, from them, enveloped Meena.

She reached up to trace the stars that looked much like the ones she'd glued to the ceiling of her childhood bedroom. Space was infinite and empty, but her father would say that it was full of matter. Meena had interpreted that as meaning it was full of what mattered. Tears froze on her face as they slid down her cheeks and continued to flow as she walked into her hotel and up the steps to her room. For the first time in a long time, she allowed herself to miss them.

Half an hour later, stripped of her outer layers, Meena lay on her bed and stared into the darkness. It had been a rash thing to do, escape when she was faced with the truth. It felt childish. She wasn't sixteen anymore. She'd traveled the world. She'd gotten to know people, the ones she worked with and the subjects of her stories. She'd formed bonds in tough situations, but she hadn't let people in. Not in any substantive way. She'd listened to stories of hopes, dreams, fears, and loss, but rarely had Meena shared hers with anyone.

She felt raw and needy. Maybe she'd felt exhausted on arriving in Boston not because she was tired of traveling, but because she was weary from keeping her memories contained. She had dealt with the loss of her parents with two years of therapy right after they'd died. But she'd left it all behind when she went off to college. Never looked back. Never gone back. She'd made a promise to herself that she wouldn't let anyone matter that much to her ever again.

As she drifted to sleep, she heard Odkell's words again and again: *You will survive it.*

CHAPTER FIFTEEN

Meena jolted awake from a nightmare that had her pinned against a wall by a giant ceramic fish while squat trees advanced on her like an arboreal army. She rubbed her face and rolled onto her side to give her sore back relief. The couch was losing its comfort, her body discovering the lumps in the cushions. She should use the bed, wash the sheets, maybe splurge on a new comforter and pillows. The sofa had become a way to keep things impermanent.

In the end, she knew she needed to see this through. It was less than two months until Christmas. She would take the time, stay off the road, and stay in Boston to clear out the apartment. She'd get it ready and find ways to feel out the aunties so that in April, one of them might want it. After that, she'd get back to work. It was a solid plan.

Meena padded to the bathroom and then the kitchen for a cup of tea. Had it been only a month since she'd done the same her first morning here?

She hadn't known about her roots then. Her brown skin came with expectations. People wanted to know her ethnicity, her origin. When she'd say she didn't know, some were offended, as if she purposefully did not want to answer. Others, thinking they were being helpful, made assumptions. She'd learned, in her travels, how ingrained some beliefs were.

At least now, when she looked in the mirror, she could see the markers of similarity between her and the aunties, between her and Sam. They had different shades to their skin, but the shapes of their brows, the bone structure. It was hard to describe that while they did not look alike, there was a familiarity in their looks. She was part of a race, a culture. There was a specificity she could acknowledge. It was a blood-and-bone connection.

She knew nothing about the rest of her heritage except the westernized versions of foods, the little pockets of Indian culture in movies and books. She knew what a sari was but had never worn one. And likely never would. She wasn't here to learn how to be Indian. She was here because . . .

What would it be like to belong?

The thought broke in, unbidden, while Meena made a cup of tea. She squeezed the tea bag and tossed it in the bin.

Ignoring the thought, she ran through her mental checklist: supermarket for fresh staples to offset takeout. She didn't cook, but she could make a decent salad with a few fresh ingredients and a lemon-mustard dressing. She opened the cabinets to take inventory. If it wasn't expired, she would use it. Hannah Dave had not raised a wasteful daughter. There wasn't much. A few dishes and bowls. Not a lot of cookware.

On her way back to the living room, Meena jostled the notepad attached to the fridge, and it fell to the floor. As she picked it up to put it back, she saw a little pocket on the cardboard where the magnet was attached. A slit, a sleeve. She picked at it until she freed what was inside. Two business cards, for an electrician and a contractor, respectively. On the back of one, though, the small, crisp handwriting.

The English language is complex and simple at the same time. It's the meaning of the word that matters. Language lives and evolves with every utterance. Does it matter where the apostrophe goes if you understand the meaning from the sentence? And the labels. Noun: a person, place, or thing, but not always. Hope is a noun. So is murder.

CHAPTER SIXTEEN

A day after she'd come back, she'd run into Sam and Wally. He'd taken her departure and return in stride, had asked a few questions with genuine interest, and had asked her to dinner.

A few days later, Meena met him in the foyer. The slim side table held a fresh bouquet of purple and white dahlias. There was a hint of cinnamon in the air from the potpourri bowl next to the vase. Meena gave Sam a slight wave as he stepped out of his apartment. In a simple pale-blue sweater, dark-brown jacket, and jeans, he was casual. This time his hair wasn't slicked down, just brushed back, the curls falling as they wished.

"Sounds like Wally doesn't want you to leave," Meena said.

Sam sighed as he closed the door behind him. "We both need some time away from each other. He'll settle. I gave Tanvi strict instructions not to bring him out of his crate."

"Tough love." Meena felt bad for the puppy and for Sam.

"The training videos on YouTube say it's good for him. We don't want him to have separation anxiety every time I leave him home."

"You think the aunties will stay away?"

"I can only hope."

It was dusk, even though it was just past five thirty. Tonight the clocks would change. She used to hate it when daylight saving ended.

Remembered leaving school in the dark even though it was barely four. Perpetual darkness. She never liked this side of fall and winter.

"How was your trip?"

"It was good, productive."

"Iceland bars. Sounds fun."

She told him about the people she'd met and repeated the joke Odkell had told her.

"Tanvi mentioned your door was locked again," Sam mentioned. "That's how she knew you were back."

"I haven't seen them yet," Meena said.

"Everything OK?"

"What do you mean?"

"You seem, I don't know, sad?"

She gave him a wobbly smile. "I'm tired. I've been wrestling with some things, and I can't seem to stop thinking about it."

"I'm a good listener," Sam offered.

"I know," Meena said. "I'm still sorting out the words to explain when I don't know what's going on myself."

"I get it."

"It's not that big of a deal." *Just a career crisis and finding my birth mother, who is dead, while finally mourning my real parents, who died when I was sixteen.*

They walked for a bit, and Meena appreciated that Sam didn't have the need to fill every pause. As they neared the Public Garden, the street was busy with people cutting through on their way home from work or to meet friends. A few who didn't mind the crisp chill in the air sat on benches. She wondered if Neha had spent much time in the large park in the middle of the city.

"I looked up Neha's obituary," Meena said.

"I was the one who wrote it."

"Not the aunties?"

"Sabina planned the funeral, Uma took care of the food, Tanvi the flowers. Their husbands performed the rites, and I wrote the obituary."

"You each had a role."

"We went with our strengths."

"What about her parents?" *My grandparents?*

"Sabina reached out to them," Sam said. "Neha didn't have much of a relationship with them. At their age, they weren't up for a long flight from Nairobi."

"The aunties must miss her."

Sam gave a short laugh. "Probably. They had their challenges."

"Neha wasn't part of their trio?"

"Not like they are to each other, no."

They walked through the lush colors of the Public Garden and over the footbridge. As dusk gave way to night, Boston's skyline gleamed through the yellowing weeping willows. Leaves crunched under her boots. She tucked her hands into the pockets of her jacket. The brisk air was cool and comforting on her face.

"This used to be the world's shortest functioning suspension bridge, until the 1920s," Sam pointed out.

"Interesting."

"I didn't say that to impress you. A few friends and I belong to a pub trivia league, and I know a lot of random facts."

"This isn't something you learned on your annual walk of the Freedom Trail?"

He laughed. "I will have you know that we aren't currently on it. If you look down and see red lines, that's the marker."

"I know." Meena recalled the long bus rides as a kid. "We used to come to Boston on history school trips."

"I remember those," Sam said. "I can't tell you how many times I've been on the USS *Constitution*."

"And the Bunker Hill Monument."

"In all your travels, what's been your favorite place?" Sam asked.

They crossed over from the Public Garden and headed into Boston Common. Meena thought about his question. "That's tough to answer. It depends."

"On?"

Meena looked over at the white gazebo as the footpath sloped up. "The assignment. I love the wildness of Scotland, the people of Vietnam, the expansiveness of Alaska. There's always something about a place."

"What about just to be, to go on vacation?"

"I've never taken one of those."

They crossed Beacon Street and headed up Beacon Hill. The architecture changed. The streets became narrower, the row houses smaller. The streetlamps gave the area a Victorian feel. She could almost hear horses clomping through the street.

"Why not?"

Meena shrugged. "I guess since I'm always on the road, it never occurred to me."

Sam sighed. "That makes sense, just extend time wherever you are to explore or relax."

Meena let him assume. Relaxing wasn't something she did well. That was why she meditated. She couldn't imagine lying on the beaches in Indonesia without purpose. The next thing was always waiting. Maybe that was all she needed. A long vacation. Except she couldn't get away from her thoughts. "What about you? Your favorite place?"

"I like London," he said. "I spent a couple of years there working. I traveled a lot when I was based there. Spain, Belgium, Sweden."

"I'm based there—in London," Meena said. "Well. Sort of. I was in Seoul before that."

"Where's home?"

"I don't have one." It was a reflex answer. The truth, that her home had exploded when she was a teenager, wasn't something people responded well to.

"I can't imagine what that would be like," Sam said. "I need a home. One place. I like knowing my neighborhood. The bakery, the restaurants where I've eaten so often they don't even hand me a menu. I like the change of seasons outside of my window. The daily routine, the steadiness."

"I like having to think for a few minutes when I wake up about where I am and why. The unpredictability of what's ahead is energizing."

They crossed through Beacon Hill and turned right on very busy Cambridge Street.

"Here we are." Sam stopped in front of the restaurant. "Tip Tap Room."

It was noisy, and there were large and small tables scattered throughout the big room. They followed the hostess and passed the long bar full of people, pints in hand, laughing and chatting away. As she took the menu from the server, for the first time in a while, Meena felt a little lighter, less tired from the weight of her listlessness.

"This is nice," she said. "I'm glad we decided to go out."

He raised his eyebrows.

She laughed. "You know what I mean."

He laughed. "I'm glad to have dinner, not a date, with you."

She hid her sheepish smile behind the giant menu. A trio played pop in the corner, the singer vocalizing over the din of the crowd. The air was heavy with the smell of fried food and hops. People around them laughed and joked, some singing along. She couldn't remember the last time she'd enjoyed someone's company in such a relaxed way. Her camera was a mile away from here, and to her great surprise, she didn't mind at all.

CHAPTER SEVENTEEN

In chair pose, Meena squatted and reached her arms out. She'd been practicing yoga since college because it balanced her and helped her stay strong. There weren't many yoga poses she could do with a cast on one arm, but she liked the practice of strength and stretching. She'd never been a runner, or an athlete of any sort. Built like bones over skin, she'd been called Skeletor by childhood bullies. She liked that with yoga she could increase the strength of her small muscles *and* rest her noisy mind.

Yoga was an ancient Indian practice, and she wondered if she was genetically inclined to bend and flex in such ways. In the past few days, Meena had come around to the idea that it would be good to learn a little more about India. From the aunties, she'd learned some in-culture things like that Indians do not say *naan bread*. Naan is a type of bread like a bagel or baguette. And it's not *chai tea* because *chai* literally means tea.

She'd even downloaded a language-learning app to see if she could pick up some Hindi words, if her tongue would form the sounds. She wasn't in the weeds reading ancient texts, but more at the Wikipedia level of knowledge, just learning enough to get a taste. She didn't *feel* Indian, if that was a thing.

A loud thud in the hall jolted her. She came out of her pose and opened the door.

"Everything OK?"

"Oh, fine." Tanvi moved two large, flat, square marble tiles on either side of Meena's doorframe. "It slipped, they're heavy."

"What are they?"

"Decorative," Tanvi explained. "It's for Diwali. I create the rangoli for all our entry doors. Uma secures electric votive candles on the stairwell and front porch. Sabina cooks all the food."

Meena understood about a third of what was said. "Do you need help?"

"Let's see how artistic you are."

Crouching, Tanvi pushed forward a tray filled with small bowls of powder in blues, greens, reds, oranges, pinks, yellows, and white. She took a pinch of the white and made a small circle in the center of the other marble tile. It had a rim, so the powder would likely stay if it wasn't jostled.

Meena sat next to Tanvi to watch her work. Tanvi added other colors, and an intricate design took form, a small paisley shape with little flowers surrounding it, all created with silky dust. "You have a very delicate hand. Steady."

Tanvi beamed. The bangles on her wrist jingled as she continued to work. "Thank you. I paint, sculpt, and even have a pottery wheel. This is simply another medium."

"I see," Meena said. "And this is part of the celebration?"

"The festival of lights." Tanvi drew an outline with white powder. "The culmination of good over evil. Some Hindus celebrate Diwali as a season that can last multiple weeks. In Gujarat, for example, it starts with Navratri; then there are also days in between that are celebrated by different observers of different gods and goddesses. It all culminates with the Indian New Year."

Meena knew a little about Diwali, but not much. "Is it a religious holiday?" She had been raised Catholic. Faith had been a ritual in her childhood, Easter Mass and Midnight Mass. She'd been baptized, received Communion. It was important to her parents, and she'd participated. She hadn't set foot in a church since her parents' funeral. What good was God if he couldn't prevent a home explosion?

Tanvi laughed. "It's all a mix of things. During Diwali, some people, like Sabina, fast and go to the mandir, do all the religious rituals. Uma celebrates by eating and making special food, snacks and sweets, things like that. I like the color, the lights, the community, the socializing parts of it."

"Are most Indian holidays like that?"

"Yes," Tanvi said. "Even Raksha Bandhan, a day a sister celebrates her brother. You tie a raakadi, a bracelet, around your brother's wrist and do a little religious pooja. Then everyone eats and enjoys being together."

"What if you don't have a brother?"

Tanvi winked at her. "There's always a cousin around. We don't have a word for cousin in Gujarati. Everyone is brother or sister, no matter how far or distant."

"Just like everyone is uncle or auntie," Meena said.

"It doesn't matter if you share blood or not. Everyone is related."

"What did you call this?" Meena asked, gesturing to the marble.

"Rangoli," Tanvi said. "In India they use flower petals as well as powders. In ancient Hindu epics, it was written that rangoli was used by unmarried girls as a way of praying for a good husband. Speaking of, how was dinner with Sam last week?"

Meena laughed. She admired Tanvi for her determined matchmaking.

"It was only dinner," Meena stated. "Nothing more."

"I used to have dinner with my husband." Tanvi grinned. "Before he proposed."

"You're not funny."

"And you're not seeing what is right in front of you. You are both single, around the same age, well educated, and about the same level of attractiveness. Not to mention that I've noticed the little looks between you, the way you smile when you're around each other."

"Can I try?" Meena asked.

"Fine. Change the subject." Tanvi held out the tray.

Meena took a pinch of green between the fingers of her uncased hand and gently drizzled it in the empty space, mimicking the pattern Tanvi had created. "This is very cool. The powder is so soft, like silk." Her fingers were covered in green, and she shared the damp towel Tanvi had used to clean up between colors, then chose bright orange, a bit of gold, and white to finish the slab. "The marble is interesting. It holds the powder well."

"It's the same type used to build the Taj Mahal," Tanvi said. "I had it shipped over from Agra when I went for a visit about a decade ago. Ten squares, two for each door. Then I treated it, roughed it up a little to make the texture grainy enough to hold powder."

"It's beautiful."

"Have you been?" Tanvi asked. "In all of your travels, did you ever go to India?"

Meena shook her head. She wondered if she would have found a sense of belonging if she'd gone. "No. I've been to a lot of countries in Southeast Asia but never had an assignment in India."

"Your work sounds so glamorous."

Meena laughed. "The opposite. It's a lot of couch surfing, traveling in coach, and squeezing in as much as possible to meet tight deadlines."

"Then this must be nice," Tanvi said. "A little break."

"Yeah." It was turning out to be a little more than that, but she'd stayed put, and that was something.

"You need to explore," Tanvi exclaimed. "Go out and make friends. Date Sam."

"You're tenacious."

"Start small, then. Sabina has a big Diwali dinner for all of us. Put it in your calendar."

Meena nodded. "Did Neha help decorate?" She bit her lip. The curiosity would not leave her.

Tanvi glanced at Meena. "You want to know about her."

"I'm staying in her home." Meena shrugged a shoulder.

Tanvi sat down, her back against a wall, her arms around her knees. "I'm not sure how to describe someone I've known my whole life. She liked to dance. Garba. It's part of the Gujarati pre-Diwali festivities. For nine nights, we dance during Navratri. Neha liked to go to the suburbs on the weekends, where people hosted dances in high school gyms."

"Alone?"

Tanvi laughed. "Sometimes. Uma and I went with her a few times. She had a lot of stamina. Garba starts late, around nine at night, and doesn't end until one or two in the morning. But she loved being on that hardwood floor all night, continuously dancing in circles."

The door across the hall opened, and Wally charged at the two of them. Tanvi screeched. Meena caught the puppy with her good arm and held him against her. He yipped. His body wriggled for freedom.

"Oh no." Sam ran out the door. "I'm so sorry."

"It's OK." Meena grabbed the runaway dog with her free arm. "I got him before he did any damage."

"Tanvi auntie?"

"I'm fine." Tanvi held the tray of powders out of reach. "You're going to have to carry him around from now until after Diwali. Or he'll be covered in color like Holi."

Sam reached down and scooped Wally up. "I didn't know it was that time."

"We're a little late in decorating. Diwali is early this year." Tanvi looked at Meena. "And we had to finish Halloween."

"You didn't call me to get the marble out of the basement," Sam said.

"I made Pi do it." Tanvi waved his comment off. "That was his contribution this year. Meena, I will need you later when I do the lights outside."

"Text me," Sam said.

"I was just asking Meena about your date, Sam."

Meena's eyes widened. This woman was relentless. "I explained that it was dinner."

"We had a good time." Sam shoved his hands in the front pockets of his jeans.

"Don't encourage her," Meena groaned.

"That's good." Tanvi wiped her hand on the artist's apron she wore. "When is the next one?"

Meena turned to Sam. "See what I mean?"

"I was actually coming to ask about that." He laughed.

"Oh, isn't that nice." Tanvi winked at Meena.

Meena glared at Sam. He smirked.

"A few of my friends and I are doing an escape room in the North End this weekend, if you'd like to join us."

"He means you." Tanvi nudged Meena. "But Sam, a group date? Aren't you too grown up for that?"

"I'm taking things slow," Sam clarified. "Meena's skittish."

He seemed to be teasing, or at least Meena hoped so. She didn't like the idea that he might want to pursue her in any real way.

"So, want to come?"

"Uh."

"Sunday afternoon."

"She's free," Tanvi answered on Meena's behalf.

"How do you know?" asked Meena.

"You never leave your apartment."

"I could have plans." Meena tried to think of a way out of the invitation.

"Do you?"

"No."

"Great," Sam said. "I'll knock on your door around two. Enjoy decorating. Tanvi auntie, can you make sure my designs are more . . ."

"Geometric," Tanvi finished. "I know. I know."

"Thank you."

He walked outside with Wally in his arms.

"He does not like the paisleys and flowers," Tanvi said. "Grids, squares, triangles, sharp angles. I don't mind because it challenges me to make something pretty using straight lines."

Meena followed Tanvi's pattern on the slab on the other side of her door. She let out a long breath. This was more relaxing than meditation. Tanvi was fun and chatty. Whenever Meena made a mistake, Tanvi didn't scold her, only went over her work and fixed any flaws. Finished with hers, they moved across the hall to Sam's slabs. Tanvi hummed under her breath. Meena asked her about the tune, and Tanvi began to sing a Hindi song in response. They worked together until they finished the slabs in front of each apartment.

"Thank you," Tanvi said. "You're not too bad at this."

Meena laughed. "Because you cleaned up a lot of what I did."

Tanvi stood, tray in hand. "Still. It was nice to have your company."

"I had fun." Meena waved goodbye and headed back down to her place. She grabbed her camera to take pictures. She felt a little thrill of energy, the joy of seeing art through her camera—not for an assignment, but for herself, for the pleasure of marking the moment, making note of a memory. Riding on the high, she decided to send a few pictures to Zoe as a way of saying hi and checking in.

She went inside to search for her phone and couldn't find it. Thinking back to when and where she'd last used it, she retraced her steps to the side chair where she'd left her external hard drives. She felt around between the back and the cushion. "Aha." She pulled out the phone. Beneath it she felt paper. It could be the cushion tag. She tugged at it. The papery plastic came off in her hand, and she flipped it over. Meena sighed. Neha's handwriting, in black marker.

Sam is my favorite. Of all who have come and gone, he's the one who gets me. He lets me be. Right now, he's helping Sabina with the roses in the back garden. They must be just so, and never a twig out of place. She's dictating the perfect height of the grass. Sam is following her instructions. He has patience I do not possess. I would prefer the back garden to be messy and grow wild. There is beauty in chaos.

Meena shoved the note into the envelope. *A little too on the nose with this one, Neha.* She ignored it. There would be another one. Of that Meena was sure. For now she wasn't going to let Neha's little notes take away from her cheery mood. She went back and snapped some photos with her phone and sent them to Zoe.

Finally it felt as if she was on a break.

CHAPTER EIGHTEEN

Meena walked alongside Sam's friends Ava, Dinus, Luis, and Xenia as they wound their way through the North End after a victorious escape room adventure. The narrow streets intersected with each other without rhyme or reason. The buildings all touched, and all housed apartments on top, small restaurants at street level. Even on a crisp mid-November evening, the odor of seafood fried in garlic lingered in the air.

Two hours trapped in a room full of puzzles wasn't something Meena had thought she would enjoy. Surprisingly, it had been fun. Sam's friends had all gone to MIT, so she'd puffed out her chest a little when she'd solved the final puzzle to unlock the faux prison. They'd all surrounded her in a group hug she'd strained against. She wasn't used to casual hugs from people she'd just met. In her travels she respected and took part in cultural norms like double cheek kisses in Europe and bowing in Asian countries. And hey, this was the American way to celebrate a win, right? What was the harm?

They walked through the North End to go to the Bell in Hand, an old pub around the corner from the famous Union Oyster House.

The bar was quiet for a Sunday evening. It was entirely made up of wood, from the floor to the tables to the bar. A few people stood around in the open floor space. Ava passed them and grabbed a tall table along the windows, and half the group went to the bar to get drinks.

Once they'd settled around the table, they rehashed the game, bragged about solving the hard puzzles, teased each other for missing the easy ones. Their rhythm was based on familiarity. Meena wished she had her camera with her. No. She would just be. That was her new thing. No camera, no work, no thinking. Just living in the moment.

"Where are you off to next?" Luis asked Meena.

"London."

"Or you could stick around for a while." Sam shrugged.

His face was open and earnest. He meant it. "My work isn't suited for that." What she really wanted him to understand was that she wasn't the type to stay in one place, not in a forever sort of way. Even if she didn't sell the apartment, if she made it her US base, she wouldn't really live there. Not in the way most people lived in a place.

Ava jumped into the conversation. "You should definitely stay. Boston over the holidays is amazing. Skating on the Frog Pond. The tree lighting at Faneuil Hall. The Santa Speedo Run. The Holiday Pops at Symphony Hall. The library and Copley Square decorations."

"She gets the idea," Xenia said. "You don't have to be a real-life version of the Boston events website."

"Pshaw." Ava waved her hand. "I know more about secret Boston than you will ever find on the internet."

"I make cookie tins for everyone," Dinus boasted. "This year, in Meena's honor, I'll do cookies from around the world. If you stay, you'll get a special batch."

A memory flashed in her mind and cracked open her heart.

Make sure you dunk your mom's cookies in milk for at least thirty seconds so you don't break a tooth. The memory was so vivid Meena could hear her dad's voice, one she hadn't heard in years.

Jameson Dave, do not fill your daughter's head with such things. The cookies are meant to be hard. Then her dad would take one and exaggeratedly try to snap it in two. Meena would giggle quietly so as not to hurt her mom's feelings.

One memory slid into another. She remembered the ice rink and skating while holding her dad's hand. Every year they would drive to Boston and spend the night in a hotel so they could go to the symphony for the Holiday Pops.

"Meena might want to spend time with her family," Luis said.

The pain of the past was so sharp Meena clutched the edge of the table with one hand.

Sam put his palm against her back. "OK?"

She nodded and toyed with the roughened edge of her cast. She tuned in as they chatted about painting, robots, and video games. They teased each other and shared embarrassing stories of their past adventures. Sam was in the middle of it all. Meena on the edge. Without her camera, the aloneness of the life she'd built around her became stark. She'd been at similar tables with other photographers, but they usually talked about work, gossiped about who was good to work with and who was sleeping with whom.

These five weren't colleagues. Each had a different career. What connected them was their relationships to one another, their friendship and loyalty. She could see that they were close enough to have shared vulnerabilities, that they gave each other support, a comforting shoulder. She'd had opportunities to build friendships like these, even on the road. Her work was inherently collaborative. But she hadn't.

They spent another hour in the bar before putting their jackets on and wrapping up in scarves. They said their goodbyes out front, each group heading in different directions.

"Want to walk? It's about twenty minutes, and it's a nice night," Sam suggested.

Meena shoved her hand in the pocket of her jacket. She was cold but she agreed. She turned her face up to let the air caress her skin.

As they passed various landmarks, Sam added historical sound bites. "The Old State House is the oldest surviving building in Boston."

Meena took in the brick facade and the white roof as they walked on a cobblestone path away from the busy Downtown Crossing shopping district.

"Will you be expecting tips in cash after this personal tour?"

"Yes. And I hope you're generous," Sam said. "Between Neha's Freedom Trail lectures and the pub trivia league with Ava, I'm an excellent personal tour guide—at least for Boston."

Meena laughed. "Your friends are great."

"Yeah. I'm lucky."

"It must be nice, with your family so far away."

He was quiet for a while as they crossed Boston Common.

"I have the aunties," Sam said.

There was something in his tone that piqued her curiosity. Instead of prodding, she stayed silent as they walked.

The path to the stairs of the Engineer's House was lit with little electric votive candles on metal posts stuck into the ground. The stairs had twinkling white fairy lights wrapped around the iron railings.

"Festive," Meena commented.

Sam unlocked the front door. "Are you coming to Sabina's for Diwali dinner on Sunday?"

"Tanvi mentioned it." But Sabina hadn't extended an invite.

"You know, there's been talk."

Her back against the closed door of Neha's apartment, Meena raised her brows. "Talk?"

"More like intensified curiosity." Sam closed the distance between them. Faced her. "You keep to yourself. Is it because you don't like us?"

The hall was silent. She focused on his face, his lips. They were full and well moisturized. She pursed hers and ran her tongue over them to make sure they weren't dry, that her reapplied gloss was still in place.

"I like you," she said.

"You do?"

"Plural." Meena smiled. "All of you."

She would never have believed that the faint scent of cinnamon and pine from the potpourri would be arousing, yet here she was, locked in on Sam. She saw the rise and fall of his chest. Relieved that the tension wasn't all hers, she raised her free hand to his chest.

He'd unbuttoned his black peacoat, a gray scarf hung around his neck, and the pale-blue sweater he wore underneath was soft cashmere. Maybe it was the two pints, maybe it was his kind eyes, his open expression, the prominent chin dimple. She let impulse take over. Meena stepped closer.

"Want to come inside?" she asked.

He waited. The quiet became oppressive, and Meena regretted her invitation. But she stood firm. He would have to reject her. She wasn't going to give him an out. Mostly because she could see in his eyes that he wanted to say yes.

"Another time."

Meena dismissed her disappointment.

"Another time." She turned and opened her door.

"After a date." Sam grinned.

Meena turned her head, raised her brows. "I see."

"Just want to do things in order," Sam said. "With you."

The smile fell. She faced him again. "Sam."

"I'm not asking for anything except a night out," Sam said. "The two of us. One where we both agree that there is something interesting between us and see where it goes."

Meena took a breath. "I have to go back to my regular life soon."

"The thing about the word *regular* is that the constant pattern can change," Sam said. "Can be redefined based on circumstances."

"Did Neha teach you that?"

"I learned all of my vocabulary from her," Sam said. "Think about the possibility."

He leaned down and pecked her on the cheek before going to his apartment.

Meena let out a long breath before going inside hers. She hung up her coat and flopped on the couch. She put her small cross-body bag on the coffee table. The strap got caught on her cast, and the bag fell under the sofa. Meena sighed and knelt on the rug to pull it out, and it was stuck to something. She used her free hand to pat the underside of the couch to figure out what it was. The thing wouldn't come loose. She pulled with all her effort, and her elbow caught the side of the coffee table. "Soap on a stick!"

She distracted herself from the pain by glancing at what she'd yanked out. A book, of course. *The Glass Castle*. And inside it two fortunes, the kind found inside cookies. Neha had written over the originals in red ink.

There is no order to life. While time is linear, we do not have to live within its confines.

The second one: *Expectations of how things must be are an anathema.*

Ugh. Enough with the riddles. Meena added them to the growing stack of notes. Frustrated, she sat on the couch. She was beginning to think Neha was messing with her.

She grunted. "Just say what you want to say, Neha."

She sighed and got ready for bed. She'd deal with it in the morning. She changed into her pajamas and tucked herself under a blanket on the couch. Her cased arm lay heavy on her stomach after she turned off the lights. It wasn't just the cast; exhaustion weighed her down.

Dust it off. Her mother's favorite saying. Hannah had been pragmatic to a fault. Meena hadn't gotten the part she'd wanted in the school production of *The Nutcracker? Move on. Find something else.* Hadn't gotten on the gymnastics team? There were other clubs. If something hadn't worked out, Hannah hadn't seen the point in dwelling on it.

They had been so different, Neha and Hannah. There had never been any meandering to Hannah's practicality. Always straightforward, always efficient. Neha had hidden little notes in odd places, notes that had no dates, no timeline, no logic. Like a jigsaw puzzle Meena wasn't sure she wanted to solve.

CHAPTER NINETEEN

Daylight fading, Meena huddled in the garden with a red and green checkered blanket she'd found in the bottom drawer of a large antique cabinet. She'd been relieved not to find a note. They were starting to make her twitchy.

She crossed her legs and put both feet on the metal bench so they were tucked under the blanket. The lights in the back garden gave off a soft glow. It was pristine, even as fall closed in on winter. The bare branches and twigs were trimmed. The sturdy winter plants bloomed, arranged in a row of pots that were color coordinated from deep red to light pink, like ombré but with planters. Even the rocks around the large dogwood in the corner were in immaculate order, each piece the exact same size and shape as the one beside it. There was too much symmetry. Too little color now that the leaves had been cleaned away.

Sam and Wally came out of the house. Wally, off his leash, charged toward her. Put his front paws on her lap. Meena gave him the requested scratches. He tried to climb on her, but Sam directed him down.

"He's not allowed to jump up." Sam spoke to Wally: "OK, pal. Go do your business."

The dog left her to sniff the ground.

"He's starting to listen to you," Meena observed.

"When he feels like it." Sam sat next to her.

They watched Wally take a sniffing tour, going wherever the smells led him.

"It's a nice garden."

"Sabina's mother was the previous keeper, her grandmother before her. It's changed little with each generation."

"It's Sabina's even though it belongs to the building?"

Sam shrugged. "It's communal, and she's the caretaker."

"And no one minds?" Meena asked. "Like what if I wanted to replace those rocks with daffodils or plant a large tree in that empty corner? Do I have to get permission?"

Sam laughed. "You wouldn't get approval."

"Then it isn't really communal."

They watched as Wally lifted a leg to water a rosebush.

"Neha must have hated it," Meena mused.

"She avoided the garden," Sam said. "Preferred the inside to out. That didn't stop her from needling Sabina or making snippy comments about the lack of wildness."

"Sounds like they had an interesting relationship."

"That's probably the best word to describe it. To some extent, it was like that with all three aunties. There was an age difference, with Neha being older. She wasn't part of the trio, but when Neha was left on her own, the aunties became self-appointed caretakers. Not that she wanted or needed it. Neha liked to complain, indirectly, about everything."

"You were the one she vented to."

Sam gave her a sad smile. "I think she was lonely. She wanted to be left alone but didn't like that she'd been left, if that makes sense."

"In a way." It was something Meena was starting to think about. Aloneness was a choice, but loneliness felt different. A disconnection from others that felt more like a condition of how she lived her life. Meena was beginning to relate to Neha.

"What about you?" Sam asked. "You must know a lot of people, though you only ever talk about Zoe."

Leave it to Sam to ask a question she didn't have a scripted answer for. "I haven't really thought about it. My work, there are a lot of people involved. Yes, it's me and the camera, but there are editors, sometimes assistants. There are other journalists, a network of hundreds. You can't be lonely when you're out in the world surrounded by people living their lives." A lie she'd been telling herself for a very long time.

"Right," Sam said. "I've looked up some of your work. It's fantastic. The photo of the kayaker in that small village in Norway is unforgettable."

She'd spent two weeks in the Lofoten Islands, waited out three storms. "I took that from a bridge to get the wide shot. I wanted to show the tiny village that had survived for hundreds of years against this massive backdrop of rocks and water." *Now,* she thought sadly, *it's overrun by tourists who want to stand in front of the red wooden houses for their Instagram followers.*

"I added it to my list," Sam said. "Of places to go."

"I thought you were a homebody."

"I am. That doesn't mean I don't like to travel. We used to take two family vacations every year. One in the summer and one over winter break. My brother likes to ski and scuba dive, so we went to places where we could do those things."

"What about what you liked to do?"

Sam kept his attention on Wally. "I don't mind skiing. Though if I don't dive again, I won't miss it."

That wasn't what she'd asked. "You don't talk about your family much."

He shrugged. "Two parents still married. A younger brother, also married, with three kids. The usual."

He talked about them as if he were an outsider looking in. "And you."

"And me," Sam said. "We're not close. I don't think they even know what I do or have seen the movies I've worked on."

"What happened?"

"Sibling rivalry gone to DEFCON one. My brother and I had a falling-out, and my parents chose him." Sam glanced toward his dog. "Wally, leave it."

The dog gave Sam a look to ask if Sam was sure that was what he wanted Wally to do. Sam gave him the command again, and Wally dropped the rock from his mouth.

"I'm sorry," Meena said.

"I hear you're coming to Diwali dinner on Sunday."

"Anything I should know? To prepare myself."

"Don't eat beforehand," Sam advised. "There will be a lot of food. You're not going to need to order out for a week after."

"What do you have against me and takeout?" In America it was cheaper for a single person. Thanks to portion sizes, she got two if not three meals out of one order.

"Too much sodium?" Sam grinned.

"My blood pressure is fine," Meena said.

They watched Wally start battles with stationary objects, then become distracted by other things. In this moment, with Sam next to her, Wally zooming around them, Meena realized she wasn't lonely.

"About the other night . . . ," Sam began.

"It's fine." Meena had already relived her attempt to kiss him and his rejection. She didn't want to dissect it with him. It had been an impulse. "Too much beer and the homey scent of potpourri."

He glanced at her. "Cinnamon does it for you, huh?"

She laughed. "Who knew?"

"It wasn't that I didn't want to kiss you," Sam said. "I want to make that clear."

"It's fine." She reached over and put her hand on top of his. "Forgotten. No hard feelings."

He glanced down and flipped his hand to hold hers.

She tugged her hand out of his. "It's better to not complicate things. It's been nice to hang out in Boston, but soon . . ."

Sam finished her sentence. "You go back to your life."

"Exactly." Though she wasn't sure what that meant anymore.

"The thing about complications," Sam said. "Avoiding them doesn't always work."

"I don't know." Meena wiggled the fingers of her casted arm. "I've kept it simple so far."

He nodded. "No ties. No knots."

It was a gut punch. So succinct and so true. "It's getting cold." She stood and, on her way back to her apartment, gave Wally a few scratches. The dog looked at her with adoration. He accepted her love. Without thinking, she gave the pup a kiss on the top of his head.

Once inside, she looked out into the garden. She'd gotten scared. On that bench, next to Sam, she'd started to want.

CHAPTER TWENTY

As Meena climbed the stairs, she could hear the lilting sound of a clarinet coming from the top floor. She wore her nicest and only dress, a simple black sheath, and her serviceable ankle boots. She clutched the bottle of white wine in her hand. Nerves fluttered in her belly. She didn't know why. She'd been to dinner parties before, and she knew at least a few of the guests and liked some of them. Tanvi and Sam would be there to ward off any awkwardness.

It wasn't as if she were intimidated by Sabina. Meena had rafted through Class IV rapids. This one stern woman was nothing compared to that. But it was a holiday event, a part of a culture that was Meena's by birth, yet she didn't know the rules, the rituals, and it wasn't as if the internet could teach her the nuances. In her work Meena could often stay detached; here she was going to mingle, be social. That shift was uncomfortable.

The door to Sabina's apartment was bright white, a garland of red roses hanging from the top of the frame. Meena heard the din of conversation on the other side. She adjusted the strap of her small crossbody purse. She hesitated before knocking. It would be OK. She was here to learn a little bit about this holiday, about what it meant to Indians, and get to know Neha better through the aunties. No big deal.

It wasn't that Meena didn't know she was a woman of color. The world made sure it was at the forefront of her mind. She'd been called everything from exotic to dirty. What she didn't have was a community she could turn to, one that was tied to her ethnicity.

A part of her wanted to dive in, embrace this chance to learn more, maybe even become a part of this group. The aunties would love to teach her how to cook, make chai, and do all the other things they did together. But she hesitated. Did exploring this part of her make her disloyal to the traditions she'd been raised in, the ones her parents had given her? Neha had given Meena up. Not even to another Indian family. Had it been a conscious choice on Neha's part to give Meena to a non-Indian couple? Was there a reason Neha hadn't wanted to give Meena even that basic knowledge?

With three deep breaths, she centered herself and knocked with her uncased hand.

"Meena," Sabina greeted her. "Welcome. I'm so glad you decided to join us."

"Thank you for inviting me." Meena slid off her shoes, as was custom. The huge living area was full of people. Her gaze found Sam and her nerves settled. It had been a while since she'd seen him not in his usual rugby shirt / sweatpants combo. Today he wore a soft blue sweater with dark jeans. He seemed different and yet familiar. She was glad for his presence as she scanned the room full of people. The aunties and their husbands were there. So were a few younger people—most likely their children.

"You made it." Tanvi reached out and took both of Meena's hands in hers and squeezed.

Meena said her hellos and handed Sabina the pinot grigio she'd bought from the wine shop a few blocks away. People were scattered around, seated on formal furniture. Meena's socked feet sank into the thick rug, as white as fresh snow. Sabina's home spanned the width of the building, and the rooms were grand in their scale and decor. The bottom halves of the walls were paneled in rich, warm walnut-colored wood, and a creamy white paint coated the tops up to the crown molding. Meena would be hard pressed to find a scratch or a scuff anywhere. The seating was deep and tufted, in warm tones. The rich, dark wood tables sported gold hardware. To one side she could see a formal dining table, the chairs in creams and yellows complementing the tabletop. A crystal teardrop chandelier gave the room a sense of austerity.

Candles lay everywhere, from the large cylinder on the dining table to the pillars on the end tables. There was a hint of vanilla and clove in the air.

"Come," said Vin, Uma's husband. "Let me introduce you."

Meena didn't quite grasp all the names, but Tanvi's son was there, as were Sabina's son and daughter.

"My daughter couldn't make it," Uma said. "She's in Boulder."

Meena found an open spot next to Sam on the long white sofa. It was surprisingly comfortable. There was a stark difference between this home and Neha's. Sabina's was more like her childhood home, not in the elegant and moneyed sense, but in the pristineness of it all. Hannah Dave had not tolerated clutter or color.

Meena's childhood home had been simple, in whites, grays, and wood. Two throw pillows, one on each end of their three-seater sofa. There hadn't been candles, but her father would bring home fresh flowers on occasion, and the vase would be the centerpiece on their scarred and well-used coffee table.

"So you're a famous photographer," said Jiten, Sabina's husband.

They complemented each other. Sabina's style was formal, her hair tied back in a long, ruler-straight ponytail. Her red silk sari was embellished with gold embroidery around the edges. Jiten was a few inches shorter, leaner, with thinning hair. He wore a shirt and a sport coat in a way that signaled casual wealth.

"A photojournalist and not famous." Meena clasped her hands together.

"Journalists stay in the background," Vin pontificated. "They're not celebrities."

"Tell that to cable news," Uma argued.

"My wife hates those channels."

From there the conversation carried on, fast and chaotic, from pundits to current events to the butterfly migration and the hoped-for return of bees. Meena couldn't keep up as people talked over each other while also having side conversations with others. Meena was pulled into a few, but she could barely focus on a topic before it changed.

"What are we having for dinner?" Tanvi found the one topic that paused the chatter.

"Malabar fish curry, dal makhni, paneer tikka, puri, jeera rice, raitu . . ." Sabina continued to list off items.

"Which is why I'm here." Sabina's son patted his flat stomach.

"And because it is an important holiday for us Hindus," Sabina added.

"Don't start." Then he turned to Meena. "Mom's mad because I skipped the mandir this morning."

Meena watched the slight pursing of Sabina's lips. Tension enveloped the room for a few moments. There was a similar stubbornness between the two. Meena's money was on Sabina to come out on top when these two clashed.

"Is all of this traditional Diwali food?" Something compelled Meena to break the standoff between mother and son. "Like turkey for Thanksgiving?"

"No," Uma said. "Thanksgiving is in two weeks, and we'll have turkey then. This is just food. In abundance. Diwali is our eating holiday."

"There are some dishes we usually eat during Diwali," Sabina expounded. "Mathia, ladoo, mawa kachori. In India people drop in and out of each other's homes, so these are the snacks on hand. For us this dinner is festive and a way to keep our culture going, instill these traditions in our children."

"The menu changes depending on what we ask Sabina to make and what she feels like cooking," Tanvi jumped in.

Meena had come to see that Sabina was the alpha in this group. They all deferred to her, even as they believed they were all equal. Meena glanced at her. This was Sabina in her element, people around her in her showcase home who would dine on her food and eventually shower her with praise.

"And this year we don't have to cater to . . ."

"Jiten," Sabina admonished.

"It's OK to talk about Neha," Uma said. "She was a part of this building. And she was difficult. Took pride in it, and I'm glad for that. She was a nonconformist."

"And a pain," Jiten mumbled.

"Last Diwali." Uma explained, "Neha brought a bowl of macaroni and cheese for herself because that's what she'd wanted on that particular day, and she didn't care if it was a major holiday."

"From a box," Sabina added.

Meena gave a mental high five to Neha. Staying in the apartment, reading the notes, Meena had come to understand that Neha did what she liked. Meena could relate to that. While she wouldn't have described herself as odd or quirky, she chose her own path on her own terms. She paused. Personality wasn't genetic. Meena had been raised to follow convention, to be polite, to eat what was served. It wasn't until she'd had to make her way on her own that Meena had chosen the life she had.

"There were some Indian dishes she liked." Uma interrupted Meena's thoughts. "Dal makhani was her favorite."

"And Sabina auntie's is the best in Boston," Sam commented.

"Best in the world," Jiten added.

Sabina's face lit up in a bright smile, and there was a hint of bashfulness mixed with pride. It was the first time Meena noticed her beauty. When Sabina's features—bright black eyes, high cheekbones, thick arched brows, and full red-painted lips—were relaxed, the woman was stunning. Meena fiddled with the zipper on her purse. Sam helped her open it, and she took out her phone. It had been hard to leave her camera back in the apartment, but she'd been invited as a guest.

"Do you mind if I snap some pictures? Everyone looks so great," Meena asked.

The aunties were dressed in saris, with Sabina in red, Uma in an eggplant color, and Tanvi in bright pink.

"Later." Sabina waved her off. "Sit and talk with us. This is not work."

Meena did as told and tried not to put her back up at Sabina's stern tone. It was her party, her rules.

"How are you settling in?" Jiten asked.

Meena gave a rote reply, then decided she needed to be a better guest. "You have a lovely home."

"It's my wife's main passion." Jiten patted Sabina's knee. "Not just our apartment but the Engineer's House. To preserve its history falls on her shoulders. It was her grandfather who bought this building in 1932."

"He was part of a contingent of Indians who came here from the 1920s to the late forties," Sabina said. "Over a hundred of them came to study at MIT right before the fall of the British Raj in India. My grandfather's uncle was one of the first."

"I didn't know."

"Not many do," Uma opined. "Even Indians who've been born and raised here don't know about it. Mostly people assume Indians came here in the 1970s."

"Once the quotas opened up in sixty-five, more Indians began to migrate here," Vin said. "But before the end of colonialism in India, this group of mostly Gujarati men came here to study. They were in civil work in India, working for the British, but they did not want to go to the UK. They came here instead, knowing that the Raj was coming to an end because of what Gandhi and others were doing. They paid their own way and studied engineering at MIT so they could go back and rebuild India. They aspired to remake the country."

"It wasn't easy for them." Sabina's face softened. "They were a different kind of foreigner. They had wealth, but because they were not white, they had very little community and faced a lot of discrimination. So my grandfather bought this building, through a trust, and invited his fellow Indians to live here while they were studying. He stayed instead of going back, to oversee a sort of dormitory, make those that came feel a sense of home."

"Most went back," Jiten added. "Except five."

"At first they stayed as constants, welcoming new students as they came. Helping them adjust," Vin said. "Then they stayed to make a go of it in America."

"They turned this building from a single residence into five separate apartments." Sabina's chest puffed with pride. "Like the communal homes in India. They lived separately and collectively. Open doors between the families, no need for formal invitations. They went back to India to marry and started their families here. The children, our parents, were raised by all of the adults."

Meena finally understood the symbolism of the unlocked door. She hadn't welcomed them freely into the space they'd been used to going in and out of their whole lives, as a matter of tradition. She'd been keeping them out.

"And the same for us, and our children." Tanvi smiled. "Right, Sam?"

"It took an entire year of my meager ten-year-old allowance to pay Uma auntie back for breaking her window with a baseball," Sam said.

"You were a good kid," said Uma. "Each generation assimilated more and more within American culture, but we kept a lot of our heritage, our traditions. Our parents taught us. We teach our children."

Meena caught the pointed look Sabina gave her son. "Our parents didn't have easy access to Indian groceries. It is only in the last twenty years that all these Patel Brothers opened. Before, they would bring suitcases full of masala and dal and nuts, everything they could, from India. Then each family would share with others."

"Did Neha have a large family?" Meena wanted to know if there were others, if she shared DNA with anyone else.

"She was an only child," Sabina said. "Her parents moved to Nairobi after Neha received her master's degree from Harvard."

"They left her the apartment?"

"It goes to the eldest child," Sabina explained. "At twenty-five."

"She wasn't married when she took it over?"

"No," Uma said. "It's not a requirement. Neha put it off for as long as possible. Then, in her early thirties, she agreed to an arranged marriage with Kaushik."

"What happens if there are no children?"

Silence enveloped the room.

"Neha was the only one, to date, who did not have any." Sabina sipped her drink. "I spoke with her about the future, offered to buy her unit. You can only sell if it is to one of the descendants of the original five. But she was stubborn and refused me. Several times. She wanted to decide who to leave the apartment to. I finally agreed to it with the caveat that whoever inherited the apartment would have the option to sell it to one of us after a year if they chose to do so."

They all looked at Meena. She didn't know if she was supposed to agree or disagree to whatever wasn't being directly asked. She chose to stay quiet.

"We've spent some time discussing how the apartment came to be yours," Uma stated.

Meena tensed. She wondered if this was why they'd invited her. For a face-off of a sort. She didn't belong in this building full of history and legacy. Meena glanced at Sabina. It had to be her doing. The woman had kept her distance, where Tanvi had welcomed Meena. She squeezed the strap of her purse to steady herself for whatever came next. If they confronted her over her right to the apartment, Meena would fight them. She'd inherited it, legally. Neha had wanted Meena to have it, and she wasn't going to go away quietly.

"We believe Neha knew your parents." Tanvi's voice softened. "That there was some connection. She was erratic, but she did love her apartment. She wouldn't be so cavalier in giving it away."

Meena bit the inside of her lip. No, Neha hadn't been cavalier. "And she had no descendants." She waited to see how they would fill in the blanks, wondered if they would acknowledge the possibility that Meena was more than a daughter of a friend.

"It should have reverted back to her parents," Sabina opined. "Neha didn't want them to have it. I did a background check on you, your family."

Meena clenched her jaw. The gall of this woman.

"We think she knew your parents through her job," Sabina continued. "Her office was in Springfield, an hour from where you grew up. She often spent weekends in Northampton. She would talk about the college there, Smith. We think she must have met your parents there. It's not that big of a town."

"She didn't have many friends," Tanvi added. "Any, really—just us. But it's possible that she could have known your parents. Maybe you might have even met her as a child and don't remember."

Their theory tracked, at least as far as how Neha had found Meena's parents. She wasn't ready to admit that Neha was her birth mother, not to a roomful of people, some of whom she'd just met. She also didn't want to reveal Neha's secret. Neha had chosen to not mention anything about her pregnancy to these women, had found a way to hide it. Seeing how judgmental some of them were, Meena didn't want to add to their dislike of Neha.

"Regardless," Sabina argued. "As you can see, this building has a purpose and a legacy."

And as far as they were concerned, Meena wasn't a part of that.

Sabina didn't want Meena here. Meena's back went up. Meena wasn't going to make it easy for her. She did belong; this was Meena's birthright. At least one thing became clear: Meena wasn't going to sell the apartment to Sabina. She'd keep it out of spite.

"But it is done," Tanvi offered. "You're here now, and you're a wonderful addition to the Engineer's House."

Meena gave a wide smile to Tanvi. "*You* have been so very kind."

"Enough talk." Uma stood up. "Let's eat."

Everyone moved at once. Tanvi reached over and patted Sam's shoulder. Sabina gave Meena a glance, just a small raising of the eyebrow. Meena understood that this wasn't over. Not by a long shot. She felt energized. She would be ready for whatever Sabina tried.

CHAPTER
TWENTY-ONE

The dal makhani was creamy, spicy, savory. The fish curry had a tang and a kick. The food was passed around, everyone serving themselves. A lot of the conversation centered around complimenting Sabina on the food. Meena begrudgingly admitted that the praise was well deserved.

"Meena." Vin turned toward her. "Have you managed to clear out all of the excess furniture?"

"And the books," Pi added. "Some are rare collectibles, so be mindful if you are going to get rid of them."

"I'm working on it," she replied. Though she wasn't. Not really.

"No you're not," Uma argued. "She's not even sleeping in the bed. That couch is going to break your back."

"It's comfortable." Meena didn't want to be on the defensive. She had her own reasons for her choices. "I've slept on plenty."

They all stared at her.

"I travel a lot." That should be enough to convince them.

"Don't worry," Tanvi said. "I cleansed the place thoroughly with sage. Neha is not haunting you. She has moved on to her next life."

Except through her notes. Neha had wanted to be present in that apartment long after her death, and she'd found a way to do it.

"I feel for the next body she's reincarnated into." Jiten swirled the whisky in his glass. The large cube of ice clinked as it touched the sides.

"She's likely going to be a grump," Vin joked. "Or a helpless and spiteful person."

Meena didn't appreciate their humor. She knew that Neha had had her quirks, but she didn't like that the aunties would talk about Neha in such a mean-spirited way. "You didn't like her?"

"We loved her," Tanvi said. "The men joke because they didn't spend time with her."

"She didn't like us." Jiten drank the last of the liquid in his glass.

"Neha wasn't a fan of people in general," Vin said.

"The feeling was mutual."

"She had other interests." Meena jumped to Neha's defense. "Like reading and learning languages. She seemed to like her work too. A person isn't unlikable because they prefer hobbies to people."

"How do you know these things?" Sabina asked.

Meena shrugged. "I've been living in the apartment for almost two months. I'm a journalist. I picked up on a few things." Then, because she wanted to needle Sabina, she added, "Neha left journals in her desk, and a few index cards lying around."

"Yes," Sabina said. "We came across her workbooks when we cleaned."

Meena mimicked the slight raise of the eyebrow back at Sabina and reached for another serving of cumin rice and two more deep-fried balls with a savory mash of peas stuffed inside. She was full, but the food was delicious and a solid distraction until the group moved on to the pros and cons of a local nonprofit.

Sam leaned over to Meena's seat. "You defended Neha." His voice was quiet, an aside just for her. "Does that mean you're starting to like her?"

"It's hard to like or dislike a dead person." Meena tilted her head closer to his. "I thought they were being rude."

"Good job," Sam said.

"Thanks." His praise made her sit up taller, her smile wider. "I could have really let them have it, but since I'm a guest . . ."

"I can't imagine you getting mad."

Meena glanced at him. Of course she got angry. "Remember when you told me I smelled and commented on my messy hair?"

"That was frustration," Sam said. "When was the last time you were full-on mad? Hot face, inability to form words?"

Meena put down her spoon and wiped her mouth with the edge of her napkin. The incidents that came to mind involved something more along the lines of irritation. Missed flights, bad editors, lost photos. "I've had my moments." The very last time she could remember had been when she was a teenager. She'd wanted to go to a party. Her parents had said no. Something about how college campus parties with alcohol were not for high school students. Frustration and anger had made her bury her hot face into her pink pillows. She'd thrown her stuffed animal across the room, refused to go down for dinner, and given them the silent treatment for two days. Two precious days. Her anger cooled and things returned to normal. They didn't talk about it. Just a simple "Please pass the toast" and it was over. Three days later everything was gone. Pink pillows. Stuffed animal.

"Are you OK?" Sam asked.

She nodded.

"Then maybe ease up on the napkin." Sam laid his hand on her. "Sabina might not appreciate you ruining her linen."

Meena flicked off his hand and smoothed the napkin out over her lap.

"What are you two whispering about?" Tanvi rested her elbow on the table. "Secrets?"

"Napkins," Sam quickly replied.

"I bought these for Sabina when Vin and I went to Italy a few years ago, and we found them in Ravello on the Amalfi Coast." Uma stroked the lace on the napkin she held out.

"Speaking of," Sabina said. "We need to plan our next girls' trip."

"I want to see the northern lights." Tanvi turned to Meena. "It's been on my list forever."

Uma shook her head to disagree. "Somewhere warm."

"Every year, in January, the aunties take a trip," Sam explained.

"It's always in a warm place." Tanvi glared at Uma. "Because she hates the cold."

"I spend six months freezing in Boston, sometimes eight," Uma said. "By January I just want to sit on the beach with a fruity drink in my hand."

"And I think beaches are boring." Tanvi waved her hands around. "I want discovery, culture."

"Alcohol," Uma said.

They all laughed.

"This is why it's a girls-only trip," Pi offered. "They go. They come back. We do not ask for any details."

"Last year we went to Cartagena," Uma said. "Beach plus culture."

"More like shopping culture." Tanvi wiped her mouth. "Just because the stores are in old buildings doesn't make them historical."

"Did Neha join?" Meena leaned into Sam.

"No," Sam said. "She didn't like to travel."

Or the aunties never invited her. Meena was beginning to understand why Neha had been the way she was. It must have been difficult to break into this trio. Especially if Sabina wasn't welcoming.

As they finished up dinner, the group shifted back to the living room, and Meena grabbed her phone and purse. She'd enjoyed herself, but dinner had been long, and she'd had enough of people. She paused. Maybe there were some similarities between her and Neha after all. "Thank you for including me. The food was delicious."

"I'm going to go too." Sam joined her by the door. "Need to take Wally out. And I know this begins the drinking portion of the night."

"You will never learn to keep up," Pi teased, "if you don't practice."

"You just need a lightweight you can make fun of." Sam closed the door behind them.

"Did you enjoy yourself?" Sam asked Meena.

She walked down the deep-red-carpeted steps, her shoes in her hand. "The food was incredible, and I learned a lot."

"About?"

"The history of this building." The stairwell was elegant with its Victorian filigree wallpaper, wood trim, and dark, polished railing with ornate balusters. An abstract painting in a detailed gold frame hung on the wall of each landing.

They stopped in the foyer in front of their apartment doors.

"Do you like living here?" Meena asked.

Sam slid his hands into the pockets of his jeans. "I do."

"Because of its legacy?"

"Because it's home."

Meena admired the simplicity of the statement.

"The next big event is Thanksgiving," Sam said. "You should prepare yourself for tandoori turkey."

"The social calendar of the Engineer's House is very demanding," Meena said.

She wanted him to step closer. But Sam kept firmly to his side of the hall.

"Good night, Sam."

He gave her a slight nod.

Meena went into the apartment and leaned against the closed door. She took a few breaths. The evening had tired her out in many ways. It was hard to acknowledge that she wasn't wanted here. The purpose of the history lesson hadn't been to impart information but to solidify why *they* belonged and *she* didn't. Tears welled in her eyes. She cleared her throat and glanced around the apartment. It had been Neha's place. Now she would make it her own to show Sabina that she was ready for a fight.

CHAPTER
TWENTY-TWO

It was time. The cast was off, and she could put some muscle into finally clearing the apartment of Neha's things. She would empty out a few drawers and put away her own things. The rest she'd figure out. If she could afford it, she could keep the room in Zoe's apartment for assignments closer to London. Most of her winter gear was there. There were details to sort out. She sat on the couch and stared at her sloppily folded clothes on the suitcase. Now that the cast was off, she could do a better job.

She was her mother's daughter, and she'd been taught to fold things and put them away, never a stray sweatshirt on the floor. *When you don't have a lot, you take care of what you have.* Hannah would not have appreciated all this stuff.

With her mom's voice in her head, Meena went into Neha's bedroom. The room was spacious even with the massive bed centered against the left wall. Twilight came through the wide french doors. She'd memorized the number of chimney stacks, had been here long enough that the view was now fixed in her mind.

Meena sat on the bed and rubbed her eyes. She looked around for a clock to figure out the time and turned on the lamp. She hated how dark it got so early in the day. Next to the lamp was a copy of *The Merriam-Webster's Dictionary*.

Meena groaned. "If this was your bedtime reading, Neha, I'm sure you were out like a light every night."

She picked it up and thumbed through it. A postcard was wedged in among the *m*'s.

"Of course," Meena said. "I've looked in this room dozens of times. Never noticed this dictionary. And now I'm talking to myself."

She put the book down and flipped over the card to read the familiar handwriting.

Advice to a young person from an old person:

1. *Bravery isn't in big battles; it is in small acts.*
2. *Once you are over the age of 30 you can no longer blame the past or your parents for the way you are. Fix yourself, it's within your control.*
3. *There is always money in the banana stand. Sam has told me this is from a television program. What I infer from it is that subtext is often more telling than text.*

Meena put the postcard on the table and lay on the bed, curled into herself. What would it have been like if Neha had kept her? What kind of parent would she have been? Probably an uninterested one. Maybe that's why she'd given Meena up. She'd known she wouldn't make a good mother.

A tear dropped on the soft pink pillowcase. She missed her mom. Her real mother, Hannah, her practicality and her love. If Meena was sick, her mom would stroke her hair until Meena fell asleep. When no one had asked Meena to the freshman formal, her mom had bought Meena a pretty dress and the three of them had had their own dance in the living room. Her father had put on a clown tie over his dress shirt for effect.

Meena laughed as she cried. They would have never left her notes, not like this. Her dad would have left her a journal to fill with her dreams, her mom a list of advice along with a book of prayers.

Meena stared out into the dark, clear night. Tufts of smoke wafted from chimneys. It was quiet in here. The street noise was on the other side of the apartment. Her eyes fluttered closed. She felt the support of the mattress. The pillow emitted a faint scent of lavender, her mom's signature scent.

Fix yourself. Neha's advice. Meena had. She'd done the requisite therapy in high school. She'd put herself through college with help from her parents' life insurance. She'd built a career. She was good at what she did. But something was missing. This last year when she'd run herself ragged from job to job, it was to fill an emptiness that had begun to grow.

She closed her eyes and allowed herself to let the memories of her parents fill the hollow.

CHAPTER
TWENTY-THREE

It was early, barely six thirty in the morning. But Meena wanted to do this before anyone saw her. Under the cloak of darkness. She slipped through the french doors of the bedroom and down the steps of the small veranda, then surveyed the back garden for the perfect spot. She walked the length and width, taking in the empty spaces.

The dewy grass squished under her sneakers as Meena tightened the scarf around her neck. She rounded her lips and breathed out, watched as the warm air met the cold to create a stream of condensation. She'd loved doing that as a kid, and the plume from her mouth was still satisfying. She smiled into the quiet dawn, energized because she had a mission.

She searched for the perfect spot, one that wouldn't be too obvious at first. Only when it was too late would anyone notice. And by *anyone*, she meant Sabina.

A large tree at each corner gave the garden symmetry. Planting there would require too much effort because there wasn't enough space between the tree trunk and the stones surrounding the area. The best place would be the fence that separated their garden from the one to the left. Neha's side of the building. Meena used her phone's measuring app to work out the available space. She could figure out the plot size once she had a rough idea.

"What are you doing?"

Meena jumped. "Sam."

He raised his brow and waited for her answer. Wally sidled up to her more slowly than usual.

Meena bent down and scratched behind the puppy's ears. "Hi, Wally! Why are you not running around?"

"He's got a funny tummy," Sam said.

"Oh no." Meena gave Wally a sad frown. "Poor puppy."

"He's going to be fine," Sam said. "As long as he doesn't eat things that aren't food."

Meena gave him a few more scratches.

"Well?"

Meena straightened and tucked her phone into her jacket pocket. "Right. Um." She should tell him. He might not like it or agree with her. He could tell on her and jeopardize the whole thing. Then she thought about it. Sam wouldn't do that. While she wasn't sure he was the type of person who would help her commit a felony, in her gut she knew he wouldn't snitch.

"I'm taking up gardening?" Meena said.

He swallowed his laugh. "Is that a question?"

Meena straightened her shoulders and shook her head.

"Do you know what you're doing?"

"I've done a lot of research on the internet," Meena said.

"Did the World Wide Web tell you that it's almost winter?" Sam asked. "Probably not the best time for planting."

Meena gave him a smug look. "Not for what I have planned. It's the perfect time."

He frowned. "And you've talked to Sabina about it."

Meena glanced at Wally, who sat with his chin on his paws. The poor dog looked so pitiful.

"Meena."

"It's a communal garden, right? Besides, it's on this side of the building. I'm not going to mess up anything she's doing. I just want to claim this little patch of grass." She'd spent a lot of time thinking of ways to wage a silent battle against Sabina. Maybe too much time, but Meena couldn't let go of the fact that Sabina didn't want her here. And that she'd likely made Neha feel the same way. It was for Neha that she was doing this. Neha would have appreciated Meena's efforts.

"To plant what exactly?"

Her eyes lit up as excitement coursed through her. "I watched a lot of gardening videos. Did you know that the easiest things to grow are wildflowers? And they all have these incredible names like yellow rattle, red clover, and Yorkshire fog. And what even is a lady's bedstraw? According to the Gardening Guru YouTube channel, you get the seeds, push them into the earth in the fall. And let nature do its thing. When spring comes around, they'll start to sprout, and by summer, it'll be a full-on wildflower patch right here. Chaotic and unruly."

Sam paced with Wally to get the pup moving. "And you're going to tend to it? Take care of it?"

Meena shrugged. "That's the best part. It doesn't need tending. It can be left alone, and the seeds will do their thing."

"I see," Sam said.

"I'm not doing anything wrong." Meena tucked her hands in the pockets of her jacket. "This garden doesn't have to be only what Sabina wants; it could be for everyone. I bet even Tanvi would love wildflowers."

"And what's to stop Sabina from mowing them down?"

Meena's excitement was dampened. "I haven't thought that far ahead. I'm kind of winging things." She wiped her hands on the front of her jeans, unsure what to do with them.

"This isn't natural for you, is it?"

She laughed. "Not even a little. But hey, it's never too late to learn a new thing."

"But that's not the only reason," Sam said.

Meena shrugged. "I think Neha would like it too."

"Why are you trying to get under Sabina's skin?"

Meena began to walk toward the porch. "I should go back inside, make coffee."

She heard his sigh. Somewhere along the way, they'd become friends, or at least become friendly with one another. She stopped and walked back to him. "I'm trying to settle in. See what it would be like to make this place one of my bases."

"When's the last time you lived somewhere?" He sat down on the short iron bench.

"College, I guess." She sat next to him.

"It's not so bad here."

She looked at him. He'd thrown a coat over his green-and-black-and-gray flannel pajama bottoms, hair wild as if he'd just gotten out of bed. "No. It's not bad at all."

"Maybe you're ready to put down roots," he said.

Meena stood up and paced. She took the leash from Sam and led Wally to a sniffing spot. "I was in Romania one summer, six years ago. Most people think vampires when they imagine Transylvania. But there's a region nearby that had the most incredible wildflower meadow. I was going through photos of it recently, and I thought, *That would be nice here.* Not on that scale but just along the fence. To muss up some of the perfect landscaping."

He stayed quiet. She liked that he didn't push. It was his superpower, really, because it made her want to talk, reveal things she rarely did. "I don't know if I'm the type to stay in one place. I keep busy, keep moving. If I'm not doing . . ." She didn't know how to finish that thought. "I'm just wired to stay on the move, I guess."

"Have you tried self-help books?"

She laughed. "No. I had my fair share of therapy after I lost my parents."

"They say therapy is a lifelong endeavor," Sam said.

She'd been raised to believe that she was responsible for solving her own problems. Even Neha had said that after thirty, you shouldn't blame anyone. She'd fixed herself. "If I were a less nomadic person, maybe."

"Already planning your next trip?" Sam asked. "Don't you want to see the wildflowers bloom or at least see Sabina's reaction?"

"That would be fun," Meena said. "But I won't be around much after the holidays. I might be gone for months."

"Guess I'll have to record Sabina's reaction."

"I'd love that."

"You don't like her."

"I don't like that it all has to be her way."

"Problem with authority?"

"Who made her boss of this building?"

"History, legacy, and a lot of paperwork," Sam said.

Meena sat down next to him and crossed her arms to create some warmth in the cold.

After a few minutes of comfortable silence, Sam took Wally's leash from her and unclipped it from the collar. Wally lay on the cool grass by Sam's feet.

"You might consider adding a few bricks around your wildflower bed, so the lawn mower doesn't destroy your vision."

"Yeah, that's a good idea."

"Mahoney's Garden Center," Sam offered up. "The best nursery in Boston. The Brighton one is close. You can probably get your seeds from there."

She tucked her hands into her jacket pockets again. "Thanks for the tip."

"If you want," Sam said, "I can drive you."

"I appreciate it. But I can manage now that the cast is off."

"Right. You don't need any help." He gave her a small smile. "I need to get Wally inside."

That was abrupt. She didn't know what she'd said. She didn't need help, not with small things like going to a gardening store. "I hope he feels better." She moved over to her patch of land, finished jotting down the measurements, and went inside to look up the garden center Sam had mentioned. She picked up the postcard she'd found in the dictionary. *Bravery is in small acts.*

Meena rolled her empty suitcase into the coat closet. She'd unpacked and put things away in drawers.

She brushed her hand through the clothes that hung in Neha's closet. The woman's style was one of comfort over trend, with bold colors, patterns, and prints. Even her coats were bright. The rain jacket in royal blue, the winter coat in lemon yellow, the spring jackets in red. The shoes were the only plain things Neha owned. Serviceable, in black, brown, and sneaker form.

So far Meena had cleared out a few drawers in Neha's bedroom. Neha didn't need them anymore. She'd packed their contents in large bags for donation and stuffed what couldn't be donated in trash bags to take to the bins in the basement. The aunties' husbands took turns putting the garbage out on Wednesday nights for pickup early Thursday morning. She'd never spent time anywhere long enough to know the day-to-day way of things.

Meena made herself a cup of instant coffee and strolled around the apartment. So much stuff. Furniture with things crammed in each drawer and cabinet. A quilting basket on the floor next to the big chairs that faced the fireplace. Candles. Lamps that were more decorative than useful.

She noticed a drawer at the bottom of the bookcase next to the fireplace. It was slim, and if you looked quickly, it could appear as if it were the base slat instead of storage. She crouched down to see if the little knob on it would let her pull it open. It took a few tugs before the drawer slid out. Inside was an old photo album. Meena carried it to the couch. She put her mug down on the coffee table and held the album in her lap.

The pages made a scrunching sound as she forced them open. The plastic film over the photos was permanently stuck to each picture. The photos on the first page were all black and white. Men in suits and ties stood in front of the building. There were twelve men, likely previous residents. Meena looked to see if there was a resemblance, a face she could recognize. Maybe one of them was her grandfather.

The next page held an assortment of baby pictures. They were slightly brownish, like many photos taken in the 1980s. The snapshots showed children and adults on various group outings. New York City. Niagara Falls. Disney World. A group of teenage girls in front of the Engineer's House: the aunties. There was an older girl, possibly college age. Meena looked closer. Could it be Neha? She pulled out the photo with some effort to see if there was anything written on the back. Nothing.

Meena flipped through the rest of the photos, studied them, and started to recognize the aunties and the person Meena assumed to be Neha. There were wedding photos of couples Meena didn't know. Aunties' baby showers. Early Halloween costumes. She looked at them again: when Neha was even there, she was off to the side. By choice? Or was that how Neha felt—a part of the group but not quite? Maybe Meena was reading too much into it and it was simply that Neha had been the photographer.

She got to the end of the album, and there was a little pocket. Meena stuck her fingers in and pulled out a single picture.

Two people in front of the living room fireplace in this apartment. The woman, Neha, resembled the college student in the earlier photo. The man next to her might have been her husband. They stood side by side. Not even their shoulders touched. Neither smiled. The man was in a white shirt and black pants. He had a beard. Thick eyebrows. Neha was in a long skirt and a patchwork sweater. Her hair was short, cut just below her ears, and in waves. Her lipstick was bright red, her eyebrows shaped into thin arches. Meena looked closer. Her eyes were as flat as her expression.

Meena couldn't see familiarity. Neha's nose was a little wider than hers, the forehead smaller, the chin narrower. They could have been the same height. Meena was barely five eight. She'd hoped for recognition, to see herself in someone else, to know that even though Neha was dead, Meena was a part of the legacy of the Engineer's House, that she had a familial history. She ran her finger over the face. Neha had had everything many strived for—wealth, marriage, a passion for her vocation. Yet something seemed to be missing. Then she saw it in Neha's eyes, staring back at Meena. A wave of recognition washed over her.

Loneliness.

This was what she had in common with her birth mother. Meena flipped the photo over, no longer able to look at it. Stuck to the other side was a folded-up piece of paper. It was from a notepad with a Merriam-Webster letterhead.

I do not know the meaning of love. Even its definition is abstract. "Strong affection based on kinship." My parents are my kin. If providing for me is considered strong affection, I suppose I have that. But I do not feel anything for them except that I came from them. If it is sexual desire, I have that for my husband. But have no other use for him. What does it mean to hold someone dear? I've concluded that I do not care for it. Let it exist for others. I'm enough without it.

Meena's heart broke for Neha. To think that this woman had gone through the whole of her life not knowing love. A second wave crashed over her. That last line. It was what Meena had said to herself for the last eighteen years. She'd known what it was to hold someone dear. Didn't need to anymore. Except that wasn't true. Meena knew love. Had been cradled within it, until she'd lost it. The truth was, Meena was only enough without it because she hadn't wanted to replace what she'd had. Or lose it all again.

If she took a photo of herself, Meena knew she'd see the same bleakness she saw in Neha's eyes. She held the album in her lap and mourned for this woman she was starting to know. She looked at the photos of the aunties again. The love and friendship among them were so obvious in the way they smiled, the way they wrapped their arms around each other. They hadn't included Neha in the trio. Was it because that was how Neha had wanted it? Or had inclusion not been offered to her?

Neha was only her birth mother, but Meena hadn't felt this link with anyone, not with a sense of deep familiarity. Whether she felt the link because of living here or through the notes or these photos, Neha mattered.

CHAPTER
TWENTY-FOUR

The four frothy concoctions were as festive as the decor in the dark lounge. The leather furniture, the rich wood of the tabletops, the paneled walls were made cheerful with gold metallic garlands, red-and-white ornaments, and white lights.

"These are almost too pretty to drink," Tanvi said. "Not that it's going to stop me."

"I'm going to start with the spiced Mexican chocolate," Uma said, "then work my way down."

"I'm going in the opposite direction," Sabina said. "Peppermint first. I like to end with a kick of heat."

Meena listened to them debate about the hot chocolate flight in front of them. Four tall mugs, bursting with whipped cream at the rims, each topped with something unique—from a burned-marshmallow skewer to a gingerbread cookie to a candy cane. Each laced with Baileys or vodka in a complementary flavor.

"Which one are you starting with, Meena?" Sabina asked.

Even her simple questions sounded like an interrogation to Meena. "The dulce de leche."

Sabina shook her head. "That's the best way to end. Before we go to the Oak Long Bar for cocktails."

All three aunties wore matching snowflake scarves and red-and-green earrings that Meena was sure held real rubies and emeralds.

Meena joined them with a raised glass as Uma gave a toast to bring on the beginning of the holiday season. They'd talked her into joining their day-after-Thanksgiving tradition: a hot chocolate tasting at Buttermilk & Bourbon, martinis at the Oak Bar, and dinner at Deuxave—all in their Back Bay neighborhood. While the Engineer's House was on a quiet street, each street away from the Charles River was busier, more crowded with shops and offices than the one before.

The aunties took turns splurging for the day. This year it was Uma's treat, and she got to choose the dinner restaurant.

"Drink up, ladies," Tanvi said. "Hot chocolate is best when it's still hot."

Meena sipped her second mug while the aunties had moved on to their last. She'd joined them because they'd asked. More than that, she wanted to get to know them. Pry into their lives and their relationship with Neha. A part of her also wanted to see if Tanvi and Uma shared Sabina's dislike for Neha and if they also wanted Meena gone. She didn't want to believe it of Tanvi, but Uma was a wild card. She also wanted to know if there was a possibility for genuine friendship.

"How long have you been doing this?" Meena asked.

"It's one of our more recent traditions." Uma licked a dollop of whipped cream off the candy cane. "The summer of 2013. After the marathon bombing, there was an effort to support the Back Bay businesses, and we wanted to do our part. As we spent the day from brunch to bar to dinner, we came up with this idea."

"All week we prepare for Thanksgiving." Sabina gesticulated. "Friday after is our day while the husbands clean."

"Did Neha ever join?" Meena asked.

Tanvi shook her head. "We used to invite her, but she always said no. After a while we stopped asking."

"Neha preferred to spend time with her books," Uma said. "She always had a few open she would switch between and would jot down notes, dog-ear pages."

"It was just as well." Sabina sighed. "Neha wasn't a joiner. She thought getting together, doing things with each other, was a waste of time."

Meena kept quiet and sipped her drink. Part of her wanted to tell them that maybe they could have tried harder. Ask them if they'd noticed whether Neha wanted to be alone or was lonely. "I get the feeling that she spent a lot of time by herself."

"That's what she wanted," Tanvi said.

"Sometimes people say that because that's all they have." Meena stared at the empty mugs in front of her. The hot chocolate sat warm in her belly, and she didn't mind the aftertaste of vodka anymore. "Wow. These drinks are potent."

"How are things between you and Sam?" Tanvi dipped a finger into her empty mug, scraped off the remaining whipped cream, and licked it.

Meena shook her head. "We're friends. I like his dog."

"And his handsome face," Tanvi said.

"It's not a bad match," Uma added.

Meena finished the last of her drink. "Where to next?"

"To the Oak Long Bar." Uma raised her arm and pumped her fist.

Tanvi linked arms with Meena as they walked down Dartmouth Street and crossed Boylston. The cool air cleared Meena's head. She could see the wreaths being placed on the beautiful old building that housed the public library. Groups of tourists posed for photos on the steps next to the two sculptures—both of women, one holding a globe and the other a paintbrush and palette. Carved into the stone facade were the words FREE TO ALL.

She'd been inside a long time ago, on a sixth-grade class trip to Boston for the day. Sadly, she couldn't remember any of the building's history. Sam would know. If he were here, he'd narrate random facts in his deep voice that caused her stomach to flip over. *Whoa.* She caught herself. *Where did that come from?*

A frigid gust whipped around Meena as they approached the entrance to the Oak Long Bar.

Inside, the chandeliers, high ceilings, and large leather armchairs were all designed to make the wealthy feel comfortable. The hostess led them to their table, and Meena sank into a chair that belonged in a living room instead of a restaurant.

"There is an extra-cold, extra-dirty martini with my name on it." Uma sat across from her. "If you're looking for recommendations."

"Or she could look at the cocktail menu," Tanvi said. "I prefer to be more adventurous than order the same drink every time."

The waiter took their orders, and Meena listened to their stories of past vacations. They talked over each other, teased each other, and laughed. A lot. Three cocktails in, Meena had learned a few things about herself. One, the Autumn Star was her least favorite drink. She didn't mind the apple brandy, but vermouth was disgusting. Two, gin, which she didn't often drink, was her liquor of choice. Three, she preferred the Bee's Knees over the gimlet.

"OK, enough of our stories." Uma sipped her third or possibly fifth martini. "Your turn, Meena. Tell us something about you."

Her brain was foggy as she tried to remember something interesting. "I have been to base camp of six of the Seven Summits."

"That's boring." Tanvi frowned. "Give us something juicy. Like a torrid affair, a horrible heartbreak."

Meena toyed with the lime on the rim of her glass.

"Forget heartbreaks," Uma said. "Have you ever killed anyone?"

Meena snapped her eyes to Uma. "I don't think so."

The aunties burst into laughter.

"If you do, we'll help you bury the body," Uma offered.

She wanted to believe them. She wanted to belong among them, be a part of the building. She could admit that only because alcohol flowed through her bloodstream and jostled her brain into wishing for things. She looked at Sabina, who stayed quiet at the idea of helping Meena in any way. A knot formed in her throat.

There was Zoe, of course. Zoe would be there for her and always had been. It was Meena who kept the friendship at a remove. The truth was that she hadn't been part of a friend group since high school. She and her best friend, Holly, had been inseparable from kindergarten. But Meena had shut her out after everything happened. Hadn't stayed in touch after the funeral. Holly had said her parents would come get Meena so Meena could spend weekends at her house, but Meena hadn't called. She didn't want to go back to that town, see others there living their lives when hers was gone.

"Can I ask you something?" Meena hesitated.

"Oh Lord. We really are going to have to bury a body," Tanvi said. "Uma, you're the muscle. Sabina, you're the brains."

Meena shook her head. The room spun just a little. "No. Nothing like that. I want to know why you didn't like Neha." She couldn't believe she'd blurted it out.

"What makes you think that?" Tanvi asked.

"The way you talk about her," Meena said. "Make fun of her. Like yesterday, during dinner, your husbands were complaining about having to take a plate to her every Thanksgiving or holiday dinner when she wouldn't join. You all were talking about how she would snap or lash out if someone said something she didn't want to hear. The three of you are so close. It seems like Neha wasn't a part of your group."

"Because she wasn't." Sabina munched on the salted almonds that had come with their drinks. "She was older than us. Didn't grow up with us."

"But we did like her," Tanvi said. "We took care of her because that's what we do. Everyone in the building is family, and that included her."

"She wasn't one to mix easily." Uma took a healthy sip of her drink. "She was also a jerk most of the time."

"That's not nice," Tanvi said.

"Just because she's dead doesn't mean we make her into someone she wasn't." Uma's voice rose. "And honestly, the feeling was mutual. She didn't like us either. Only Sam. And that's because she could take advantage of him. Use him whenever she felt like company."

"She left him a dog." Sabina sneered. "To get back at me."

"Exactly." Uma pointed at Sabina. "That's who Neha was. You'd think she was doing something nice, but there was always another angle."

Subtext is often more telling than text.

"She tolerated us because we did things for her," Uma said. "Like filling her fridge with food or reminding her to go through her bills. Sabina did a lot of that, almost like she was Neha's assistant at times."

That surprised Meena. "Why did you keep doing it?"

"Because we take care of our own," Sabina said. "That was the foundation for the Engineer's House. Our grandfathers took care of those that came and went. We look after each other."

"That includes you now." Tanvi reached over and patted her hand. "Neha left you the apartment for a reason. She wanted you to be a part of the Engineer's House."

"That's not how things are done," Sabina explained.

"Sabina," Tanvi said.

"Unless she's a direct descendant," Sabina argued. "It would be best if Meena sold the unit. To preserve our history."

"Let's not get into this." Uma squashed the topic. "This is Friday Fun Day."

Meena excused herself to run to the bathroom before she yelled the truth to Sabina. Neha had wanted Meena to have the apartment. If she couldn't be a mother to Meena, maybe she had known that Meena needed a family again. She ran water over her face and looked at herself in the mirror, searched for a resemblance to the woman in the photo. She couldn't see it, but she could feel it.

CHAPTER
TWENTY-FIVE

The steps. There were four of them or six. Meena couldn't count. *I can do this.*

"Ay, why are you standing there?" Sabina asked.

Meena focused on the steps. Sabina, Tanvi, and Uma were behind her.

"Hello."

Sam. Beautiful Sam. At the top, in front of the big black doors.

"You OK?" Sam asked.

"I tried to keep up."

"I can see."

"She did great," Tanvi said.

Meena grinned wide. "I did."

"Need help?" Sam asked.

"Is it three steps or five?"

"Four."

"Oh."

Meena braced herself. Right leg. Up. Left leg. Right leg. Up. Left leg. She made it. She lifted both arms in victory. "Ta-da."

Sam laughed. "One more to go."

"Oh," Meena said.

Her toe caught the lip of the last step, and she fell into Sam's arms. His strong arms. She clutched at his biceps. Held on. The muscles were small, but she could trace the ridges.

"You broke her." Sam glared at the aunties.

"Nonsense." Uma shook her head. "We brought her out of her shell."

"Give her to us." Sabina reached for Meena. "We'll take her in."

Meena rested her face against Sam's chest. His wool coat felt warm and soft against her skin.

"Let Sam take care of her," Tanvi said. "She wants him."

Meena nodded. "Yes."

"She needs water, Sam," Sabina instructed.

"So do the three of you," he said. "Careful climbing up the steps."

"Who do you think you're talking to?" Uma put her hands on her hips. "I have climbed these stairs since I was a baby. I will climb them when I'm ninety. Don't think I'm too old to go up the steps. I could run up them if I wanted to."

"Not old," Sam said. "Drunk."

"I can hold more liquor in my left leg than you can in your whole body," Uma argued. "Let's go, Sameer: you, me, and a bottle of Johnnie Walker Blue. Right now."

"More like you, Tanvi, me, and a jug of water." Sabina let the two of them away.

Meena opened her eyes. She was on the couch. Sitting down. Thank goodness. The living room was slightly tilted or spinning. She blinked to clear her vision. Sam sat on the coffee table in front of her.

"Sip this." He held out a glass.

"If it's vodka, no thank you."

"It's water." He nudged it into her hand.

Meena cupped it and sipped. "It tastes so good."

He smiled. "Did you have fun?"

Meena laid her head against the back of the couch. "I can't feel my face. Is it still there?"

"It is."

"I need to reapply my lipstick."

"Maybe later," Sam said. "Your lips are fine."

She sat up. "So are yours. They look soft." She reached up and stroked her fingers over his lips. "They are. You must use lip balm."

"Carmex."

"Good for you." She smiled widely. "You're so pretty, Sam."

"Drink a little more water," he said.

"The aunties," Meena whispered. "They are so nosy. They asked so many questions. And they're filthy. The jokes from dinner . . . whew. Not that I'm a prude, but I learned some new words today. Do you know *gaand* means *ass*? That's a weird word to say. *Gaand*. Apparently I have an accent. The aunties are going to teach me Gujarati and Hindi. They think I should know. And they're right. I have a secret. I didn't tell them, but I want to tell you."

"After you sober up," Sam said.

"I'm Indian." Meena added, "Not bland Brown."

"Meena."

"*Fart* is *paad*," Meena said. "I don't curse. I say *wiener schnitzel* or *lollipop* because my mom never wanted me to curse and so I don't. It's a sin, you know. But is it cursing if I'm only learning curse words in another language? Did Neha curse? She liked language, so she probably used better words, not curses. It's another thing we might have in common."

"Finish your water."

Meena obeyed. She handed him the empty glass.

"Why are you trying to find things in common with Neha?"

"Because everything I've learned about her," Meena said, "is so different from me, and the notes are so confusing."

"Notes?"

156

Meena stood up. A wave of dizziness hit her, and she held on to Sam's shoulders for balance. He stood with her and held her at the waist. His warm hands made her body tingle. She leaned her face toward him, and he leaned away from her. Meena stepped away from him and went to the other side of the coffee table. "I'm sorry. I keep throwing myself at you even though it's a bad idea."

Sam grinned. "We'll talk about it tomorrow, or maybe the day after, depending on how long it takes your liver to recover."

"I had vodka, and gin, and wine." Meena couldn't believe how much she'd drunk.

"You're going to feel awful tomorrow," Sam said. "I don't want one of the reasons to be about us or this conversation."

"I think it might be a little late for that," Meena muttered. "I've probably said a lot. That's why I don't get drunk. It's like my brain forgets and says things I don't want to share. Like now the aunties know how many people I've had sex with. That's private; they shouldn't. But I had a glass of cabernet and I told them. Also I tried duck for the first time, and it is gross. Very slimy. Tanvi was upset that Uma ordered it because ducks are cute, but then Uma said that God made them cute to hide how mean they are. What were we talking about?"

"Take off your shoes and head to bed," Sam said.

"Notes." Meena went to the desk and grabbed the envelope she'd stuffed them in and handed them to Sam. He didn't open it. "Did you know Neha hid notes all over this apartment? In the most random and annoying places. There's no order to them. Like a puzzle with a lot of missing pieces."

"Did she write them for you?"

Meena shook her head. It hurt, so she stopped. "Yes. Sort of. I mean it's not like she starts with 'Dear Meena.' But I know they're for me."

Sam closed the distance between them. He gave her the envelope back. She hugged it. He led her to the bedroom, sat her on the edge of the bed. He knelt in front of her to take off her ankle boots.

"Scooch back." He turned over the comforter and helped her into bed. "Lie down."

"Thank you," Meena said. "For this. I don't have anything like what the aunties have. They're a solid unit. You have that with your friends. But I don't."

"Why not?"

Meena stared at the ceiling. "Because it's better not to have anyone care about you, so you don't have to care about them."

"What's wrong with caring?"

"Because when you lose them, it can break you." Meena spoke aloud what she'd been holding in for years.

He sat on the bed next to her. "You survived a big loss. You could see it as a sign of strength."

Meena reached up and stroked his face. "Don't give me more credit than I deserve."

"I will. For now," Sam said. "Until you start giving yourself some— then I'll back off to keep your ego in check."

She wanted to kiss him. But she couldn't want Sam. He wouldn't be a distraction or a temporary person. He would expect more than she could give. Meena dropped her hand, rolled over on her side, and closed her eyes. A few minutes later, she was warm under a blanket.

CHAPTER
TWENTY-SIX

Meena knocked on Sam's door and waited. Nothing. She knocked again. He was likely out. Instead of walking away, Meena tried the handle. Of course it was unlocked. Still she hesitated. It was odd to walk into someone's home without an invitation. Meena ducked her head in and said hello into an empty room. Slowly she entered, leaving the door ajar.

Sam's place was very different from Neha's. The living room was small, cozy, though the high ceilings gave off the impression of roominess. The walls were painted in a soft gray. The art mostly black-and-white lithographs. The furniture erred on the side of comfort over style. The gray pillows on the sofa were lumpy, and she could picture Sam on the couch with his head against the arm, watching the big screen hanging on the wall facing the front door.

Noting the quiet, she was about to leave when Wally burst through the small entryway to the left. She crouched down as the pup ran into her and began his usual jumping and scrambling to try to get as close as possible.

"Hi, Wally, hi." Meena gave him all the scratches he requested.

"No jumping," Sam called out.

Meena put his paws on the rug and frowned into the pup's face. "Sorry, Wally. We have to follow Strict Sam's orders."

He yelped and stared longingly at Meena.

She gave him scratches behind his ears. "Blame him. Not me."

"You and the aunties are why he's spoiled and hard to train," Sam said. "Wally, go lie down."

The dog looked at Sam, then turned away, resting his head in Meena's lap.

"Wally." Sam's voice took on a stern tone. "Bed."

The dog blew out air from his nose in frustration.

She heard a matching sigh from Sam. He went over to a small jar on the little table by the door. Wally's ears perked up. Sam pulled out a tiny bone-shaped treat. Wally jumped up on all fours and went to Sam.

"Bed," Sam said.

Wally stared at the treat.

"Bed," Sam repeated.

Wally slowly moved to the dog bed next to the couch and sat. His tail wagged back and forth as he waited eagerly for his treat.

Sam went over to him. "Lie down."

Wally finally lay down, his face resting on his front paws. Sam gave him the treat.

"Hopefully that occupies him for a bit," he said. "Hey."

"Hi." Seeing him reminded her of the way she'd been with him, and her face flushed with embarrassment. "Sorry, I knocked but didn't hear you. I, uh, should have come by later. When you were back."

"I'm back now."

He was in black sweatpants and a long-sleeved T-shirt. His hair was shiny at the tips, likely from his being out in the snow.

"Do you want tea?" Sam asked. "Don't tell the aunties, but I use tea bags for a quick hit. Chai is too much work."

"If you don't tell them I drink instant coffee," Meena said.

"If you want coffee," Sam offered, "I can make you an espresso or a latte."

"That's not too much effort?"

"Touché," Sam said. "Come back to the kitchen. Maybe with us gone, Wally will nap."

Meena followed him through the short hallway to the kitchen. Beyond were a few doors. Likely bedrooms. The kitchen was a little bigger than hers, with a small round table against the windows that overlooked the back garden.

"What's your preference?" Sam asked.

"There's no need to . . . espresso." She was here to talk to Sam, apologize about yesterday, thank him for taking care of her. She could do that over coffee. "I stopped by to say I'm sorry. I know they shoved me into you yesterday, making my drunken state your problem. And I just . . ."

"You weren't a problem." Sam grinned. "I enjoyed drunk Meena."

She groaned. "My tolerance is no match for theirs."

"I can't believe you didn't pace yourself. It was the one piece of advice I gave you at Thanksgiving."

"I don't know what happened," Meena said. "We were having spiked hot chocolate, and the next thing I know I'm capping off the night with an Irish coffee."

"You had fun." Sam handed her a small teacup of espresso.

"I did."

She shifted. She had to get through the hard part.

"I, um, also wanted to say sorry for, if, uh, I tried to kiss you." Meena mumbled out the words while staring out the kitchen window.

She looked back when he placed his hand on top of hers. "There is nothing to apologize for or be embarrassed about. You had a good time. Don't feel bad about that."

His palm was warm against her hand, and she stilled so he wouldn't remove it. She wanted to stay like this, feel him on her skin.

"You told me about the notes," Sam said. "The ones Neha left you."

"You didn't read them."

"I didn't know if you wanted me to since you handed them to me in a liquored-up state."

She flipped her palm over and squeezed his hand. Feared he would remove it from hers.

"I want you to read them," Meena said. "Fill in some of the blanks."

"What do you know so far?"

It was snowing harder now, and the grass was quickly disappearing from the white coating.

"She mentioned her work, that her husband left her, the relationship she had with the aunties . . . why she left the apartment to me." Meena braced herself. "I'm not . . . she . . ." The words were stuck in her throat. The word *mother* didn't fit Neha.

Sam said nothing. His face was clear of any emotion. He didn't prod her or urge her. Simply waited for her to continue, for her to decide what she wanted to say and not say. It comforted her.

"I'm . . . she was my birth mother."

His hand tensed in hers. She let it go, sat back, and crossed her arms. They had been friends, Sam and Neha, and he was likely shocked. He might feel betrayed or angry with Meena for not telling him sooner.

He ran his hand through his hair. "Is that what she wrote?"

"Not in so many words," Meena said. "She isn't one to spell things out. She goes on tangents, speaks in circles, implies. I've reread them. It's the most obvious connection, even though I didn't want to admit it."

"She didn't come out and say so, though."

"I'm a smart person. I put it together. She left me this apartment. She wrote notes to help me get to know her. It all fits," Meena said. "I was adopted, Sam. My parents were white, I didn't look like them. I didn't know what my ethnicity was, but I knew I wasn't theirs. And a place like this doesn't just go to a stranger. Didn't Sabina say each apartment gets passed down to the next generation?"

Sam took her hand again. "Listen."

She pulled out of his grasp. "I'm sorry I didn't share all of this with you before. I have a hard time talking about my past and my parents." She toyed with the rim of her cup. "They used to tell me I was a gift."

"Meena."

"Hey, it's fine," Meena said. "I was surprised to know all of this, but it's also good, you know. A solid piece of information about my genetic background. And I can be part of a culture, a country. I'm beginning to develop a taste for chai and paratha, though I will have to work on my tolerance for spice."

"It's not that," Sam objected.

"I know I should have told you sooner," she interrupted him. "Except, well, I had one foot out the door for a while, and then I didn't know how."

"You needed to trust me," Sam said. "I get that."

"Wally," Tanvi's voice rang out. "Where's your papa?"

"We need to finish this conversation." Sam stood.

Meena nodded.

"Oh, here you two are." Tanvi showed herself into the room. "Sam, I made your favorite. I was craving fried food, and Sam loves batata vada, so I brought you some. Now you can share with Meena."

"You wanted it because your body is still trying to soak up all the alcohol," Sam said.

"Our Sam is such a good boy." Tanvi cupped his face. "His aunties are always doing things he doesn't approve of. I remember a few drunken stumbles from you in your twenties. If you joined us, you would have remembered when you were fun."

"I would be too busy trying to keep you out of trouble." Sam wrapped his arm around her shoulders.

"This one." Tanvi leaned into him. "Maybe you can loosen him up, Meena."

The overt matchmaking was embarrassing. "I need to go." Meena stood. "Check my emails. Finish some things."

"Meena, wait," Sam said.

"Later." She rushed out. She'd shared enough, told him everything. But she didn't want to get into any of it with Tanvi or the aunties. It had been a long day, and she was still hungover. Meena needed to lie down and sleep for another day. Maybe two. Then she'd think about how much to share with the aunties and what any of this meant.

CHAPTER
TWENTY-SEVEN

There is a tree in the back garden, a red dogwood. It's at the far corner of the fence. My grandfather planted it. In the spring the twigs are green, the blooms white. In the fall the tree turns bright red from twig to leaf. It is spectacular. My ashes will be in the earth beneath the tree.

She'd found the stationery paper folded up in a freaking cookie jar in the shape of a dinosaur jammed in the back corner of the pantry. All she'd wanted was to make a pie because sometimes baking helped her think. Whenever she was challenged by a story, an angle, a source, she could take a walk. If she had a gnarly problem to figure out, she'd bake. For Meena, baking was an example of something difficult that eventually produced something great. While reaching for the flour, she'd knocked a ceramic container over. The small dinosaur-shaped jar had shattered, and in the middle of the wreckage, a note had appeared.

"Meena?"

Sam. "In the kitchen."

"Uh, what happened? Did you hurt yourself?"

She squeezed the piece of paper in her hand. "I'm trying to bake."

"And is sitting on the floor with flour on your pants part of your process?"

"Ha ha." Meena stood and wiped off her black yoga pants.

"I thought you mentioned that you were using the laundry," Sam said.

"You're on a bad-joke roll today."

"I'm in a good mood," Sam said. "I just finished a grueling project. Forty-eight straight hours. Then ten hours of sleep. I was heading out to grab dinner and thought you could join me."

So that was why she hadn't seen him since Saturday. She'd worried that he might have been upset about her revelations. Or that Neha had kept this secret from him. She'd seen him with Wally here and there on short walks but hadn't had the nerve to pop her head out or wave to him.

"Congratulations," Meena said.

"There's a Thai place nearby, it's not bad."

"That doesn't sound like a solid recommendation."

"I haven't been to Thailand, and you probably have, so it's fine for me, but maybe not up to your standards, so not bad."

"I could eat. Give me a few minutes to clean up," Meena said. "Put my face on."

"When did you take it off?"

Meena tilted her head. "Did you get like a bad-joke-a-day calendar or something?"

He laughed. "I have dozens more. Just you wait."

"I guess I'll suffer through it for a good plate of *som tum*."

Meena ducked into the bedroom to change into jeans and a black sweater and sat at the vanity to put on her makeup. *It's not a date,* she needed to remind herself. It was dinner out. With a friend on a random Tuesday night in early December. There was no occasion or anything remotely special. Her head and heart were already jumbled; she didn't need to add Sam into the mix. He was being a good friend. That meant more to her than anything else.

She added dark-red lipstick to finish off her look and unknotted her hair from its bun. It was nice to have the full use of both hands again, especially to manage her hair. She'd put it up wet, and it fell around her in waves. She fluffed it a little, smacked her lips to seal the color, and grabbed her cross-body purse.

⁓

"For the record," Meena said, "I've never been to Thailand."

Across the table Sam put his hand on his heart and feigned shock.

"There are a lot of places I haven't traveled to," Meena added. "I keep a list of places I want to see just to see them."

"Like where?"

"Nebraska." It was the first place that came to her mind.

Sam laughed. Then stopped. "You're serious."

"I just have this generalized image of cornfields and big blond farmers. And the only city that's ever mentioned, Omaha. I want to see what it's really like."

"It's not that hard," Sam said. "I'm sure it's easier to get there than Mongolia."

Meena chewed on the tangy green papaya salad she'd ordered along with three other things. She was ravenous, and the food was better than not bad. "It's not level of difficulty. I've gone everywhere for work. And I have yet to get an assignment there."

Sam put a spring roll on her side dish before helping himself to one from the shared plate. "You never go anywhere for the sake of it?"

Meena shook her head. "I travel when I can get paid to do so."

"And what do you do with the money?"

"Pay bills, replace equipment, buy expensive lipstick."

"I am definitely a fan of the lipstick."

His eyes twinkled. Or was it the way the muted light hit his face as he talked? Meena glanced away from his lips. He was flirting, and she didn't want to encourage him, but she liked it. Too much. She changed the subject. "I found another note."

"That's why you were sitting on the kitchen floor."

"She told me her ashes should be buried under the big tree in the backyard," Meena said.

"Yeah," he said. "I was the one who took care of it."

Meena nodded. "I was baking a pie when I found it."

"What kind?"

"Apple," Meena said. "Tanvi brought me a dozen Granny Smiths from the farmers market on Sunday. That's not the point. I want to know more about her, Sam. Not as a replacement for my parents, but to understand who I came from. Do I resemble her in any way? Am I like her? I know she liked to be alone, and so do I."

"You're not like Neha."

"Really?" Meena frowned. "I can be cranky."

"So can I," Sam said. "All of us can be certain ways at different times."

Meena didn't know how to voice it, this desire to find a connection with someone she'd never known.

Sam leaned in over the table. Reached for her hand only to stop at touching the tips of her fingers. "I tried to tell you on Saturday but didn't get the chance."

Meena put down her fork.

His voice dropped lower, to a whisper. "Neha wasn't your birth mother."

Meena stilled. The synapses in her brain zapped around. Made it difficult to think. She took a breath. Then another. And calmed. She put her hand over his. "I understand. You were friends and you can't see this side of her. Maybe you're upset that she kept this a secret from you."

"That's not it," Sam said. "She probably had secrets. This isn't one of them."

"How do you know?" She believed Neha. Needed to believe her. Wanted this connection to the house, to a legacy. She wanted to belong somewhere. No, not just somewhere, but in the Engineer's House. "I have the notes."

"Does she say it explicitly?"

"She . . ." Meena mentally ran through the clues. "I'll show them to you. Let's go back. I've been through them over and over again. She defined my name. Then there's the apartment. She left it to me, the next generation." Meena called over their waitress and asked her to wrap up their food. "I know her. I can feel it. I wouldn't just believe something like this. She wanted me to find out."

The server brought empty containers. Silently they packed up. Sam had to be wrong. Or he wasn't convinced. Had she misread the notes? No. She'd been so hesitant to admit the possibility when she'd arrived. And she wasn't impulsive, not by a long shot.

He paid their bill as Meena wrapped her scarf around her neck and buttoned up her coat. She walked out of the restaurant and took long strides back to the apartment. Once Sam read the notes, he would see that Neha wasn't a stranger. Neha was the answer to a question she'd stopped asking. Neha was an anchor.

CHAPTER
TWENTY-EIGHT

Meena chewed on the loose cuticle of her thumb as she watched Sam go through each note, from index cards to fronts of fortunes from cookies. They were scattered on Neha's scuffed coffee table. She sat on the floor opposite him with Wally, who'd been freed from his crate after their silent walk back to the Engineer's House.

Meena knew she was a good journalist. She didn't jump to conclusions. She'd kept her mind open, allowed the story to unfold instead of forcing it together. The threads were all there, the inheritance, the messages Neha had written specifically for her. Meena stroked Wally's fur as he chewed on a toy that might have once been a raccoon.

"Well?" She ran out of patience.

He dropped the note in his hand on top of the others and removed his black-framed glasses. "I can see why you may think—"

She cut him off. "It's not an assumption. It's a conclusion."

"She doesn't explicitly make that claim."

"Why is this so hard for you to believe? Is it me? You don't want me to be here, like Sabina?" Meena heard the hitch in her voice and cleared her throat.

He reached for her. She shifted away from his touch.

"There are more notes," Meena argued. "They pop up all the time. So far the pieces fit."

"Because you want them to," Sam said.

Need them to. But Meena couldn't voice that. She wanted him to see the rational truth, not an emotional wish. "You don't get it. You think because you knew her, she would have told you all of it. But she wasn't the type to care about people. She had no use for a husband and likely didn't think she would be a good mother. What if she couldn't tell anyone and kept it a secret? Maybe she thought this was the only way to acknowledge me."

Sam rested his elbows on his thighs and clasped his hands. "When we don't understand the whole, we tend to fill in the missing pieces, like a sentence you can read even when it's missing all of the vowels."

"Don't patronize me."

He stood and ran his hands over his face. "She told me."

Meena stilled. "About me?"

"In a way," Sam said. "Not by name. Parts of it. She was thirty-four when you were born. Married for two years."

"She didn't want to be a mother." Meena's voice was flat. "There are many women who don't. You all said, over and over, that she didn't like people. She wasn't a nurturer."

"And what? She hid the pregnancy from her husband?"

"Stop." Meena didn't want logic. She couldn't have been wrong.

"Neha and I used to play chess." Sam softened his voice. "Whenever she felt like talking, she would set up the board. Not often. I learned quickly that she wanted someone to listen for a few hours."

Meena closed her eyes. She didn't want to hear what he had to say.

"About three years ago," Sam said, "she told me that she'd had a rough day. That she'd noticed the date. August sixth. She was restless. She'd been holding a secret that had become stuck in her throat. She wanted to say it out loud. She wanted to tell it to me."

"August sixth is my birthday." She knew she had to hear him out.

Sam nodded. "Now that I've put the pieces together, I know."

Meena sat on the couch and hugged her knees into her body, wrapped her arms around them. Wally wedged his face between her thigh and stomach. She loosened her grip and relaxed her legs. Wally climbed into her lap and nuzzled her. "That's when she told you about me?"

He shook his head. "Not you specifically, but about the time you were born. She'd been approached by a teenager who needed her help. Neha had been excited to help, proud to be of use to this person. Neha told me she'd helped the girl hide her pregnancy. Found a family to adopt the baby. The girl was so thankful, she'd let Neha name the baby."

Neha had named her. Her heart cracked. It was as if she were losing someone again. Someone she'd let in, not even all the way in, and still it was painful. "She was talking about me."

"I didn't know," Sam said. "At least not for sure. I wondered, but I didn't know how much I could say. It wasn't until you told me the other night. Even then I wasn't sure how to tell you about this."

A tear escaped and she didn't wipe it off. Another joined. She swallowed to stop the flow, but her heart needed the release and wouldn't let her brain stay in control. It wasn't until she felt Sam's arms around her that she steadied herself. Moved away from him. "Don't."

She went to the desk and stared out the windows that overlooked the back garden. The patch of dirt along the fence was covered with a layer of snow. She'd planted the wildflowers to annoy Sabina, but, in a way, Meena had been claiming her rightful space. "Did she say anything about the pregnant girl? Did Neha know her? Was she a relative?"

"She didn't say much more than that," Sam said. "I didn't think to ask questions. She was like that, told stories when she was in the mood. Mostly about herself, her family. Things like how she'd stopped learning to cook at fifteen because she'd decided she didn't want to become like her mother, working during the day, cooking and cleaning after her family on nights and weekends. Most of them were complaints disguised as stories. She was angry at her circumstances, yet she still reveled in what she'd made of her life."

"I guess I'm not as good at putting a story together as I thought," Meena said.

"I'm sorry." He came over to her and put his hands on her arms.

She turned around to face him, shifted out of his grasp. "Thanks for telling me."

"Meena."

"I don't want to talk about it anymore."

I believed I had found somewhere to belong.

"I know you're hurting," Sam said. "You don't have a good poker face. I'm a friend."

She bit her lip to keep from crying out.

She looked around the living room, surrounded by the things that belonged to the woman she thought she'd come from. Meena couldn't stop herself from asking, "Do you believe her? Could she have been lying to you?"

He gave her a sad smile. "The timeline. She was of an age where she could have taken care of you."

Meena nodded and rubbed her hands over her arms. "Do the aunties know too?"

Sam shook his head. "I don't think so. She barely told me. And even then in pieces."

Meena nodded. "You must think I'm such a fool."

"No." Sam took her hand in his. "You just didn't know the whole of it. I'm here for you. Whatever you need."

She nodded. "Thanks."

He leaned over and gave her a light kiss on the cheek. The faint contact made her yearn for more. That was the problem. Wanting. Needing. Yearning. Those words had seeped into her vocabulary these last few months. Her life didn't revolve around people or a place. She'd been free. She knew what she had to do. Leaning on Sam wasn't it.

When Sam left, Meena rushed into action. What she'd thought she'd found here wasn't real. She couldn't stay. Once Sabina learned of the loose link between Neha and Meena, she'd find a way to take the apartment. Meena couldn't stick around and watch Sabina win. Plane tickets, assignments, discovery—those were her life. Living everywhere was what suited her.

She reached for her backpack, which she'd left on a side chair by the fireplace. As she dug out her laptop, Meena noticed the small round table next to it. It was gray, made of iron, suited for the outdoors. A lot of knickknacks sat on top. An old-school wooden alphabet block caught her eye, the kind she'd played with in kindergarten. There was only one. The letter *M* in bright yellow.

She picked it up. Felt the weight of it in her hand. She clasped it tight until the edges left dents in her palm. She ignored the burn and ache of the wood against her skin. Then she turned and flung it into the fireplace. It didn't even nick a brick, which meant the throw wasn't as satisfying as she'd needed it to be. She picked the block up from the stone floor, where it had landed next to a fake giant decorative plant. Inside the plant's vase, she noticed a silk ribbon in pale pink. She tugged at it, pulled it from the fake brown branches. She unknotted it where it had gotten tangled up in the white and pink silk flowers.

On the other end was a small yellow envelope sealed with red wax. She lifted it, ripped the edge around the seal, and pulled out a folded letter. The paper was old, pale brown.

I don't travel. I know what the Eiffel Tower looks like. I do not need to stand in front of the Taj Mahal. Everything worth seeing can be done through photos. When I want to be somewhere other than this apartment or my office, I stay at a little bed-and-breakfast in Northampton. The main street has curious shops, and the people are average. There is nothing particularly spectacular there, and that's what I like about it.

She wanted to cut the note into little pieces. Neha was taunting her from beyond the grave. These notes weren't cute little fun facts—they were designed to manipulate and mislead. If she'd found this note earlier, she would have thought of it as further proof. Reading it knowing what she knew now, she saw it had been written to confuse, to make her wonder. Just enough information for Meena to believe something that was and wasn't true at the same time.

Meena added it to the pile and shoved the full envelope into her backpack. She'd had enough of being toyed with.

CHAPTER
TWENTY-NINE

The train was crowded with passengers and suitcases, and she was glad she'd found a little corner in which to stand, away from the doors. Meena read through a dozen text messages on the tube from Heathrow to central London. The aunties were tenacious.

Where are you? Sabina.

Emergency? Uma.

Next time leave more details. Sabina.

Come back for New Year's Eve. No, come before then so we can go shopping for a dress. One that will make it impossible for Sam not to kiss you at midnight. Tanvi.

It's been two hours. That's too long not to respond to a text. Uma.

We are worried you've been kidnapped even though Sam says that's unlikely. Tanvi.

On and on they went. Twenty texts later, Meena glanced around to see if the private investigator Uma had threatened to send was looking for her on the train. She slid the phone back into her backpack. She didn't want to miss them. They were the past. She had a life to get on with. Meena was hit by a wave of unfamiliar guilt. She shouldn't have worried them, at least not Tanvi and Uma. Should have left more than a terse note—*Off to London for the holidays. Apartment is unlocked.* They'd been kind to her and deserved more, and so did Sam. Except it was taking all her strength to push away the loss of what she'd thought she'd found.

Her phone rang. It was Tanvi. She ignored it. Put them in the rearview. Except she was weak. I'm fine. Just busy. She texted, then put away her phone.

She rubbed her forehead. She wrestled with the familiar tiredness from travel. She was ready to crawl into her twin bed at Zoe's and acclimate. She wanted a cup of coffee and a warm blanket.

She wondered what Sam was up to, if Wally was behaving. She could text him. She fiddled with her phone. She didn't know what to say. A simple "Hi" would be too vague and put the burden of conversation on him. She could explain why she'd left so suddenly, that she always chose flight over fight. It had not been a great way to leave, Meena acknowledged. She should have at least told Sam. As a courtesy. He had been a good friend, and she'd left with a generic note on the door.

She would apologize to him. Eventually.

The train stopped at South Kensington Station. She exited and caught the bus to Battersea. The small apartment with its closet-size spare room was empty. She sent off a text to let Zoe know she was there so as not to surprise her friend, then curled up in the twin bed she rented for under a hundred pounds a month and closed her eyes.

It was better to leave things as they were with Sam. It wasn't as if she were going to see him again anytime soon.

CHAPTER THIRTY

Meena huddled in her coat as she crossed over the Battersea Bridge into Chelsea. London was familiar and unfamiliar, a feeling Meena grew accustomed to in her travels. Each city had its urban centers and its suburbs, its shops and drinking establishments, its special corners for when locals wanted to keep away from tourists. There were areas of density, areas of luxury, and areas of inequity. The ethos of each city, however, was unique.

London was steeped in power, the rule of a few over many, the idea that some blood was better than others. It had evolved from lording over land to amassing wealth through financial markets. Underneath there were unwritten norms of politeness and etiquette. To exist in London was to conform to its essential Britishness. Boston was a distant cousin of London, more tenacious, more rebellious, and constantly on the lookout for a fight, as if its first battles against British tyranny had formed the nature of the place.

She'd been in this city a dozen times, knew its streets and sidewalks, but she never saw it as hers. In all her travels, she'd kept herself apart from the city. Always the observer. She wouldn't allow herself to be immersed, to feel a sense of belonging, a sense of home.

Every adoption starts with a loss. A woman who ran an orphanage in Wuhan had said this through a translator when Meena had been on an assignment covering Western adoptions. It had resonated as she took photos of infants and toddlers with their new, mostly white, parents. She'd thought of the loss for the little ones, even as they'd found families. Their names would be changed; some would know only that they looked Chinese or Asian. They might never speak their birth language or acquire a taste for the food of their ethnicity.

For the last few months, she'd believed she'd found herself. That she was part of a culture. She'd warmed to chai and paratha, to the snippets of language the aunties had taught her. She'd liked living with people who resembled her, as in the shape of Sabina's thick eyebrow, in the texture of Tanvi's long black hair, in the full bow of Uma's lips. When Meena was in the fourth chair at the dining table, she wasn't alone in her look, her shape, her laugh. While she didn't always understand the aunties, she wasn't dissimilar. For a couple of months, she'd grown to like being a part of a group, a building, one with history. Her history. She'd been so naive.

Meena navigated her way around a couple in matching Santa hats who stumbled out of a black cab. The woman, in a bright-green coat, held on to her partner as she navigated the steps to the bar in her stiletto heels. Meena smiled as they wished her a happy Christmas, a tacit apology for inconveniencing her. She nodded in acknowledgment to absolve them.

The street changed from the chip shops and working-class pubs of Battersea to the posh stores and upscale restaurants of Chelsea. Her surroundings changed from the gray-and-brown dullness south of the River Thames to the blue-and-white sparkle on the other side of the water.

Her mother used to say that people who lived near water were more kind. *When you make your own home, try to have one near a river.* The Engineer's House was two short blocks from the Charles River. Maybe that was why Tanvi and Sam were so nice.

Meena walked through the doors of the Builders Arms, a cozy pub on a short street that was more an alley than a thoroughfare. It was warm and crowded. She navigated past the long bar to the back, to where Zoe and her friends sat at a table against the wall. Zoe waved her over and patted a large red chair with a straight back.

"Saved this just for you." Zoe and Aiden, her boyfriend, were on the dark-brown leather couch tucked against the blue wall. Zoe's three friends were on stools around the large scuffed wood table.

Meena unwrapped her scarf and tugged off her coat. She recognized the faces—Fiona, Paul, and Bernie, Zoe's longtime friends. From the way they laughed and joked, they were more than a few pints in. Zoe poured a glass of prosecco from a bottle chilling in an ice bucket and handed it to Meena.

"It's so nice to see you again. How long? Last year?" Paul was Zoe's friend from childhood. He and Zoe had been neighbors and schoolmates in East London. He was an investment banker by day and a sax player in a trio in the evenings, and he was always friendly. He was as handsome as he was kind. And dressed sharply to complement his dark skin and deep-brown eyes.

"No," Zoe said. "She's missed the roast the last two years. She popped by in April to drop off a few things."

"I am sorry," Meena said. "I've apologized by stocking your fridge with champagne."

"How long have you been here?" Paul asked. "Where have you come from?"

"About two weeks. And Boston." Meena sipped the prosecco.

"A toast. Happy Christmas," Zoe interrupted. "May we all get exactly what we deserve."

They clinked glasses. This was Zoe's annual tradition, one Meena had participated in once or twice in the past. The pre-Christmas Sunday roast at the pub. Meena loved this quintessential British custom. A lazy Sunday, the quiet hum of the crowd, a crackling fireplace on the other side of the room, and platters of roast beef, chicken, or salmon with potatoes, cabbage, and carrots. The best part was the Yorkshire pudding drizzled with gravy. It all ended with sticky toffee pudding.

"How was it, besides cold and dark?" Paul asked. "Shoot anything fun?"

"It wasn't for work," Meena said. "Took a little break. Fall in Boston is beautiful."

"And the men?" Fiona was an old work colleague of Zoe's, petite and cheerful in her Santa hat and bright-green dress.

Meena shook her head.

"Are you sticking around for a bit?" Paul asked.

"Through the New Year," Meena said. "Then I'm in Seoul for a quick feature."

She'd pitched a few stories while she'd been in London, and one had been picked up by an editor for *Rolling Stone* magazine. It would be good to get back to what she did. Next year at this time, the memories of these past few months would have faded.

"No work talk," Fiona ordered. "We need to drink and party."

"Speaking of." Paul cleared his throat as if to make an announcement. "I'm playing at a little place in Islington on New Year's Eve. Will add you to the guest list."

"Thanks," Meena said. "That sounds fun."

"They've added a new drummer." Fiona licked her lips. "He's deliciously beautiful."

"Fee." Paul turned to her. "You know the rule: no dating my bandmates."

"It's not my fault," Fiona said. "Add some undatable men and I'll keep away."

Paul wagged his finger at Fiona.

"Zoe has Aiden," Fiona argued. "Bernie and Louise are moving in together next month. You've got Andrew. I'm the last of our group; all of you need to be on the lookout for me."

"I'm doing my best," Zoe offered. "I even have a date for you for New Year's Eve. He's a creative at my agency and very fun. At the holiday party, he led the whole office in karaoke to 'Dancing Queen.' It was hilarious."

"Sounds like a keeper." Bernie nudged Fiona with her shoulder.

"What about you, Meena?" Fiona asked. "Any New Year's Eve dates? Did you bring a burly Bostonian with you to spend the holidays?"

"Leave her be. She's perfectly happy on her own," Zoe said.

Meena poured herself more prosecco and tried not to think about Sam. At least he wouldn't be described as burly in any sense of the word. Geeky, charming, casual, kind. She took a sip and returned her focus to the conversation that continued around her.

"Who are you thinking about?" Fiona asked.

Meena touched her cheek. "No one. It's warm in here."

"No it's not." Fiona pointed her glass toward Meena. "Spill."

"It isn't like that," Meena said.

"Now I'm curious." Paul leaned toward her. "Tell."

"Nothing to talk about," Meena said. "Besides, my arm was in a cast for the last two months, and I was stuck inside. It wasn't as if I could do much."

"There are many interesting possibilities with one hand." Bernie smirked.

A quick laugh escaped her. They were being so nice, she didn't want to be churlish. "There is someone. Maybe. I'm not sure."

Their silence was quick and acute.

Meena awkwardly kept going. "He lived, uh, lives, across the hall from where I was staying in Boston. He's nice and cute. And he has an awesome dog."

"I love a man with a dog," Paul said. "I want one, but . . ."

"It's a big commitment," Aiden added.

"Forget the dog," Zoe said. "Tell me more about the neighbor."

Meena laughed. "We became friends."

"Name," Paul said.

"Sam."

"Profession."

"Special effects," Meena stated. "For movies and television."

"Good kisser?"

Meena blushed. "We didn't . . . uh, it wasn't like that."

"But you wanted to." Zoe grinned.

"Yeah," Meena said. "It got complicated."

"Always does." Bernie sighed.

"Besides," Meena said, "I'm on the road. He's the type that enjoys being in one place. We're very different."

"But you like him," Fiona said. "I can hear it in your voice."

Meena touched her warm face again. "It's like I'm a teenager with a crush."

Zoe touched her knee. "I hope we never stop being fifteen when we like someone."

Meena gave her friend a wide smile. "Yeah."

"Ask him to come join you for New Year's Eve," Paul urged.

"Like a grand gesture," Fiona said. "Buy him a plane ticket, get him over here."

"That would be very premature." Meena couldn't imagine ever doing such a thing.

"Show us a picture, then." Bernie waved her hand for Meena's phone.

Meena opened the gallery app and handed it to Bernie.

Paul looked over Bernie's shoulder. "These three women are magic."

"The aunties run that building. In a way they are the building."

"Is this the guy?" Fiona asked. "A disheveled man in a tux is really sexy."

"He dressed as James Bond for Halloween."

"I'll swap you," Fiona suggested. "You with whoever Zoe has me with, and your James Bond with me to ring in the New Year."

Meena felt a twinge of possessiveness for Sam. She wanted to be the one to kiss Sam at midnight.

She put away her phone as their meals were served. Meena dug in. The beef was perfectly cooked, dark on the outside, pink on the inside. The gravy with the Yorkshire pudding was made to be sopped up. Meena didn't feel like an interloper. Today, for this brief time, in this red chair, she felt she had a place at this table among these people.

As the afternoon wore off and the gray sky turned dark, Meena huddled back into her coat and scarf. She said her goodbyes and headed back to the apartment while Zoe went to Aiden's.

Her head was full in a good way as the prosecco bubbles traveled throughout her body and gave her shimmery warmth on the inside. She walked over the bridge back to Battersea behind a couple who were arm in arm, and in that moment, though she was wistful, she didn't feel as alone as she normally did. She grabbed her phone from her coat and scrolled down to Sam's name.

She didn't quite hit the call button. What was there to say? She could ask after Wally, or just say hi. But it was awkward. Although, knowing Sam, he would take it in stride. Silly. They'd been neighbors for a few weeks, friends. Nothing more.

Meena tucked the phone back in her pocket and continued on her way.

CHAPTER
THIRTY-ONE

Meena clasped her hands in front of her as the toned, slim woman on the television said, "Namaste." She exhaled as Zoe turned off the yoga class.

I'm Indian. I'm allowed. It was one of the first things Sam had said to her. To know something that basic—she'd never realized what a luxury that was. Most people took it for granted.

"I needed that." Zoe patted her face with a towel. "A good start to dry January."

"Every year . . . ," Meena began.

"I know, I never make it to the end of January." Zoe cut her off. "I lack discipline, but one of these times, I will finish the whole month. The fridge is stocked with veggies and fish, brown rice is the only carb in the house. I've got plenty of herbal tea. No caffeine. No alcohol. No food that's not on the list. And no fun."

Meena scooched back on the yoga mat to lean against the navy couch. "At least you have company with Fiona and Paul doing the same."

"And we made a pact to stay away from Bernie, who will always order all the things we cannot eat," Zoe said. "I swear Bernie tests us to see which one will break first."

"I won't do that to you." Meena rolled her shoulders. "I'll even make us salads for lunch."

"Today," Zoe said. "Three days into the cleanse. But you leave tomorrow—then what?"

"You'll be fine."

"What happens after you go to Asia? Where to then?"

"Once I finish up in Seoul, I'm going to hang around there and see if I can snag a couple more assignments in South Korea." Meena picked at a loose thread on her black yoga pants. "To be honest, I'm not very excited about going back on the road."

Zoe sat up and crossed her arms around her bent knees. Her short, curly blonde hair had fallen out of the clip during their yoga session. "Why not?"

"I don't know." Meena felt the tension she'd just released creep back in. "This is what I do, right? It's my career. My life. I want to go to these places, tell these stories."

"Makes sense," Zoe said. "You've been at this since we graduated college. You've been able to make it work."

"But?"

"We're in our thirties now. It's OK to assess if this is what you want for the next ten years and beyond."

"I've never thought that far ahead." She had adopted the Buddhist philosophy of staying in the present.

"That's fine. But don't you worry that if you don't think about it, you might wind up somewhere you didn't want to be in twenty years?"

Meena smiled at her friend. "I'll always have my camera and a way to put food on my table. That's enough."

"I know this is a touchy thing for you," Zoe said. "But you did tell me about why you thought that woman left you the apartment."

"And it turned out to not be true."

"But you found it exciting," Zoe said. "You liked knowing where you came from."

Meena shrugged. "I don't need to know my ethnicity. I belong in the world. I guess that's enough. After all, I have you and a few new friends. I can be a part of a group with people I know."

Zoe took a sip from her water bottle. "You're different. More . . . I don't know if *open* is the right word. But something."

Meena nodded. "It hurt finding out the truth. I ran because I realized how much I wanted that connection. I know I've . . . kept people at a distance." Meena cleared her throat. "Including you. I'm going to try to find a balance, figure out who I am after this speed bump."

"More like a giant hill to jump over," Zoe said. "You're lucky I don't let people leave me. It's my baggage. Thanks to divorced parents with their new children, I collect people who I want in my life and make sure they're never allowed to drop me the way my parents have done."

"I promise not to resist," Meena said. "Not as a resolution or anything. I want to be as good of a friend to you as you are to me."

"Does that mean you'll now have a five-year plan? Remember birthdays, share your accomplishments and your failures?"

"I don't know if I'd go that far."

Zoe threw a present at her and Meena caught it. It was the same present Zoe gave her each year. "This time don't treat this like a collector's item. Use it. It doesn't have to be five years."

Meena flipped through pages of dates and times. "I guess I could write in my dates for assignments. Roughly plan out a week or so to come back here."

Zoe took it from her. "You're doing it wrong." She grabbed a pen from the desk. "This is a passion planner. It's about visualizing your future, putting it on paper, and committing to it. Let's see. We're going to start you on baby steps. What do you want out of the next three months?"

"Work."

"Besides work."

Meena was at a loss. She shrugged. "What are you writing down?"

"Date someone," Zoe stated. "That's your goal. Not to go on one date but see someone for at least three dates."

"That's ridiculous," Meena said. "I'm going to be working, I don't know how long I'll be in one spot."

"That's the beauty of this." Zoe pointed her pen at Meena. "If you commit, you have to find a way. Plan for it. How long is your assignment in Seoul?"

"A week."

"Then you're going to be there for a few more, right? Build in a little time to socialize. Or reconnect with your network there. Maybe you can see someone you already know in a different way. You don't have to fall in love. You just go on a first, second, and third date with the same person. That's nothing. Baby steps."

"It's not feasible."

Zoe plopped on the couch and curled her legs under her as she crossed out what she'd written. "Let's see, what's even a smaller step than that? Got it. The guy you met in Boston, the one across the hall, your goal is to text him."

Meena shrugged. "I can do that."

Zoe looked at her. "Not just a text; you have to flirt with him. If he flirts back, you must keep at it. For three months."

"What's the point?" Meena asked. "I'm not sure when I'll be back in Boston. It's not really fair to start something . . ."

"You are practicing," Zoe said. "Not diving into a relationship. Just see what it's like."

Meena closed her eyes. The thought of flirting with Sam over text, she liked it. Too much.

"It's not a big deal," Zoe said. "Ask him about his dog, tell him about wherever you are. Send a selfie, ask for one back . . . I mean, you have interacted with the male species. It's not that complicated."

Meena chewed on a cuticle. "He did say he was interested in me."

"There you go. He's not an idiot," Zoe said. "Do something about it."

Meena stood and stretched. "I'll *think* about it."

"I've written it down in here," Zoe argued. "This means you have to do it."

"If you make it through all of your January cleanse." Meena crossed her arms. "I'll do it."

"You're not waiting until the end of January. And this time I will make it."

Meena took the planner from Zoe. Flipped to where Zoe had written things out. "There's one-year and five-year goals in here too."

"We'll fill those out after you finish this one." Zoe stood. "I'm going to shower. You're on salad duty."

On impulse, Meena leaned in and gave Zoe a quick hug. She laughed when her friend stood there in shock.

"I'm practicing," Meena said.

She went to the kitchen and thought about what she would say to Sam as a first text. "Happy New Year" felt a little too late. She chopped carrots and let herself think about him. His face was kind. She could hear the deep timbre of his voice. She thought of how sometimes he wore glasses, square black frames, and other times nothing blocked the deep-brown eyes. He touched easily, a gentle palm on top of her hand, the warmth of his skin on her arms as he tried to comfort her.

She didn't deserve him. He was meant for someone as uncomplicated as he was. Not the internal mess Meena had made of her life. She put the chopped veggies in a bowl and cut a lemon in half. It was best to keep moving, to put him in a slot as a casual friend. Seoul was next, and she wouldn't think beyond that.

CHAPTER
THIRTY-TWO

Seoul. It was a young city built atop ancient culture. The city was uniform, organized with precision without sacrificing the past. Tall, gleaming structures sat alongside Buddhist temples. Hypertechnology was the marrow that allowed this city to overperform in education and conformity without sacrificing its traditions. It was a city of contrasts that fed off one another, the tensions not obvious.

It was the middle of the night, the bass thumping heavy under techno pop, giving the crowd on the dance floor a beat. Multicolored laser lights flashed in rhythm to the music as DJ Tyno mixed on a platform overseeing the party scene. Club NB was ranked one of the best clubs in the world. Located in the exclusive neighborhood of Gangnam, it was the mecca for K-pop fans around the world.

Meena snapped a few shots of women in tight dresses and shirtless men who switched from dancing to downing shots. Then she headed back to a table in the VIP section.

"This is where I feel most at home." Kini, a woman with pink extensions, raised her glass of champagne. "It's expensive, but I save up for nights like tonight."

Meena took another photo of the group around the table. Five women from Chicago, LA, and San Diego had moved to Seoul recently. Their jobs were remote. They'd known each other for three years after meeting online as fans of the K-pop band BTS.

"Some people say we're Koreaboo, like we're too obsessed with Korean culture in a negative way." Jennifer touched up her dark purple lipstick. "But it's not like that. We're fans of Korea, especially BTS, but we're expats who want to be a part of this culture."

Lauren, a paralegal, said with a thick Chicago accent, "I still vote in the US, and my family is there."

Kini and Jada worked for Google; Jennifer and Tasha were in website development.

"OMG," Jennifer screamed. She ran from the table to the railing to dance in her red heels and sleeveless white dress. "This is my favorite song."

"She's a V fan," Kini explained. "He's in BTS."

Meena nodded and took photos of Jennifer singing into an imaginary mike. "Do you understand Korean?"

"I'm conversational in it." Jada stopped singing to respond. "I started learning it a few years ago, as soon as I discovered K-pop. Living here, it's gotten a lot better."

Meena took notes along with photos. This was her last shoot for her *Rolling Stone* assignment on American women living in Korea, motivated by their love of K-pop. She'd been with these five women for a week, in their homes, at their workplaces, on dates with their Korean boyfriends, and out in clubs. In their late thirties, these women had found something they'd been missing. Permission.

"We're not embarrassed or ashamed that we like a boy band," Tasha said. "We own it. Like, who decided we had to outgrow our teenage selves? And let's be clear, I'm not chasing boys. I love their music, yes, of course I find them sexy, but not in a way that's icky. I have an age-appropriate boyfriend. And part of me is like, *This is what I want to do, and you can suck it if you don't like it.* It's like BTS gave me this confidence where I live on my own terms."

It was four in the morning by the time Meena left the club and headed back to her hotel. She'd wrapped up what she'd needed, and after a few hours of sleep, she would edit and caption her best images before sending the whole set to the photo editor. She would also let the writer of the piece know she'd filed her pictures. Then she would find a place to stay and be on the lookout for more work. As she packed away her camera, she scanned her phone. Tanvi continued to text regularly, and while Meena's texts back had been sporadic at first, the woman had worn her down. Tanvi had a lot of questions and wanted to live vicariously. So Meena had sent short videos of Korean street food, which Uma had taken up as a challenge to re-create it. Now Tanvi was asking about the club.

Meena sent a short video of the dance floor and the maniacal strobe lights and hit send. In the cab ride back to her hotel, she rewatched the last video from Tanvi, who had recorded Wally chewing up one of Sabina's slippers. The attached text said, **He's such a good boy.** Meena missed the little puppy.

And Sam. She wanted to text him, talk to him. Instead of letting him fade from her memory, each day that passed without contact, she missed him more. The longer she put it off, the more overwhelming the need became. She hadn't stayed in touch. She didn't know if the aunties gave him updates on her. And in a way it would be worse if they did. She didn't know why she was acting this way. Sam was no different from Tanvi. *You can't lie to yourself.*

Once in her room, Meena brushed her teeth, washed her face, and applied moisturizer before climbing into the small bed. This was her life again. Prioritizing her work above everything else. The new was becoming old. Even after a few months off, she was already tired.

Because she wanted to be somewhere else. She wanted to live somewhere. Not as a base, not as a flat share, but as her own place.

An idea stirred her. A new goal to write down in the passion planner Zoe had given her. One year—not six months—to unpack her things, have utility bills in her name. The obvious place was the one she already had, her inheritance. She had three months left before she was even eligible to sell the apartment. Three months until Sabina would inevitably demand that she do so. She smiled as she thought about her wildflowers. She really wanted to be there when they bloomed in a few months, wanted to see Sabina's reaction. It wasn't going to be pleasant. She got up and grabbed a pen and the planner from her backpack. She also took out a small wooden elephant she'd taken from Neha's apartment on an impulse. It was like a talisman, and rubbing it helped her think.

Back on the bed, she wrote down her three-month goal. *Keep the apartment and make it mine.* She'd fight Sabina if she had to. She didn't know the rest. She looked at the "flirt with Sam" goal. She was going to keep that one too.

She was giddy with the energy that came from being overtired. She grabbed her phone before she overthought anything.

Hey. It's Meena. Sorry it's been a while. Hope you had a good holiday. Give Wally scratches for me. I'm in South Korea by the way. Feel free to text. If you want. She deleted the last line. **Would love to hear from you.** She deleted that too. **Take care.** She hit send before she could change her mind.

As she lay down to sleep, she rubbed the wooden elephant as if it were a worry stone. In the early-morning light, she examined it as she'd done countless times. It was as big as her hand, with a heavy, round belly that protruded at the bottom. There were sharp edges around the ears and face, roundness around the thick trunk. There were a lot of details, lines carved to show wrinkles around the ears. Nails drawn on the toes.

The elephant slid out of her hand and fell on the tile floor. Meena reached over to pick it up and saw a crack in the belly. No, not a crack but a little slit, one she hadn't noticed before. She picked at it with her nail. It unlatched from the top of the protruding belly to reveal a small pocket. There was a roll of paper wedged in. She unfurled it. A CVS receipt that had been written over in dark-blue ink in Neha's handwriting. The receipt ink was faded, and it was hard to read what the purchases had been, but the blue ink was clear and unsmudged.

Sex is a man's pleasure. A woman's burden. A man can implant his sperm into a womb and move on. Careless men do not even consider consequences. Your father is such a man.

Meena clutched the note. It wasn't addressed to her. It could refer to anything or anyone. She had to keep a clear head and not jump to conclusions. She'd gone down the road of assuming before, and she had to be more cautious this time.

He took his pleasure with a young girl, then went back to his privileged life. That he was also young is no excuse. But he was my family. His mess was mine to clean up.

Numb, Meena rolled up the note and slid it back into the elephant. *A woman's burden.* She'd been so focused on her birth mother, Meena hadn't given much thought to her birth father. Could her link to Neha be through her biological father? Would that mean the apartment was her birthright after all? She felt the ache to belong in the Engineer's House deep in her stomach.

She closed her eyes and recalled the living room. The dark bookshelves and the bright furniture belonged to Neha, but the structure, the walls, the hardwood floors, had been passed down to Meena—maybe not through Neha's guilt, but because it was rightfully hers.

She wanted to be back there, not in this tiny room six thousand miles away. The knowledge was frightening and exciting. Meena jumped out of the bed again. Sleep wasn't going to happen right now. She had clarity. She had ties that she wanted to build on. She had a home to make for herself.

It felt wrong and right. To help her anxiety, she checked the balance in her savings account. She would be OK. She lived frugally; she could take a little more time off to sort all this out once and for all. Then she booked flights.

She looked over at the elephant and pulled out the note. Neha had called the man who'd impregnated the young girl her family. She hadn't had siblings, but that didn't mean she hadn't had other male relatives, a distant cousin perhaps. It was a lead. Meena could track him down. Not for a reunion or even an acknowledgment of who they were to each other, but a confirmation. She wouldn't assume this time. She would verify.

CHAPTER
THIRTY-THREE

The apartment was quiet, as was the building. Meena let herself in, no key necessary, and pulled off her hat and scarf. It was cold, and she checked the thermostat, which had been adjusted from seventy to sixty-five. Still in her coat, she wandered around the living room, through the bedroom and the kitchen, then sat on the familiar yellow sofa.

It was different now. This was hers. Until now she'd seen this as Neha's apartment. She'd been reluctant to accept it, admit that she wanted to keep it. Even though her chest was tight at the thought of having a home, she wanted to make one for herself. Here, in a building with history, community, and . . . she let out a nervous breath as she thought of Sam. Maybe more. First things first, she turned the knobs on the radiators to warm the place up.

She could take the time to figure out what to do with all the stuff. She didn't have a lot of money to spend, but she wanted to make this place hers, not Neha's. She'd even gotten some links from Zoe to sites on decorating with a small budget. Crowded as this place was, it was a blank canvas. She had no idea what she liked and didn't like when it came to having a home of her own. Color? Not this much. Minimalism? Probably. Art? Definitely not the naked man made of bottle caps that currently stared at her from one wall. She would keep some of Neha's things, practical things, like the blue wingback chairs by the fireplace.

It had taken two weeks to get here from Seoul. Meena had finished the *Rolling Stone* story, then spent a couple of days in London, then spent a few days in New York, finally catching up with editors she'd rescheduled with in the past. It was important that they know she was back in the US for assignments. She would still go anywhere, but for a little while, it would be nice to cover Sturgis or the hot-air balloon festival in New Mexico if the opportunity came her way.

It was exhilarating, the idea of doing things she'd never done. She'd made notes in her planner about switching over the utilities currently being paid for by the estate once the year was up. There was a lot to do, from her driver's license to tax things. It was daunting, but she was without the undercurrent of exhaustion she'd been carrying. She smiled to herself. It felt good. She'd made a decision, a choice.

Meena was startled when the door opened. She couldn't believe she hadn't locked it behind her when she'd come in. Then she laughed as Wally ran in and jumped on her, his front paws on her thigh. He nudged her for more.

"Hi, buddy." Meena scratched behind his ears. "Do you remember me? I missed you so much." Wally jumped again. "You got so big. You want up?" She pulled him into her lap, and he pawed at her thighs and chest, his face all over her.

"Wally, down."

The pup looked up, and Meena braced against Sam's stern voice.

"Wally, down," Sam repeated.

The dog nudged his face into Meena's armpit. She stood and put him down. "I see he's still having issues with authority."

He gave Wally an exasperated look. "He's stubborn."

"A dog with his own mind."

"He's made some enemies. Sabina hasn't forgiven him for ripping up her slipper, and Uma still glares at him because he chewed up her laptop charger."

Meena went down on her knees and cuddled Wally. "Oh no, Wally." Then she whispered in the puppy's ear, "Good job on the slipper."

"Fair warning," Sam said. "Don't take your eyes off of him."

Meena stood, and Wally went over to sniff her backpack. She followed him and pulled out a little gift she'd gotten on impulse. "Smart puppy." She handed him a big bone. "Here, is this what you smelled?"

The dog took it out of her hand and moved to a sunny corner by the window and gnawed.

"I hope you don't mind," Meena said.

Sam shook his head. "It'll occupy him for an hour, tire him out. I'm thankful."

She tugged off her coat. She didn't know what to say. He hadn't texted her back. Two weeks was a long time not to respond. It was fine. She hadn't been in touch for weeks before that. She hadn't mentioned her trip. "I should have told you I was leaving."

He shrugged and put his hands in the pockets of his black sweatpants. "You left a note."

"I should have texted. Earlier."

"You have your own life."

It used to be that way. Now she had people she wanted to stay in touch with, wanted them to miss her. "I'm staying."

"OK."

"You're mad at me."

"I'm not." Sam shook his head. "You've been clear that your life is fairly transient."

She gave him the truth. "I ran. I let Neha in. Thought she was, well, you know. Then she wasn't and I ran." *Because that's who I am. Who I was.*

"I get it," Sam said.

"Can you maybe not be so . . . understanding?"

"I don't have the right to be upset," Sam said. "I'm not in your shoes."

"We were friends. I didn't treat you like one when I left."

"Yeah." Sam paused. "I thought . . ."

Meena waited, but he didn't finish his sentence.

"I'm sorry," she repeated.

"Next time, add me to your group chat with the aunties."

"Are you sure about that? They send racy jokes and not-safe-for-work photos."

He gave her a soft smile. "In that case, let's keep things as they are."

She didn't like that. "I'll text you separately. Just the two of us."

His face lost some of its tension and Meena's heart sped up. She could feel him, sense that she'd hurt him. It was more than attraction. More than friendship. She refused to be scared off by it. "You can leave Wally with me if you want. I'm going to unpack."

"He's almost six months," Sam said. "You won't get anything done if he's here. Wally, come."

The dog looked up. Stared.

Sam deepened his voice and gave him the same command. This time Wally stood, bone in his mouth, and went to Sam. Sam took Wally by the leash attached to his harness and left. He closed the door behind them.

There was distance between them, but Meena wasn't daunted. She would figure out how to fix it. She rolled her big suitcase, the one she'd bought to fit more of her London stuff, into the bedroom. She would start here. She had emptied a few drawers for her things during her temporary stay, so she filled up that space. As for the rest of it, she'd keep it in the bag until the remainder of Neha's things were cleared out.

Meena heard footsteps and went into the living room.

Sabina froze, a tin watering can in hand. "Meena."

"Hi."

Sabina regained her composure. "I thought you were still in South Korea."

"I'm back."

"I see."

Meena wouldn't back down, but she didn't want to start off confrontational. She didn't know how Sabina was going to handle her decision to stay. "How are you?"

"Good," Sabina said. "Everyone is fine. Settling into the New Year."

"Right. How was your New Year's Eve party?"

"Fun. As always."

Meena rubbed her arms. "I adjusted the thermostat, but it's taking a while to heat up."

Sabina put the watering can down on a stack of newspapers on the coffee table and moved to the radiator. She crouched down to turn the black knob. "I half closed the valves because no one was here. I wasn't expecting you back."

Of course not. "Thank you for taking care of the apartment while I was away."

"It's my place to do so." Sabina rose back up. "This is my building."

Meena kept quiet instead of reminding her that this was Meena's apartment. Honey and flies and all that.

"There is a blizzard in the forecast starting later tonight." Sabina added a few more details about the coming storm. "If you need food or anything, I suggest you go get it now. They're saying eighteen to twenty-six inches."

"They mentioned it on the flight in," Meena said. "I'll run out to the market. Let me know if you need anything."

"We're fine. I'm surprised to see you back so soon. I thought you had work that takes you all over." Sabina walked around watering the few plants, holdovers from Neha.

"I do need a base, somewhere to keep my things." Meena tried to keep her voice neutral. She wanted to get along with this woman. "This is a good one. Close to New York, an international airport."

"I see."

Meena hoped she did. "Thank you again."

Sabina finished up and nodded before leaving the apartment.

When Sabina left, Meena locked the door. She knew she'd have to adjust and keep it unlocked . . . at least part of the time. But she wasn't ready for that. Baby steps.

She bundled up and headed out for storm supplies. As she turned left, she saw Sam walk with Wally down the block. They were on their way back. She switched directions and took the long way around to the small market on Newbury Street.

∾⋇∾

Neha could have outfitted a fifty-person ugly-sweater party. Meena folded a peacock-green sweater with a giant rooster embellished with glass stones. She'd already filled a box, one of a dozen empties she'd picked up from the corner liquor store during her presnowstorm supply run. She'd done it in four trips back and forth because a blizzard was the perfect time to clean out the apartment.

The wind howled, and she could see snow falling sideways through the french doors. Inside she was warm from the hiss of the radiators and her exertion. After her initial encounters with Sabina, Sam, and Wally, the previous day had been uneventful. No aunties had run into the apartment with a thermos of chai and conversation. Instead she'd sat in her designated chair at the dining table and eaten a solitary bowl of canned soup.

Funny. A few months ago, she'd craved time alone. Thought the aunties barging in for visits was intrusive. Now she kept waiting to hear footsteps. When she did, she'd hold her breath for a knock on the door.

But the only visitors she saw were a snow-removal crew coming to clear out what fell to keep up with the blizzard.

Meena closed one box, shoved it to the side, and grabbed an empty one. The bedroom closet and dresser were going to use up all the boxes she had. But looking around, she saw she'd already made a difference in the room. This apartment was no longer a shrine to Neha and her belongings. Meena would ask the aunties if they wanted anything before donating them.

She had also decided to deal with the books last, if ever. Tanvi's husband was interested, so she would have him take what he wanted. She might leave the rest, as they gave the living room a studious vibe.

She hopped up as she heard a knock on the door.

"You're back." Tanvi enveloped Meena in a hug.

Meena was stunned for a second at the casual affection. For the first time since she'd been back, she felt welcomed. She stepped back from Tanvi, who was dressed in a long purple skirt with matching tights and a white wool sweater. Her hair was up in a loose bun, and purple gems dangled from her ears.

"What are you up to?" Tanvi stepped around the boxes.

"Clearing out some of Neha's things in the bedroom." Meena led Tanvi back.

"I suppose it is time." Tanvi found an empty spot on the floor and sat down. "Let me help." She began folding. "We talked about it but couldn't make ourselves do it. Then you came. Then you left. How was your trip? I told Uma and Sabina that we're adding Seoul to our list of trips. I want to go to that club."

"You'll love it."

"I would never judge anyone's fashion sense, but Neha's was really out there." Tanvi held up a sweater in bright red. The front had a black felt top hat, mustache, and monocle sewn on. "I'm not sure anyone could pull this off."

Meena laughed. Tanvi joined in.

"I remember her wearing a lot of these," Tanvi said. "Uma is usually in jeans. Sabina must always have some Indian artifact on, jewelry or a kurta. I thought I was the brave one in my color choices. But Neha took it to the next level."

"You're welcome to anything you'd like to keep." Meena waved her arm over the clothes. "This is just the beginning. I'm going to donate most everything."

Tanvi nodded. "Don't donate the art. It's kitschy and weird, but some of it I made."

"I'd like to keep what's yours." She really hoped it wasn't the nude bottle-caps dude.

Tanvi gave her a big smile. "Of course."

Meena chewed on her lip. "Can I ask why no one's come by since I've been back?"

"I just did."

Meena nodded. "You didn't bring chai. And I haven't seen Uma at all."

"I see. It's not the company you're missing but the tea."

"No. It is the company. Things feel different somehow."

Tanvi crossed her legs on the floor and reached over for another empty box. "Well, we didn't know if you were coming back. You never mentioned it in any of our conversations or texts. You came back the way you left, without word. This building is like a family. Yes, it can seem a little too close with everyone in each other's business. It's what we're used to and you're not."

"I know I'm not part of the family . . ."

"I meant it's not what you're used to," Tanvi said. "You keep your door locked and come and go as you please, and that's understandable."

"You're right. I haven't been very . . . I don't know . . . involved."

Tanvi reached over and squeezed Meena's hand. "Yes. But we are here if—*when* you want to see what it is like again."

"The way I left was a spur-of-the-moment decision," Meena explained.

"Work can be like that. When inspiration hits me, I go into my studio and don't answer my phone for hours. You have a job that needs you to be somewhere fast, you go. Remember, though, we appreciate texts with some details instead of a generic note on the door."

"Got it."

"You are independent," Tanvi observed. "You don't need anyone. Maybe because you've been on your own since you were a teenager. It's also OK to rely on people, ask for help. Friendship can only work if it's reciprocated."

This time Meena reached over and squeezed Tanvi's hand. "I'm sorry for leaving like that. And thank you for helping me with all of this."

"Neha did have a lot." They folded items as the wind howled outside.

Meena chewed on her lower lip. "I don't have a lot of practice being a good friend. I have Zoe and she's great. No matter how many invitations I pass up, she still asks."

"She sounds lovely."

"She is. I'm going to be better." Meena knew she had to keep working on building and maintaining relationships. "With Zoe and with you all."

"Don't sell yourself too short," Tanvi said. "There is something you're doing right with Zoe for her to keep asking."

"More like she's as stubborn as you. Never takes no for an answer."

Tanvi bobbled her head from side to side. "Oh, I always take no. So does Uma. We respect everyone's choices."

"Sabina?"

"It takes her time to accept things that don't go the way she wants them to."

"I'm glad to be your friend," Meena said. "I'm sorry I left the way I did. Came back the way I did."

"History always starts in the present." Tanvi folded a sweater. "One warning, though. Be careful what you wish for. I'm a bad influence."

Meena laughed. "I can use a little bit of that. Though maybe baby steps when it comes to day drinking."

"That was fun." Tanvi laughed. "Right now we're drying out from last week. We took our January trip to Saint Bart's, and it was nonstop fruity cocktails on the beach, wine for dinner, and making memories we've already forgotten thanks to the constant flow of alcohol."

"I hope you took pictures."

"We never document our trips. We have no desire to be the Real Housewives of the Engineer's House." Tanvi tapped her head. "It either sticks here or it was meant to be forgotten."

Meena hesitated, then went for it. "Maybe I can join in next year."

The surprise on Tanvi's face made her cringe.

"Sorry. I didn't mean to . . . I know it's the three of you, your friend-ship bond . . ."

"As long as you promise to leave your camera behind," Tanvi said. "You're more than welcome. The rules are no husbands, no boyfriends, no cameras, no witnesses."

Meena tugged her phone from the side table and took a few pics of Tanvi. "But you're so photogenic." She snapped away, then laughed as Tanvi camped for the camera, holding up sweaters and putting the back of her hand on her forehead in exaggerated dismay.

They finished up the tops, and Meena grabbed an armload of pants still on hangers and dumped them on the bed. A few minutes later, she worked up the nerve.

"Is everything OK with Sam? He seems upset."

Tanvi sighed. "He is. Not with you. Sam has family problems. They crop up around this time of the year. He retreats into work. We used to try to cheer him up. Sam is so sweet, we realized it was painful for him to fake happiness. Now we leave food in his fridge and make sure he has clean clothes. He'll come out of it. I'm glad he has Wally. That dog came to him when he needed someone the most."

Meena was ashamed. She'd made their interaction about her without even considering that Sam had problems of his own. She hadn't even asked how he was when she'd seen him. She might not have practice with close friendships, but she was an adult, one who knew that relationships were give-and-take. She'd never wanted to take, so she'd forgotten how to give. It was something she needed to correct. Try harder with.

"And Sabina?"

"She's being Sabina." Tanvi dismissed Meena's concern. "Don't read too much into it."

"How can I not? She doesn't want me here."

"She thinks you do not want to be here," Tanvi said. "This building is her life. Her whole identity is about who she is in this house. You've been careless with this apartment. First you stayed here like it was a place you didn't want to be. You didn't even sleep in the bedroom. She thinks you don't appreciate what you've received. She'll get over it now that you're making an effort."

Meena wondered if that was it. That maybe she'd read too much into Sabina's hostility and that it was more about respecting the history for a building she deeply cared about. "Do I have to get her permission to paint the walls?"

Tanvi laughed. "Your back stiffens just like hers. No, you do not need approval. If you're painting, however, you might want my opinion. I have an artist's eye."

"I'm open to it." Meena considered the idea. "As long as color is used sparingly."

"Don't be afraid," Tanvi said. "I can see this bedroom in bright green with wallpaper of yellow daises on an accent wall."

"Absolutely not."

"Now I know your boundaries." Tanvi grinned. "I didn't think you'd be so boring about wall color."

"We'll find a way to compromise. Anything I should know about Uma?"

Tanvi shook her head. "She's prepping for the start of the semester, buried in her books."

"And you and I are good?"

Tanvi reached over and hugged her. Meena wrapped her arms around the sturdy frame. Tanvi's long hair brushed her face, and Meena inhaled the floral scent of her perfume.

Tanvi pulled back and let go. "We're OK. And you need to practice hugging along with other things. You're really clumsy about it,"

"How did I mess it up?"

"Your arms were too loose," Tanvi said. "And there was a lot of hesitation."

Meena laughed. "I guess I have a lot to learn."

Tanvi patted her shoulder. "Only if you want to. Not everyone likes to hug."

"Was that a topic in your Do No Harm Club?"

"Uma did it just for me," Tanvi said. "I'm a tactile person, and she wants to make sure I don't force myself on everyone. It's difficult, but I understand why."

Meena was amazed that these women continued to learn, to improve in ways they believed made them better. It was never too late to fix yourself.

CHAPTER
THIRTY-FOUR

Meena knocked on Sam's door. When he called out to let herself in, he was on his couch, his legs stretched out on the coffee table, a computer on his lap and earbuds in his ears. In gray sweatpants and a pale-blue long-sleeved shirt, he looked casually cute.

She looked around for Wally and found him napping in the corner. She went to him and sat down to stroke his fur as he nuzzled her, then rested his face on her lap.

"You're a tired puppy." Meena kissed the top of his head.

Sam took out the earbuds. "Puppy school is exhausting."

Meena left Wally to sleep and went to the other side of the sofa. She put a plastic container she'd brought with her on the coffee table. "I baked cookies."

He raised both eyebrows.

"By myself," she said.

He continued to stare.

"Fine." There was no sense pretending with him. "I opened a bag of presectioned cookie dough and followed the instructions."

He reached for a cookie and ate a piece. "You're a talented baker."

She threw a pillow at him. He caught it and tucked it against his side, then turned his attention back to the laptop screen.

Meena watched Wally as he snoozed. The silence between her and Sam felt uncomfortable, and Meena didn't know how to break it and get back the Sam who was friendly, chatty, and . . . took on the burden of conversation. She'd been closed off, and then she'd leaned on him. She'd thought he didn't need *her*; he had his own friends and the aunties. Meena was learning that it didn't work like that. It wasn't a cliché; a two-way street was what sustained friendships.

She stood and paced the living room, scanned the single bookshelf. She should go. It was clear that he was busy and that he wasn't the type of person to ask her to leave. Meena walked to the door. He hadn't looked up.

"Sam," she said.

"Yup." His eyes still on the computer screen.

She rubbed her arms. The chill had nothing to do with the temperature. "If you ever want to chat, about anything, I'm right across the hall."

He nodded but didn't glance her way.

Back in her apartment, she put her hands on her warm cheeks. She'd been foolish to think that a plate of cookies was the right way to break the ice. And she'd waited two weeks to do even that. The accumulated snow had melted away as January gave way to February. Apart from random hellos and waves as Sam and Wally made their way in and out of the apartment, they'd barely talked.

Meena paced in the cluttered living room. With Tanvi's help, they'd cleared out the bedroom, leaving only the bed and mattress, which she'd covered with her recently purchased bedding. She couldn't keep Neha's linens. Meena needed a bed that was hers, not a hand-me-down of sorts. She had left the armchair but not much else. The room echoed from emptiness, and Meena didn't spend much time in there, except to sleep. She went to the desk and looked out the window. The back garden was barren, the lush colors of fall long gone. The green in the grass was faded, the brown branches swayed in the breeze, and the stone around the base of trees looked dull without the sun.

She'd spent a lot of time with Tanvi but hadn't found a way to bring up the topic that was always present. She'd asked in an indirect way about Neha's extended family, only to be told that Tanvi didn't know of any and that it was likely in India or Africa. Meena had also searched for more photo albums, papers, or anything with names that could give her a lead on a relative Neha had helped. So far nothing.

She thought that if anyone in this building would know of this relative, it would be Sabina. Approaching her would require careful thought and planning in terms of how much to share. Sabina was sharp and suspicious, and she didn't like Meena. Those three things made it difficult to casually start a conversation about the past.

She turned away and walked along the bookshelves. She was restless. She could work, but she didn't really want to. She wasn't in the mood to flip open her computer and watch Netflix. Maybe she would read. Though nothing on these shelves interested her. She scanned the books on farming in Central Canada, the old novels—not classics, just well worn—and decided to pass.

On a whim she grabbed a few books in a set called *Lands and Peoples*. On the couch she skimmed through the Baltic states edition, then moved through Canada and the US. The next one was about South Asia and the Far East. Intrigued, she flipped through it. An index card was wedged in the middle. Meena sighed. These notes would never end. When she intentionally searched, she came up with nothing. Neha would never stop taunting her. She'd cleared the bedroom and had looked here and there, but nothing had turned up in The clothes or in drawers.

irregular (adjective)
1 a.: not being or acting in accord with established custom; irregular conduct
b.: not following a usual or prescribed procedure

2: not belonging to or a part of a regular organization
3: lacking perfect symmetry or evenness
4: lacking continuity or regularity especially of occurrence or activity

She leaned her head back against the couch. Meaningless or meaningful? She wouldn't know. She glanced at the shelves, looked around the room. So many hiding places. Meena thought about the boxes she'd taken down to the basement. The ones picked up by the charity. Meena had gone through every item and found nothing. How many more notes were here? Meena added it to the envelope with the others.

Someone knocked on the door. "Come in." She'd left it unlocked, as a test for herself.

The aunties walked in. Meena stood, left the books on the sofa, and met them at the table.

She'd barely seen Sabina or Uma since she'd gotten back. Tanvi had a casserole dish in her hand.

Meena greeted them. "Hi."

"Your door was unlocked." Uma came in. "Are you feeling OK?"

"I'm trying." She'd been practicing a few times a week to get comfortable with the idea.

"We're proud of you. And we always knock first. So don't worry about us interrupting anything." Tanvi put the dish on the dining table. "I made my specialty, aandvo. Come sit."

"I can make coffee," Meena offered.

"I don't drink that bitter, burned stuff," Tanvi said. "Uma will make chai."

"Do you have milk?" Uma asked.

Meena nodded.

Uma rolled up the sleeves of her bulky sweater and washed her hands. "Get a notebook, or take a video with your phone. You're going to learn, and then you're going to practice. Next time we come by, you'll be able to make it for us."

Meena was a little taken aback. Then she realized this was an opportunity not only to learn something that seemed to be part of their culture, and possibly her own, but also to find a way to bring the conversation around to Neha's relatives, or the one that could be Meena's.

"Do you have fresh ginger?" Sabina asked.

"I don't."

"I'll run up and get it," Tanvi said.

Meena leaned against the kitchen counter.

"What are you doing?" Uma asked. "Go get something to take down the recipe."

Meena grabbed her phone from the living room. "OK, I'm ready."

"The ingredients first." Uma pointed to the various tins she'd lain out. "Loose black tea. Wagh Bakri is the only brand that's worth a damn. You get it at Patel Brothers in Waltham. Don't go to any fancy tea shops. You want proper black tea for chai."

Meena aimed the camera and recorded.

"Next, this small tin has premade masala. Sabina makes hers from scratch, I buy mine. This is Sabina's she'd given to Neha. It's old, but chai and masala don't spoil." Uma sniffed. "It'll do for now. I will add more than typical because it might not be as strong as fresh masala."

"How do you make it?"

"You combine ginger powder, nutmeg, cinnamon, cardamom, and black pepper. Grind it all together."

"But Tanvi went to get fresh ginger."

"Because you can never have too much ginger in tea," Sabina said. "That's the way I prefer it."

"I add fresh tulsi, an Indian mint." Uma pulled a pot from the cabinet. "We grow it in the backyard in the summer, then dry it out for the winter."

"We all have our own preference." Sabina took milk from the fridge. "Once you have the variations, you'll find that perfect balance for you."

Meena liked the idea of having her own chai recipe. "What's the version for people who like coffee?"

"Kadak. Strong chai, brewed longer before adding milk, and then simmered for over ten minutes after," Sabina said.

"First you boil water." Uma turned the stove to medium heat. "I prefer a one-to-one ratio. Sabina does one and a half cups water and three-fourths cup milk, and Tanvi a quarter cup water and the rest milk."

"I like mine jaadi." Tanvi came back. "Fat, thick."

"Once it is boiling, one spoon of tea for each cup. We're making six, but I'm going to add five and a half. A teaspoon of masala, and a lot of freshly grated ginger." Uma used a hand grater right over the pot.

Meena recorded Uma and the teapot. The water was black, with masala and flecks of ginger among the tea. "That doesn't make sense."

"It's aashrae," Tanvi clarified. "Approximate."

"Indian cooking," Sabina said, "is about feel and instinct, not exact. Artful, not scientific. The more you do it, the better you get."

Meena filmed each woman as she spoke. She vowed to go back over the video and write the recipe down, to practice making chai until it became as instinctual for her as it was for the aunties.

"Then you add milk." Uma poured it into the pot of boiling tea, water, and masala. "Let it come to a boil. Once it gets to the point that it is going to boil over, you lower the heat and let it simmer. The longer you let it cook, the stronger the chai."

Meena recorded Uma pouring the chai from the pot into mugs through a small handheld strainer. The kitchen came alive with the warm and sweet aroma.

"When it comes to sugar, it's up to each person to add after." Sabina added two teaspoons, stirred, and handed the mug to Meena. That she remembered that Meena liked sweet chai made Meena pause.

With plates in hand, they sat around the kitchen table. Tanvi served a slice of savory cake made of rice, lentils, shredded squash, and spices and coated with sesame seeds. It was delicious. In their designated seats, they chatted. Meena told them about Seoul and K-pop, after which Tanvi added BTS to her Spotify. They told her about parasailing in Saint Bart's and Uma seeing piranhas while swimming.

For the next hour, Meena laughed, joked, and reveled in their shared memories. She held up her own end of the conversation, asked questions, told them about Zoe and her time in London. She'd settled into their rhythm and had forgotten her agenda to question them about the names of Neha's relatives.

"When do you get back on the road?" Sabina asked.

The abrupt question startled Meena. "I don't have anything immediate. I've pitched a few stories to editors in New York." And she didn't feel in a rush. It felt strange to be in this position where her career wasn't the most important thing in her life.

"Does that mean you're going to stay?" Sabina asked. "Keep the apartment?"

That put Meena's back up. She wanted to give Sabina the benefit of the doubt, but whenever she mentioned Meena leaving, her tone came across as suggesting *Why are you still here?* "Yes. I plan to make this my base."

Sabina pursed her lips. "Why the change?"

"Don't interrogate her," Tanvi said. "I told you, Meena isn't going to cut and run. She's part of this building now."

Meena appreciated Tanvi's defense. "I know you don't know me well. And it's true I've been going back and forth about keeping the apartment. But yes, I'm going to stay. You'll see."

CHAPTER
THIRTY-FIVE

The kitchen was clear. There wasn't much to clean out except the expired pantry items. The dinnerware and flatware were in good condition, as were the mugs and glasses. Meena wasn't much of a cook, but it would be wasteful to get rid of the pots, pans, pressure cooker, utensils, and the like, so they stayed in the cabinets and drawers.

She did peek into the cooker to check for a note and found Neha had written on the back of the warranty card.

> I do not agree with Julia Child. There is no joy in cooking. It is an unnecessary chore when we are surrounded by dozens of restaurants. This is a present from Sabina. She knows I hate to cook, yet she still buys pots and pans for me. She likes to goad me. In return, I gift jeans. She hates them and does not ever wear them. One useless gift in exchange for another.

Meena added it to her ever-growing stack and shoved the envelope back in the desk. She would finish the kitchen later. The biggest project was the living room and foyer. The sofa, coffee table, and desk were in good condition even with clutter on every surface and in every corner. Having read through design blogs and taken quizzes, Meena had learned that she preferred minimal and modern. Clean surfaces, structured furniture. The small stuffed parakeets tucked in between books wouldn't work with her new style, nor would the random wild animal figurines spread out on the fireplace mantel and along the end tables.

Between the fireplace and the opposite wall, there was little space. Every inch was taken up by furniture: small tables, a desk, a chair, a standing lamp, big pillows on the floor, and a huge wooden chest that looked as if Neha had bought it at a flea market. And of course, the top of the scarred chest was the perfect place for a lamp in the form of a butterfly made of stained glass.

"Snickerdoodle." Meena accidentally bumped into the lamp, and it crashed on the floor. The shattered glass flew every which way and caught the top of her foot. She yelled in frustration.

Her front door crashed open. Sam rushed in, his hair mussed, as Wally barked behind him.

"You OK?"

"Sorry," Meena said. "Keep Wally back, there's glass everywhere."

She was cornered against the bookshelf with no place to step over the shards.

"What happened?"

"I went to grab this parakeet." Meena waved the small velvet figurine. "And I knocked over the lamp."

Sam picked up Wally and plopped him on the couch. "Stay."

"I can't go anywhere," Meena said.

"I was talking to the dog."

Meena grinned. "I knew that."

He gave her a harried look before getting a broom from the coat closet. As Sam swept a path for her, Meena picked up the lamp base. Something glinted as the sun hit it. She looked closer.

"Your foot is bleeding," Sam said.

"Flying glass." Meena picked at something wedged in the black rock base. Slowly, carefully, she slid a piece of paper out.

"What's that?"

Meena knew. "Right now, it's pretty stationery paper folded up, but watch . . ." She opened it up, and it was the size of printer paper. "Ta-da! Neha and her notes." She handed it to Sam.

"You should read it," he said.

She shook her head. "Your turn. I've opened all the ones I found so far. Some turned my life inside out; others are either nonsensical or I'm completely missing the message. Honestly, go ahead. You should enjoy her shenanigans too. I've officially stopped caring."

Sam frowned. "I'm sorry about not telling you everything. I didn't . . ."

"I know, you didn't know what I knew . . ." She waved him off and stepped away from the corner as he swept up the broken glass. "Don't mind me. I'm irritated. There is so much clutter in this place."

"She liked to collect anything and everything," Sam said. "She would ask me to take her to flea markets or go antiquing in Vermont."

"Then she shoved it in every inch of empty space."

He nodded.

They were getting back to their easiness. "Thanks for coming to my rescue."

He gave her a half smile. "I heard a crash and a scream."

"And like double-oh seven, you ran in here."

He grinned. "You need to watch a Bond movie before you make a comparison."

Maybe we could watch one together, she wanted to say. Instead she nodded to the note. "Seriously, you read it. You knew her; it might make more sense."

He took the page and read it out loud.

"'*Friend* as a noun has five definitions, as a transitive verb, two. If I were to apply one to designate my relationship with the women in this building, I would use "one who is not hostile." The one I would apply to Sabina, Uma, and Tanvi, "one attached to another by affection or esteem." They have the bond from being born within months of each other. Despite their differences, they care for each other. Tighter than sisters, they often say.

"'Of course, I know that one of them has a secret. Shared only with me. Not by choice but by circumstance. Such a secret can destroy the bond they believe is impenetrable.

"'I do wish to be there for the fallout when all is revealed. I wonder if you resemble her. I hope for your sake you do not take after my cousin. He was quite unattractive in his personality.'"

Meena moved over to the couch, her mouth agape—with saying and not saying things. She closed her eyes and asked Sam to read the note again, then read it herself.

"I don't understand," Sam said.

She limped to her jacket, not caring about the blood dripping from the cut on her heel, and grabbed the wooden elephant. She'd kept it in the jacket pocket as a talisman of sorts. She took it out and unsnapped the latch as she'd done a dozen times since discovering it and took out the note.

She didn't watch him as he read it, instead focusing on the words in the new note. *Friend. Secret. Resemble.* Meena was so frustrated she wanted to throw the elephant in her hand, smash it against a wall, watch it shatter in fragments near the swept-up shards of the broken lamp. The rising anger felt right. She rarely lost control of her emotions, rarely allowed herself to get to the point of rage. Right now there was nothing but anger in her bones.

Her heel burned from the cut, and she sat down on the couch.

"Her cousin?" Sam said.

"Turns out I am related to Neha," Meena said. "Likely through my biological father."

He sat next to her.

"And now this about my birth mother . . ." She'd already made a wrong assumption once. She didn't want to chance it. "How would you interpret it?" She handed the new note back to him.

"Let's see." Sam frowned. "She talks about how close the aunties are and that one has a secret."

"'Circumstance,'" Meena jumped in. "That could be code for pregnancy?"

Sam looked around. "Do you have a dictionary?"

Meena laughed. "More like fifty or so." She took an older edition of *Merriam-Webster* from the bookshelf and handed it to Sam.

"OK, the definition is 'condition.'" Sam flipped through it.

"And *a woman in a certain condition* often refers to pregnancy," Meena said.

"Then she adds, 'I wonder if you resemble her.' She hopes you resemble her." Sam looked up at her. "If these notes are for you, and it's very likely that they are—and that there's a secret that one of them has the other two don't know, and then a direct mention of the man being unattractive."

"Just say it, Sam." Meena leaned back. Closed her eyes and let the wave of frustration, resentment, anger, irritation, grief, pain, and heartache crash through her. "Or better yet, rip it up. Destroy it."

"I think she's saying that one of them could be your biological mother, and her cousin was the one who got her pregnant."

Meena didn't want to cry. She'd made peace. Well, apart from wanting proof that she belonged here, rightfully. That was all that mattered. She didn't want to feel things. Didn't want to know that there were more secrets. That she'd been growing close to these women, and one of them could be her . . . she stopped her runaway mind. "There's a fat envelope in the desk drawer with all of the notes I've found. Take them all, light them on fire."

He took her hand. She pulled out of his grasp. Her skin hot, her heart fragile, she did not want his kindness. Her mind screamed for her to retreat. To run away. "One of them knows. Right? She *has* to know. She knows why Neha would have left me this apartment." And yet they'd let Meena believe she was a stranger, a random person who had come into their lives.

Sam put his hand over hers. This time she let his touch calm her. She wasn't going to run. She wasn't going to push away someone who was starting to matter.

Meena bit the inside of her cheek hard. "I've eaten with her, gotten drunk, I've . . . she knows . . ."

He put his arm around her. Squeezed her against him. She kept her hand in his and closed her eyes. She was drowning in betrayal as all her feelings swam around her. Every cell in her body wanted to run. She could be packed and out of there in thirty minutes.

No ties. No knots.

She stayed in Sam's arms. Let him steady her. Keep her in place.

"Don't run." Sam held her.

Her eyes clashed with his. "How do you know what I'm thinking?"

"You're not thinking, you're feeling," Sam said. "That's what you want to stop doing by running."

"Therapist?"

"Special effects engineer."

She laughed, and it helped her come up for air.

"Stay and figure it out." Sam stroked her hair. "The only way is through."

CHAPTER
THIRTY-SIX

She hadn't run. But she'd hidden. She'd avoided. She didn't want to see the aunties or sit at a table with them knowing one of them shared her DNA. The last few days, she'd tried to manage her feelings, contain her anger. She wanted to confront them but didn't know how. She didn't know what they knew, and they didn't know what she knew.

She put her palms on her warm cheeks. She had the puzzle pieces, but not the whole of it. She channeled her exasperation into cleaning. The living room was less cluttered, the knickknacks packed up in three boxes in the corner. She shook lamp bases, opened lids, and looked under every possible item for other notes. She didn't want to miss any further musings. Neha had written that the truth would be revealed. Maybe it was still here somewhere. She knew enough about Neha to know that the woman had a warped personality and a cruel streak. Maybe she'd find a birth certificate or hints of names, date of birth, place of birth. But she found nothing.

Meena had looked at archives online for people with her birthday, but without much to go on, it was too long a list. One thing was certain. Meena no longer wanted to play this game in which Neha was the only one who knew the rules. The aunties, or one of them, would have to tell her. No more notes. She didn't want to read any more of Neha's ambiguous words. She wanted someone to narrate from beginning to end. She was no longer amused by or interested in unearthing facts. This was her past, her future. She wanted it in plain, simple terms.

Meena got up from the couch. She needed to do something. Spending this much time in her head was unbearable. She flung open the apartment door. If anyone passed through the hall, she would talk to them. If it was one of the aunties, she'd face them, confront them, wait for an explanation. Flowers and hearts assaulted her, the former with their sharp scent, the latter with their overwhelming presence in the hallway.

Heart-shaped wreaths of fresh red and white roses hung on her and Sam's doors. The inside staircase was laden with small red satin hearts tied to each baluster, a large white satin heart attached to the newel. The small hall table held a bouquet of preserved red roses with a giant silver ribbon around the vase, the diffuser making the hall smell like the queen's rose garden.

Valentine's Day. Of course. There wasn't a holiday the aunties didn't celebrate. She stepped outside to see what they'd done with the exterior of the building. Shivering in only her sweater, jeans, and socks, she made it to the front stoop to take in the large heart-shaped wreaths on the doors and the twinkle lights in red and white around the iron railings before rushing back inside.

Except she didn't want to go back to the apartment. She didn't want to be alone. Arms wrapped around herself, Meena paused. Four months ago she'd never thought of wanting company. Her work had afforded her enough interaction with different types of people that she hadn't minded the time she spent alone. This was a different kind of need, though. She wanted not strangers and small talk but something deeper with someone she knew, who knew her.

On impulse, she knocked on Sam's door. He was the one she wanted. She heard Wally bark as Sam opened the door. He was rumpled in another one of his long-sleeved T-shirts, this one with an MIT logo, and gray sweats. His eyes looked red behind his glasses. Meena fidgeted.

"Didn't you hear me say come in?"

Meena shook her head. "Sorry. I was in my own head."

Sam held the door wide and Meena walked through. Wally bounced out of his crate and ran toward her. At least the dog wanted to see her. She crouched down to give Wally proper love and gave in to the need to press her face into his fur. The loneliness of the week caught up with her, and she stayed there until Wally squirmed to escape her hold. She stood, uncertain, as the pup went back to his crate and gnawed on a toy.

"Do you want to grab lunch?" Meena asked.

Sam rubbed the back of his neck. "I'm on deadline and have a lot of work."

His eyes were distant, focused on something other than her. She should go. She was bothering him.

"I'll go. I don't want to interrupt you."

He took her by the hand. "I'm sorry. You need to talk and I'm here."

She shook her head. "I was the one that told you I needed to be alone, and you respected that. I can't come in here and expect you to drop everything now that I can no longer stand to be in my own skin."

"Friends do that for each other," Sam said. "Tell me."

She paced in front of him. "There's nothing to tell. I'm still angry at Neha, at the aunties, at everything. I want to confront them and blow it all out in the open."

"Then do that," Sam said. "Don't plot or plan. Just go with the straightforward truth."

"You don't get it." Meena winced at the high pitch in her voice. "I need to know if whichever auntie it is knows. And if she knows I know."

"I'm lost."

"If I hand them all of it on a platter, they could lie. Pretend they didn't know, even if they did."

Sam sighed and sat down. "So what do you want to do?"

Meena tapped her chin. "Drop hints. Different ones to each auntie. See what sort of reactions I get."

"Are you sure you want to take the long way around?"

She crossed her arms in front of her. "I'm not sure of anything. For once, I want someone to recognize me. Tell me the truth. All of it."

He nodded and stood. "I'll help with whatever you need."

She took his hands. His eyes looked tired. There was a stain on the front of his T-shirt, maybe from coffee. She reached up and touched his face. "I'm not going to put you in the middle of this."

He put his hand over hers. "Too late."

She smiled. "Thank you."

He nodded.

Reluctant to let go, she stepped back and headed to the door. Before leaving she turned around and faced him. "Sam, I'm glad we're friends."

"Me too."

She took another breath. "I think there could be something more here, and maybe, if you're up for it, we should figure it out. If not, I totally understand. I don't have a lot of experience in this. The last time I let myself genuinely like someone, it was Jason Lee in tenth grade." She paused as a look of surprise crossed his face. She'd blurted it out, and he said nothing. "It's OK if you aren't interested. You don't have to like me back." Oh God, she was in high school again. "What I mean is, I would like us to go on a date, dinner, but this time a date. But if you don't, just let me know, I can take rejection."

Meena forced herself to stop talking. She wanted to run out of the apartment and leave the house, go for a long walk, maybe jump into the frigid Charles River to escape. "I'll go," she said.

"Wait," Sam said. "That was a lot of words, my brain is still catching up."

She put her hands on her hips. "How long is it going to take?"

He held up a finger. "*You* want to go out on a date?"

She nodded.

"First, yes. I'm saying yes so that we're clear," he said.

"And second?"

"Why now?"

Because I like the person that you are. "It's almost Valentine's Day. Maybe I'm giving in to societal pressure. Or maybe I just want to get out of the apartment and do something that's not by myself. And you're . . ."

"Convenient?"

"No," Meena said. "You're the opposite of that. If I wanted easy, I could go to a bar and find a stranger to pass the time with."

"I see."

"No pressure," Meena said. "I'm not going to throw myself at you again. And I'm not saying that to make you feel bad. You're perfectly within your rights to choose who you kiss."

"Wait," Sam said. "We're kissing now?"

She put her face in her hands. Then she heard a little laugh. He stepped closer and pulled her hands away. "I'm teasing."

Meena saw it in his eyes. They were clear, less tired, his lips in a grin.

"My turn." He kept her hands in his. "First, I have wanted to kiss you since, well, our first dinner that wasn't a date. I mean have you met you? You're smart, fiercely independent, talented, and I know you've looked in a mirror enough to know you're beautiful in an obvious way."

She pulled her hands out of his. "Obvious?"

"Traditional," Sam said. "Conventional. You're inarguably pretty. Second, I stopped because I didn't know what you wanted. It was a push-away, pull-back-in situation. I'm not good at that."

"You're a nice man."

He dropped her hands and moved away. "No, I'm not. I let people think that about me. There's a difference."

Meena noticed the slight shift as his shoulders tensed. "From where I stand, you're a good guy."

He gave a bitter laugh. "You know very little about me."

Stunned, Meena wrapped her arms around herself. He was right, she had résumé bullets and a biography filled in by the aunties and Neha's notes, an occasional anecdote about his friendship with Neha. "I'm sorry. You're right. Everything has really been about me when it comes to us."

He'd gotten her out of her apartment, introduced her to his friends, given her advice, been her sounding board. She'd taken what he'd offered but hadn't reciprocated. She couldn't think of a single time she'd centered the conversation around Sam.

"That's not what I meant," he said.

"Doesn't make it not true."

He nodded. "It's fine. You were the one with the existential crisis."

She laughed. It burst out of her, and it felt good, like a release. "When you put it like that."

Sam took her hand again. "I'm not diminishing what you're going through."

She squeezed his hands. "I know. I like your framing. Tell me why you're not nice."

"It's a long story." Sam moved to the couch and sat down.

She sat next to him. "I'm not going anywhere."

"I have to finish up work."

He'd dropped everything for her; she wanted to be there for him. "Work can wait. You don't hate puppies, you let the aunties roll through your life, you help anyone that asks, so what's the deep dark secret? Are you building killer robots in the basement? Do you litter? Hate recycling?"

"Are you done?"

She leaned back. "Yes."

They sat in silence for a while.

"I know how to build robots, you know," Sam bragged. "MIT."

"Ah, you like to mention where you went to college," Meena said. "You're awful."

"My parents would agree with you." Sam's voice softened. "About the awful part."

She couldn't imagine anyone thinking, much less saying, that about Sam, much less his parents. "You told me you weren't close to your family."

"We talk once a year," Sam said. "My parents call me every January. The first Saturday after the New Year. They ask me one question. I say no. That's the end of the call. I won't hear from them again until next year."

Meena didn't push. She knew silence was more powerful than a stream of questions—Sam had shown her that.

"They want me to give this apartment to my younger brother," Sam said. "If I was a nice person, I would. He got married young, right out of college. They have three kids. My parents adore him. It's not an assumption. The reason the aunties take care of me, that Neha befriended me, was to make up for the lack of interest my parents had in me."

Meena's heart hurt as she listened to his matter-of-fact tone.

"The entailment of the apartments in this building says that it goes to the eldest child. At the age of twenty-five. That's when I moved back from LA. My parents, brother, and his family were living here. They didn't want to leave. I forced the issue." Sam met her eyes. "What kind of man does that?"

"You kicked them out?"

"I told my parents they could stay, live with me," Sam said. "But my brother and his family should find their own place, start their own home. They fought me. Wanted to take me to court. Lucky for me, Sabina does not mess around when it comes to preserving the ways of the Engineer's House. She told my parents that the homeowners' agreement was clear, and every time the apartments change hands, the heir must sign their willingness to uphold the rules of the entailment. She showed my mother her signature."

"Way to go, Sabina."

Sam shook his head. "I took this place knowing my parents wanted it for my younger brother. I took it early, did not wait for the norm of moving in when I had a family of my own. I live with that. I knew it would mean I would lose my family, but this was more important. I traded a family for an apartment. That's the kind of man I am."

"Why?" Meena asked.

He turned his head to look at her. "Does it matter?"

"Intent and motive say more about a person than their action."

"Did a psychologist tell you that?"

"A prince who owned a Grand Prix race car. He liked power, said he needed it to protect his people. He led to keep them content. As I talked to him, I learned that his intentions were different. He liked to dominate, he liked that his people were afraid of him. Did you want this apartment as payback for your parents loving your younger brother more?"

Sam laughed. "Hell no. They are who they are, and I liked living three thousand miles from them, still do." He rubbed the top of her hand with his knuckles. "I grew up knowing this apartment was going to be mine. Not through my parents but my grandfather. He told me stories of his father, how this place came to be theirs. You know the cliché *home is where the heart is*? This was home to me, just as it was to my great-grandfather. He came to this country, by boat, in 1930, to study in a place where he probably wasn't welcome, even with his money. I was teased for smelling like curry when I was young; I can't imagine what my grandfather put up with.

"But he had this place, and other people like him. They all made it into a home where they belonged. In this house they were just men who came to get an education so they could go back and rebuild their own country after the British pillaged and divided it. I'm a part of something bigger when I live here."

"It fits you. This place."

He smiled. "It's my home. Even though it came at a cost."

"My father used to say hurt begets hurt," Meena said. "Your parents played a part in this by not stepping out of the way, by making you fight for a place that was rightfully yours."

"I didn't earn it."

"You can say the same about me. About the aunties, anyone who lived here after they did."

"Using logic against me?"

Meena squeezed his hand. "You're being too hard on yourself."

"You're only saying that because you want me to go out with you."

She shrugged. "You already said yes."

"A Valentine's Day date," Sam said. "Are you going to bring me flowers?"

"I'll grab some from the giant bouquet in the hall."

"Too easy. I want to be wooed, so I'll tell you that my favorite flower is a buttercup."

She laughed, and for the first time in her life, she wanted to spend more time with a man. She didn't want instant gratification but the slow buildup, the deepening, that would grow into something more.

CHAPTER
THIRTY-SEVEN

A few days later, Meena was still thinking about Sam. She'd spent most of her past decade surrounded by people who all wove in and out of each other's lives. Yes, she had a network she was a part of, but there was a common thread in their work. This was different. Sam didn't know about things like composition or light's many colors. Sam was grounded and knew who he was. He wasn't restless about where he belonged. It was innate. Meena was attracted to him because he was so different from her; he was a person who was strongly rooted, who didn't question his identity. He was someone who claimed his space even at a great cost. Sam embraced what she feared.

"The chai smells OK." A short knock, followed by Uma coming through the door.

Tanvi followed. "At least there's that."

And lastly Sabina.

"I followed the instructions from the video I took of you making it," Meena said. "If it's not good, it's your fault." She had a plan. Step one, poke around. See who knew what. Step two, isolate and conquer. Meena had found *The Art of War* in the process of decluttering and had not only read it but also jotted down notes. The anger was still there. She was ready to find out where to direct it.

"Or maybe you don't know how to follow instructions," Uma muttered.

"I brought cookies." Tanvi opened the tin as they took their seats around the table.

Meena poured from a teapot in the shape of a chicken she'd found while decluttering.

"You've been busy," Sabina said. "We haven't seen you so much lately."

"What do you think of the living room?" Meena asked. "It's bigger, more spacious without all the stuff."

Sabina glanced around. "It's better. Less things to dust."

"I'm glad you kept this teapot." Tanvi stroked the red beak. "I have a matching one. Neha and I bought them together at a yard sale about ten years ago."

"Ugliest thing you own," Uma snickered. "That's saying a lot since you're wearing a quilt for a dress."

"Ignore her." Tanvi rolled her eyes. "She's always in a bad mood at the beginning of the semester."

"Students complain about every assignment in the syllabus." Uma tapped her knuckles to the table with each word.

"In a month you'll love them all and brag about them constantly," Tanvi said.

"Have you always wanted to teach?" Meena knew Uma the least of the three. Right now they were subjects she was investigating. She was laying plans, as Sun Tzu wrote.

"No. I went into the research side, but as a TA while getting my PhD, I liked putting a class together, the interactions and questions from students. As they learned, so did I. It grounded the theoretical. Now I balance the two. Next time, boil the chai longer. It's not as strong as it needs to be."

Meena ignored her. "You and Neha must have bonded over books and reading. Do your collections overlap?"

Uma snorted. "Neha was all over the place in terms of what she read. She wasn't an academic. Though these books aren't for show, I'll give her that."

"Based on the condition of a lot of the books, the dog-eared pages, crinkled covers, she definitely read them," Meena said. "Did the two of you ever chat over books?"

"Our temperaments didn't suit." Uma crossed her arms and sat back in her chair.

"Two ornery people can't be friends," Tanvi explained. "They both need a foil to direct their crankiness toward."

Meena changed course. "Did you always want to be an artist?"

"Always." Tanvi's round face lit up. "When we were little girls, we would play school together. Sabina would be the self-appointed teacher. Uma would practice spelling, and I would doodle."

"She's a terrible speller," Uma griped.

"And you can't draw a straight line without a ruler," Tanvi said.

"I can't spell either." Meena wanted to defuse the sparring. "I'm happy for copyeditors."

"We have that in common," Tanvi said. "We're both visual. Your medium is photography."

If Meena was biologically linked to one of these women, she would prefer Uma. If Tanvi knew who Meena was and had kept it from her, it would cut the deepest. "I've never been a doodler or able to paint and draw, but I like to play with light and color."

"You're awfully curious this morning," Sabina remarked.

"Simply making conversation. Isn't that how friendship works?"

"Hmm." Sabina tapped her own chin. "You want to know what I wanted to be when I was a little girl?"

"Sure."

"Simple." Sabina stretched her arms wide. "This. I wanted to take care of this building, to preserve our history, to continue the legacy by caring for my family."

"And having children to pass it all on." Meena bit into a sweet, buttery cookie. "What happens when your children inherit your apartments?"

"My eldest doesn't want to come back to Boston for a while," Uma said. "She's happy in Boulder and plans to stay there."

"My son turned twenty-five last year." Tanvi rested her chin in her hand. "He wants to stay in New York City, doesn't want to live here just yet, and that's fine with me. Our parents went back to India when we inherited, but none of us plan to do that."

"This feels more like an inquisition than a conversation," Uma stated.

"Are you doing a story about us?" Tanvi asked. "The women of the Engineer's House. I would read that."

"I don't want any part in it," Uma grunted.

Meena glanced at Sabina, who raised her eyebrows.

"As you've said, this building is a community. I'm trying to get to know you better." Meena hoped they would be appeased so she could keep digging.

Tanvi reached over and gave Meena a side hug. "We're happy to be your friends."

This clearly wasn't working in terms of finding out who had the secret. Meena changed course. "What are your plans for Valentine's Day? Are you going to dress up like cherubs and shoot arrows at people walking by?"

Tanvi laughed. "That would be fantastic."

"We'd get arrested," Sabina said.

"This is a holiday we celebrate separately," Tanvi explained. "Date night with our husbands. Pi and I are going to Ostra for seafood and champagne and then a little nightcap. I ordered his present from La Perla, which is really a present for both of us."

"Vin and I are feasting on chocolate fondue." Uma winked. "We won't even make it to the bedroom."

"I'm glad for soundproofing since you live above me," Meena said.

"Jiten and I will have a couple's massage at home," Sabina added. "A catered dinner, and then we'll dance to our favorite classical pieces, and we will definitely make it to the bedroom."

"This building becomes a love den. You better have plans," Tanvi recommended.

"I do." Meena finished off her tea. "With Sam."

Their reactions were all different. Tanvi clapped her hands in excitement. Uma smirked. Sabina's face was neutral.

"He finally asked you out," Tanvi said. "I'm so proud of him."

"I asked him."

"Good for you."

"You really are settling in," Sabina observed.

Meena decided to drop a crumb, reveal a part of herself, share a bit of her truth. "I am. It feels seamless. You've all made me feel like I'm part of a giant family. I haven't had that. Not even when my parents were alive. It was just the three of us. We were close, but there were some gaps, differences in the way we looked, the way others looked at us as a family. I was adopted, and while my parents never made me feel like I wasn't theirs, there was something missing. Not love, more like grounding. I don't know if I'm making sense."

"I had no idea," Tanvi said.

"I don't really talk about it." Meena crossed her arms. "As I was going through Neha's things, I found out why she left me this apartment. You were right. She knew my parents."

"Oh my God," Tanvi said. "What did you find?"

"It's a little complicated." Meena was cautious in revealing too much. "Neha wasn't very direct about it."

"You're making assumptions," Uma argued.

"I'm putting the pieces together," Meena said. "Did Neha ever mention anything to you?"

"No," Tanvi whispered.

"Neha probably got distracted and forgot about it," Uma suggested. "She could be like that."

"She never mentioned anything about it," Sabina said.

"That's too bad." Meena was disappointed in their excuses and denials. One of them knew the truth. "I was hoping to learn more."

"Who were your birth parents?" Uma asked.

Meena decided on half truths to avoid direct confrontation. "Neha didn't leave any names, which makes it hard to research adoption records."

"What did she say exactly?"

"A few notes here and there confirming that she intended to leave this apartment to me. It makes sense since she didn't have any children of her own."

"Leave it to Neha to be so vague," Tanvi muttered.

"I never thought about searching for my birth parents. I wanted to know more about my ethnic background, but that was all. I loved my parents, and we were a family. I didn't need to know more."

"What about after they died?"

"Their death was shocking enough." She rarely talked about this. She let the grief through instead of reciting an emotionless script. "There was an explosion. Something about an underground gas leak. They were in the house. I was already at school."

"Oh no." Tanvi took Meena's hands. There were tears in her eyes.

"It was a long time ago," Meena said. "I was barely sixteen, I didn't realize what it meant to lose all the documents as well. Everything was gone, including any adoption records my parents might have kept."

"I can't imagine losing everything like that," Tanvi said. "In an instant. My heart hurts for you."

Meena cleared her throat. Tanvi's kindness made Meena's loss feel more acute.

"There is nothing left?" Sabina asked. "No link back to your birth?"

"I haven't really looked. I didn't know a lot, don't remember what hospital I was born in or if there was an agency involved. When the social worker helped me get an ID, we went through my school records, but there was no birth certificate as part of it."

"How can we help?" Uma asked.

Confess. Except only her birth mother knew. The other two were innocent. "I don't think there is much, unless you remember anything Neha might have said to you."

"She also was erratic about secrets," Sabina added. "If she wanted to share, she would. If she didn't think it was important, she would forget."

Meena nodded but stayed quiet.

"It doesn't matter how you got here." Tanvi laid her hand over Meena's. "You're where you are supposed to be."

"Be careful," Uma warned. "She's going to suggest we sit on the floor in a circle and meditate."

"Meditation is key to living a healthy life," Tanvi said.

"I agree." Meena decided to let it go for now.

"Great, there are two of you."

Meena finished her tea. She'd told them just enough. Now she would wait and see.

CHAPTER
THIRTY-EIGHT

Reservations for two on Valentine's Day were hard to come by. Luckily, Wink & Nod had had one left for 8:00 p.m., and Meena had jumped on it. It was a crisp and clear evening, and the long walk was a refreshing way to start their night.

She'd even bought a new dress. Different from her black sheath. It was a bright-blue silk wraparound that hugged her body. The cinching at the waist gave her a bit of shape. Below, it cascaded down her legs like a waterfall to midcalf. She'd paired it with tights and her trusted black boots. Meena had knocked on Sam's door with a bouquet in hand. Buttercups were rare in February, so she'd found a sunny yellow bouquet from a florist next to the Back Bay train station.

He'd laughed and happily accepted the bouquet, and Meena had given Wally cuddles while Sam put the flowers in a jug of water.

The restaurant was dimly lit, with candles on each table. The host ushered Meena into a leather seat as a couple across the narrow aisle used a cell phone flashlight to scan the menu.

"This place is known for rotating chefs," Meena said. "A speakeasy and an incubator." She saw the grin on his face. "You already know."

"I've been here a few times," Sam said. "But I liked your summary."

She wondered if he'd brought a date here or come with a friend. "The menu looks . . . eclectic."

"I'm sure you've had some interesting food in your travels."

"Not caviar panini or foie gras lollipops."

They settled on burrata, a cheese board, ahi tuna flatbread, steak pot stickers, and a few more small plates along with a California cabernet.

"How are your friends?" Meena wanted the conversation to be focused on him, not her.

"I was supposed to meet up with Dinus and Ava tonight, but they're at a pub in Somerville." Sam helped himself to a pot sticker.

"Oh," Meena said. "I didn't mean for you to change your plans."

He smiled. "It's not often I get asked out, especially not on the day of hearts and chocolates."

"I'm not sure I buy that. Attractive nerd-type men are very hot right now."

Sam sat up and rolled his shoulders back, looked around the dark restaurant. "Oh yeah, I can see so many of us here with beautiful women."

Meena glanced over as a blond male-model type passed by their table. She laughed. The man paused and winked before moving on.

"What about you?" he asked. "What's your type?"

"This burrata is delicious," Meena said.

He waited her out and sampled a few more of the items in front of them.

"I don't have a track record when it comes to relationships," Meena said at last. "I meet someone in my travels, not the subject, but either another photojournalist or a writer, artist, or someone I meet along the way. It's spontaneous. Drinks, company, and human companionship before moving on to the next place." She shrugged. "I bet you're the opposite."

"You'd be wrong," Sam said. "I had a girlfriend in college, two years, another in LA for one year. No one since I've been back."

Her eyes widened. "By choice?"

He laughed. "I date, sometimes. Go out for a month or two before it fizzles. The biggest complaint I get is that I'm not a good boyfriend."

Meena poured more wine in both their glasses. "Why not?"

"I can be forgetful," he said. "If I'm on a project, I can be in it for days, only stopping to sleep. I throw myself into it, and my brain only refocuses on the rest of the world after I'm done."

Guilt and embarrassment shamed her. Meena had assumed his distance, his distraction, had been about her, that she'd left, and he'd been upset. But he was telling her it was the way he worked, his process. "I mull. When I'm putting together a story, trying to find the right angle, I let it all swirl around in my head. Even when I was young, I'd have a history paper due or an essay to write and I'd wait until the very last minute, until the whole thing was laid out in my head, before I'd start writing it. Usually in the middle of the night."

"Your parents must have been thrilled."

"My mom would get frustrated. She would nag me to get started. She would say, *Don't think. Do.* I tried, but it's not how it works for me. I write down notes, but if I need to put pieces together, it has to connect in my head."

"And your dad?"

Meena's heart expanded with her love for him. "Whenever he saw the light on in my room late into the night, he would bring me a cup of hot chocolate and two cookies, give me a kiss on the top of my head, and tell me I was writing an A paper."

"You don't talk about them," Sam said.

"For a long time, I didn't even allow myself to think about them. I was afraid that if I did, it would be too painful." She leaned back and toyed with the handle of her spoon. "I was in geometry class, second period. They both worked for Smith College. I was learning to calculate the volume of a trapezoid. Funny, the details you remember. I got called to the principal's office. There was an underground gas leak that caused my home to explode. It was quick, they told me. My parents wouldn't have even known. They were there, then they weren't."

He reached over and took the spoon out of her clenched hand, rubbed her fingers straight.

"That afternoon, I was sent to a foster residence a town over," Meena said. "They brought me a paper bag with a couple of pairs of jeans, T-shirts, and sweaters. The only things I had left were what had been in my backpack when I'd left the house that morning."

"How did you handle it?"

She shrugged her shoulders. "I don't know. I just kept going to sleep in the bottom bunk and waking up. Then time took over. A week, a month, a year. Eighteen years. I have some strong memories, but I've also forgotten a lot. A Roma person once told me tears are wounds of the heart. I had stopped shedding them a few months after their death. I guess I didn't want to spend any more time with a wounded heart. My mom was a big believer in dusting off and moving on. She hated wallowing."

"I don't think she would have faulted you for grieving," Sam said.

"I guess I'll never know. Let's not talk about this. Tonight is for hearts and chocolate."

He grinned. "How did you know about my sweet tooth?"

"Tanvi let it slip when I told her we were going out," Meena said, "told me to bring you homemade cookies. I didn't tell her I'd already done that. You weren't impressed."

"I did finish them off."

Meena ate the little pat of goat cheese. The saltiness hit just right.

On the way back to the house, he held her hand, and Meena was happy. It was good to just be with him on this one night. His palm was warm against hers. She leaned closer, and her jacket brushed his wool coat. Couples passed them, in their own personal worlds.

Meena hadn't expected her life to take this turn, but she was glad that she'd found herself here, that she'd come back. "I'm adding an interim phase in my two-step plan."

Sam glanced at her as they waited for the light to cross Boylston Street.

"To figure out which auntie is my birth mother," Meena said. "I'm going to find biological similarities, like if anyone is allergic to bananas."

"You can't eat bananas?"

"They give me hives. Also, I'll see if there are similarities I haven't noticed yet," Meena said, "personality-wise."

"Or maybe tell them everything. Get it out in the open."

She sighed. "Only one of them knows. If I guess wrong, it could blow up their friendship. My issue is with the one who has the secret. I have to find out who it is."

"How many phases are going to be in this two-step plan?" Sam asked.

"This one, so far." Meena held up her fingers. "Step two is me spending some time with each of them one-on-one. They travel as a pack, but I'm going to divide and conquer. I'm trying to figure out reasons."

"Lean into their interests," Sam suggested.

Meena thought about it as they got closer to Marlborough Street. "How so?"

"Uma likes to teach. Tell her you want to learn something. Sabina likes to cook, maybe swap your cookie recipe for one of hers."

"Very funny," Meena said. "You know my recipe is to turn on the oven and set it to the right temperature. But I do make a great pie."

He squeezed her hand. "Sabina makes the best sabudana khichdi. Ask her to make it for you and bring me leftovers. It's my favorite. Tanvi is the easiest. You don't need a reason. She'd be happy just to be in your company."

"Yeah." Meena knew that if Tanvi was her biological mother, it wouldn't be hard to forgive her, but it would beg the question of why she hadn't shared who she was.

They took the steps up to the front door. Sam unlocked it and led her in before closing it behind them. The warmth of the hall helped relax her shoulders, which had been hunched against the cold, made the rose scent more fragrant. They stood in the middle, and Sam faced her.

"What?" Meena asked.

"I'm waiting for you to kiss me."

She smiled. "Right. Let me walk you to the door." She pressed him back against it, then rose on her toes to reach him. He waited. Up close, she could see gold flecks in his dark-brown eyes, feel his smooth skin as she brushed her hand over his cheek. Still he waited. She supposed he really was leaving it to her. She finally touched his lips, doing what she'd wanted to months ago. His taste mingled with hers, red wine and chocolate mousse. She pressed against him, and his arms wrapped around her. With layers in between, she couldn't get any closer, so she put everything into the kiss. Then she pulled back.

That his breathing was hard and fast gave her a sense of satisfaction. She leaned back as he still held her. "I guess we save the 'invite me in' part for a third date?"

He brushed his lips against hers. "If you count the dinners that were not dates as dates, we're well past third."

She tilted her head to count. "Invite me in, Sam."

He grinned wide as he opened the door and tugged her into his apartment. Wally barked his greeting and waited for Sam to let him out of the crate.

"I'm going to take Wally out to the backyard for a quick potty break," Sam said. "Lock the door. I don't want the aunties to interrupt."

"They have their own private celebrations going on."

Sam covered his ears as he followed Wally out. "Don't kill the mood. I'll meet you back on the couch, or in bed. You decide."

She wandered around his apartment as she removed her coat and boots. She peeked into his bedroom. It was simply decorated, with a bed, two bookshelves, a TV on a wall, and a desk holding computer equipment. The gray comforter was clean, and she lifted it.

"Did you change your sheets?" Meena sat on the bed as Sam came into the room and closed the door. Wally whined on the other side. "Were you hoping to get lucky?"

"Yes to both." Sam sat next to her.

Meena leaned over and kissed him, then pulled him into the bed with her.

CHAPTER
THIRTY-NINE

What she'd wanted was to spend time with Tanvi, to gently meander the conversation toward any tells. She should have known better, picked something that involved getting the two of them away from the house. Meena's error had been in not being specific. That was how she wound up standing in the bedroom like a mannequin with her arms akimbo as the aunties trussed her up in three yards of orange silk. All she'd said was that she was curious about saris and how effortless they looked even though she was sure it was more complicated. A few hours later, the three had descended on her and were using her like a real-life dress-up doll.

"Stay still, Meena." Sabina spoke with a giant safety pin between her lips. "Keep your arms spread out."

"A cotton sari would have been better. Silk is too hard for practice." Uma tucked fabric into the pale orange skirt tied so tight, it made it difficult to breathe.

"What am I, an old woman? I only have silk saris." Tanvi unfurled the pleats and started again. "And since you gave Meena such a hard time about wanting to learn these things, forcing you both to do this is your punishment."

"I didn't realize this was going to be so complicated," Meena said. They ignored her.

"Tanvi, you're doing the pleats for Gujarati style." Sabina nudged her friend. "We're showing her English style."

Tanvi sighed. "I can never tell."

Uma stepped back and sat in the chair by the french doors. "I'm going to look it up on YouTube."

"Eh," Sabina argued. "You don't have to look it up. I know."

Tanvi winked at Meena. "Sabina made us practice every week when we were teenagers."

"It's easy to forget when it's not something you do every day." Sabina turned Meena toward her. "Pay attention. There are two areas you must pleat. One in the front of the skirt, and the other is the sash. Both have to be neat and crisp."

"But you can leave the piece over your shoulder unpleated so that the fabric hangs over your arm and you carry it on your wrist." Tanvi tucked the pleats in the front, pulling the already-tight skirt and with it Meena's whole body. "I know it's uncomfortable, but a loose skirt can cause a wardrobe malfunction, and you don't want to take a few steps and find yourself naked from the waist down."

"You get used to it," Uma said. "My mother always wore saris, even in winter. She had a permanent indent around her waist from the tight cotton string that held up the chanyo."

"I'm surprised the woman wasn't severed in half," Meena mumbled.

"It's not fashion if women aren't suffering." Uma ticked off the list on her fingers. "Heels, bras, skinny jeans."

"The beauty of a sari is that it looks effortless in the way it hangs down your body." Tanvi straightened the pleats.

"Even though it's all held together by a blouse and chanyo that's tied just short of suffocation," Uma said. "That's why I never wear it."

Meena saw an in. "Did you teach this to your daughter?"

Uma shook her head. "She decided to learn from YouTube. She's a femme lesbian and loves all of this."

"I helped Kam when she couldn't figure out pleating from videos," Sabina said.

"I named her Kamaladevi after an Indian social justice warrior, and she's known to the world as Kam thanks to these two," Uma explained.

"OK, let's see how you look." Tanvi pulled Meena back by the shoulders so they could see her whole figure in the vanity mirror.

Meena didn't recognize herself from the neck down. The sari was dramatic in the way it fell around her with little peeks of skin at the waist. "How do you walk in this?"

"Carefully," Tanvi said.

Meena looked at Tanvi through the mirror, their faces next to each other. She scanned their features for similarities. The shapes of their eyebrows, the lengths of their noses, their hairlines where the forehead met the scalp. Nothing conclusive.

"What do you think?" Uma asked.

She looked like someone else, someone more glamorous, more graceful. She could see herself as an Indian woman. She fit with these three behind her. The four of them didn't look alike, but there was a similarity to their skin tones, the shapes of their foreheads, the way the bones sat in their cheeks. She blinked to clear the wetness in her eyes. "It fits."

"You are beautiful." Tanvi's eyes watered. "Made to wear a sari. Like Hema Malini."

"Who?"

"I know this is not because of your age but your lack of familiarity with old Bollywood," Tanvi said, "so I won't take offense."

"Hema Malini is not old Bollywood," Sabina argued. "Nargis was the original."

"We should watch movies with you." Tanvi clapped her hands together. "They have subtitles."

"OK, now you try." Uma removed the safety pins and unfurled the silk.

Meena saw herself in only an oversize cropped blouse made from the same fabric as the sari and a fitted skirt that brushed the tops of her feet.

"Here you go." Tanvi handed the pile of silk to Meena.

"Uh." She didn't know what to do, hadn't been paying attention.

The three of them laughed.

"I'll text you a few YouTube videos," Uma said.

"You can keep all of this." Tanvi took the silk from her and began to unfurl it.

"Oh," Meena said. "I could buy my own."

"Don't be silly. That's not how things work here. The right response to a gift is to say thank you." Tanvi made Uma hold the edges of the yards-long silk and layered it together into a neat fold.

Meena nodded. "Thank you."

"You're welcome. And don't take out the pins from the blouse when you change out of it. My chest is three times bigger than yours, so I'll sew the blouse to your size."

Meena put the armload of orange silk on the bed.

"Do you even need to wear a bra?" Uma asked. "Because if I was that flat chested, I wouldn't bother."

"You still barely bother," Sabina said. "I keep telling you that you will regret it when you're seventy and your boobs are hanging to your knees."

"I accept my body as it ages." Uma patted her belly. "Gravity can have its way with me. I'd rather be comfortable. Besides, who's going to care what my breasts look like twenty years from now?"

"Eighty-year-old men," Tanvi quipped. "Don't forget seventy is going to be the new fifty by the time we get there."

"Not according to my knees," Uma said. "I'm requesting a house with no stairs when we leave here."

The idea of the aunties not being in this place gave Meena pause. "When your children move back here?"

"We have a plan." Tanvi smiled. "A nice active adult community in New Jersey. We're going to buy homes close to each other so we can still do all the things. Sabina will choose first. She's the one who will have the hardest time leaving here."

"But I will because that's how things work," Sabina stated.

"I remember your kids," Meena said. "I met your son and daughter at Diwali."

Sabina took the sari from Tanvi and put it on top of the empty vanity table. "Yes. My daughter, Sarla, is older. I've been keeping records for her. She will take over the management of this house when she marries and settles her family here."

Meena caught Uma's and Tanvi's glances.

"Is that what she wants?" she asked.

Sabina met Meena's eyes. "It is not an option. It is Sarla's duty, her legacy."

"She's at the Air Force Academy in Colorado," Uma explained. "She wants to be a fighter pilot."

"And when she's done there, she will take over," Sabina said. "Until then I will continue to take care of this building."

The tension rose in the room. There were undercurrents Meena couldn't decipher. "Tanvi, you have a son, right? Amul."

"Yes," Tanvi said. "I tried for another, hoped for a daughter, but . . ."

"What about you, Meena?" Sabina asked. "Do you want to marry, have children?"

Meena shrugged. "Perhaps. But what I need now is to get out of this skirt before it cuts off circulation." Meena went to the bathroom, where she'd left her jeans and sweater. As she changed, she realized she was no closer to the truth than an hour ago.

She was coming to realize she was no match for them. When it came to the aunties, the conversation never went as she'd planned.

CHAPTER FORTY

This time she was smarter. She picked a time when Uma was off to teach and Tanvi was at a board meeting for an art education nonprofit. Then she asked Sabina if she would teach Meena how to make Sam's favorite dish.

"Why sabudana khichdi?" Sabina asked.

"Sam mentioned that yours is the best," Meena said, "I don't know what it is, so I thought it would be interesting, something new."

Sabina pointed to the small white balls she had drying on the center island in her pristine white-and-black kitchen. "It's tapioca. Sabudana. *Khichdi* is a catchall term, usually for a rice-and-lentil dish that's casual and comfortable. Like a stiff risotto. Sabudana is something we eat during religious fasts. But it's also delicious and satisfying on a cold day."

Meena took a picture of the tapioca spread. "Then I chose the perfect day."

"Hmm," Sabina said. "Wouldn't it be better to start with something simple like pasta or an omelet?"

Meena grinned. "I can make some basic things."

"You'd never know from the way you eat takeout," Sabina challenged.

"It's easier. Plus, I get three meals from one order, so it's fairly cheap. And cereal for breakfast is quick and simple."

"All part of a very unhealthy diet."

"I order lots of veggies," Meena argued. "In the stir-fry form."

Sabina gave a small smile. "Did you grow up eating like this?"

Meena adjusted a setting on her lens. "No. My mom cooked, but she wasn't a gourmet. She liked the convenience of cans and boxes that only required heat and water. I didn't really learn about spices and seasonings until college."

"That's a shame," Sabina said. "You don't make the full use of all of your taste buds if your only seasoning is salt."

"My palate opened up when I started traveling. The first time I had Indian food was when I went to London to visit Zoe after college. Chicken tikka masala."

"That's British food, not Indian," Sabina exclaimed.

"It was delicious either way," Meena said. "I didn't know what I was eating, couldn't identify the spices, but I couldn't stop. It was so good. I had the same thing every day for three days."

"Today you're about to have authentic Indian food, not co-opted or fused with other cultures. This is farmers' food from where we come from. Simple, hearty."

"Why are you drying the tapioca?"

"They come dry, then need to be soaked for a few hours. Once rinsed you spread them out on a towel to get rid of the excess moisture. If you cook them wet, they'll turn into mush."

"Can I try one?"

"It won't taste like anything," Sabina said. "You can help with the peanuts. I roasted them. You need to remove the skin. Take a handful, rub them between your palms, then pick the ones with no skin and put them in this bowl."

Meena put the camera down and washed her hands before doing as instructed. It was a tedious job, and she couldn't help but wonder if Sabina had intentionally left it for her.

"Sam and you, is there something going on?"

Meena concentrated on her task. "We're friends."

"You want to learn how to make his favorite dish," Sabina said. "That's very *friendly*."

"We've gone out a few times." More than that. In the last two weeks, she and Sam had had dinners in or out a few times a week that ended in sleepovers.

"Are you dating or are you boyfriend-girlfriend? I need you to be specific."

Meena glanced at Sabina. "Why?"

"Because I don't want to give Tanvi fifty dollars," Sabina clarified. "If you're only dating, that doesn't count."

"You bet on us?"

"Don't be offended," Sabina said. "We bet on everything."

"Like what?"

"How long you would stay the first time. I made two hundred dollars because I bet you'd leave before Christmas. Then Uma wagered you'd be back for New Year's Eve, so I made another hundred dollars. I also lost a hundred because I didn't think Sam was going to keep Wally. And don't give me that look. We bet on our things too, like Uma's professor ratings."

Meena let the betting slide, not surprised that they found entertainment everywhere.

"Anyway, we were talking about your upbringing, not about our gambling habit. What were some of your traditions?"

"My dad didn't like ham," Meena said. "For Easter my mom would make Reuben sandwiches. At Christmas we always had a real tree, even though the needles would get everywhere. We didn't do anything like you all do here. Our celebrations were simple."

"Have you spent any time in Ireland? I remember you saying your last name comes from Gaelic."

Meena nodded. "I had an assignment in Dublin, a photo essay on the first gay pub in Ireland."

"What part of Ireland were your parents from?"

Meena finished the peanuts and swept up the flecks of peels from the countertop with her palm. "I don't know. They were fourth-generation Americans, so they were more Irish American."

"I can understand that," Sabina said. "The earlier immigrants had to assimilate because there weren't enough of us to build a community. That's why I'm so proud of my grandfather and others who found this house, made it a home for people to feel close to who they were, where they'd come from."

"You honor them by keeping your culture, your traditions."

Sabina nodded. "The men who came here. Staying Indian was important to them, from speaking in their native Gujarati language to religious customs. A way to stay tied to their home country while making a place for themselves here."

Ties. It was like what Sam had said about keeping his apartment in this house. The links that they all shared as part of their collective history. And maybe hers. "The peanuts are ready."

"I have the other ingredients all set to go. Do you want to take notes?"

Meena held out her phone to record Sabina. She wore a long wool sweater the color of a pale sky and black leggings. Her feet were tucked into white slippers, her hair up in a large bun. She wore no makeup, her skin clear, and she needed none. On closer look there was a tiny tattoo, an om symbol, behind her left ear. "Ready."

The kitchen came alive with a warm, nutty scent.

Meena's mouth watered as the aromatic smells filled the space. A few minutes later, Sabina turned off the heat. She lifted the lid and squeezed half a lime over the contents of the pot, gave them a stir, and left the pot uncovered.

"Once it's cool enough, I'll put it in a bowl for you," Sabina said. "You can then take it to Sam, who is, as of this moment, not your boyfriend."

Meena laughed. "I'll let you know if anything changes. For now, you can keep your fifty dollars."

"He's a good man." Sabina's voice was quiet. "Have care with him."

Meena's smile dropped. She could understand Sabina's warning. And it was good that Sam had people who looked out for him. For the first time in a long time, she wished she had the same. If one of the aunties turned out to be her birth mother, maybe . . . She shook the thought away.

"I like him," Meena assured her. "I'm not looking to hurt him."

"He comes across as if he has it all figured out," Sabina said. "But inside, he wrestles with guilt and pain. We all look out for him."

"Is that a warning?"

"He's one of us."

Meena's spine went stiff. The subtext was that Meena wasn't. She gritted her teeth. Sabina didn't know that Meena was a part of this building's history too. Or if she did, this was a warning to let Meena know that she would never be accepted. Then Meena realized there was one clue she could drop. One bomb that would mean nothing to anyone except the woman who had given birth to her.

"Sam told me you throw Uma a surprise birthday party every year. When is that?"

"In July," Sabina replied. "A week after the Fourth."

"How fun," Meena said. "I haven't really celebrated my birthday in a big way. Maybe I'll throw a party this year. If you wouldn't mind helping me."

"Of course. When is it?"

"August sixth." Meena watched closely for the slightest shift in expression. A sign that indicated shock or recognition. Nothing.

"I'll check my calendar," Sabina said.

"Great." Disappointed, Meena let it go.

"Here. I'm going to put this in a container for you to take to Sam."

"Thanks." Meena had thought they'd share a bowl, continue the conversation. If only to see if she could rattle Sabina. "Can I help you clean up?"

"I've got it," Sabina said. "You might want to bring that to him while it's still warm. It tastes better fresh than reheated. You might even convince him to share."

Something was off, or maybe Meena was looking for things that weren't there. Sabina was always abrupt, wasn't she?

Or Sabina was shaken up by Meena's birthday.

CHAPTER
FORTY-ONE

Meena played catch with Wally. He loved the little stuffed porcupine she'd bought for him. For the last four weeks, she'd settled into a rhythm with Sam and Wally, so much so that the puppy came and went between their apartments at will. And while she'd tried to do more sleuthing with the aunties, there had been very little progress. What she'd learned hadn't brought her closer to the truth.

She'd watched all three eat bananas; no one broke out in hives. She'd asked them to share stories about their teenage years; none of them exhibited even an eye twitch when it came to sex, relationships, or broken hearts.

"Wally! No. Stop." She tugged him away from the ottoman, and a large piece of the fabric came off. Attached to it was a thick card, which flipped open to reveal familiar writing.

What is it about your destiny that you cannot stay where you're put?

The news came from Margaret Beaufort. I do not chitchat with my colleagues. That's not our environment at Merriam-Webster. Margaret is one of the few who chatter around the kitchenette. Once she spoke of a family who asked for prayers during Mass. They wanted God to bless them with a child. It was your fate to go to them.

When I handed you to Margaret, that was the end. Margaret has informed me of your tragedy. And there is nothing I'm willing to do.

I am a selfish person. If I were a better person, a kinder, generous woman . . . alas, I'm not. I cannot offer you my home, even though you have lost yours. The only thing I can do is leave you mine when I'm gone. It's your legacy, after all.

"What happened here?" Sam came through the door. "Wally, did you tear up the ottoman?"

Meena looked up at Sam. "He found a note." She patted the dog, who was curled up on the couch next to her. "He ripped open the bottom of that ottoman. By the time I noticed, he had a piece of notebook paper in his mouth." Meena handed it to him and bit the inside of her cheek. Her leg bounced to contain her roiling emotions. Neha had known where she was, could have found her, told Meena who she was, done something, anything. Instead she'd been left in that cold institutional home in a shared room with three others.

Two years. Lost. Grieving. Scared. Alone. Always alone. And this selfish, manipulative woman could have made it better. "She didn't have to offer me a place to stay. Even a temporary one." Her voice broke, so she bit the inside of her lip. Neha could have let Meena know she hadn't been left alone in the world, that there was a safety tether in the form of a past. Neha could have given her a foundation, roots. Tears she could no longer hold back rolled down her cheeks. She'd been adrift suddenly. In shock, she hadn't known how to manage a life that had shifted from daily hugs to no contact. From a home filled with music and noise, aromas of plain food, to one with silence and communal buffets.

Sam sat down next to her, put his hand on her knee. "You OK?"

She forced herself to stop the bouncing under his hand. If she spoke, anger would spew out at him, and he didn't deserve it. She didn't know what it would mean to loose the reins of her fury.

"Meena," Sam said, "let's go for a walk. We can skip pub trivia and just walk."

Meena shook her head. "I can't." She didn't want to hurt him, but at this minute, if he stayed next to her, was kind to her, she would break. She didn't want that. She needed to hold on to the rage for as long as possible because beyond it was a pain so big, Meena was convinced it would consume her. "You should go, though. Ava is expecting you." It was all she could manage.

"She'll be fine. I'm staying with you."

That would destroy her. "I don't know if I can handle you being so nice to me," she said, her voice sharp so she could hide her weakness. "I'm so angry."

"It's OK."

She stood and moved around the living room. "It's not. None of this is OK." She put her knuckles in her mouth, bit down to stop the flood.

He stood and took her in his arms. Meena didn't curl into him, but she didn't pull away. "It's better to be on my own. Rely only on myself."

"Not better," Sam said. "It's safer. But if you don't take risks . . ."

She cut him off. Pulled away. "Every day is a risk, Sam. Every day for the last eighteen years. I was left in a group home with others like me, and no, it wasn't the television or movie kind where we bonded and became our own family, nor were we abused or neglected. It was shelter. We left for school, came back, did homework, ate, and repeated it over again the next day, every day. Alone. Always alone. I had to figure out how to stop drowning in my tears. How to find a way to live without the only people who loved me, live without pictures or favorite clothes. Do you know what's left after an explosion? Debris and ashes. Not exactly something you can clutch at night to help you fall asleep. I had to figure it all out, from college applications and scholarships to how to freaking pay taxes once I got a job." Meena picked up the note. "Neha knew that. She knew and she left me there. Couldn't even figure out how to be human enough to come see me, talk to me, let me know that I had a connection to someone that was still alive." She wiped her face, the tears she'd held back running down her cheeks.

"I love your independence, but that's not all it is." His words were soft and gentle. "It's your shield, armor you've built over time because you had to navigate how to live by yourself. You don't need it anymore. You're not alone. You have someone."

Meena looked at him. "A woman who never wanted me and doesn't want to acknowledge me."

"I was talking about me." He stepped closer to her.

She closed her eyes. She was too raw and too fragile. If he wrapped her up in his arms, she would never want to let go, and that wasn't something she could risk. Eventually it would end because things always ended, and she needed to stay strong enough to be able to leave before he left her. "I can't do this, Sam."

"You don't have to." Sam took her in his arms. "Let me be here for you."

"I don't want to talk."

"Then we'll stand here," Sam said. "Like the last shot of a movie. A clutching couple, backlit by the setting sun. We can stand here for hours."

She laughed into his soft sweater. "I don't know any movie that ends like this."

"We'll find one to watch together."

She said nothing. The rage swirled even as she let Sam comfort her. At some point he moved them to her bed and held her with his front snug against her back. She'd run out of tears. She fell asleep in a state of numbness.

CHAPTER
FORTY-TWO

As night faded, the sun rose and Meena woke. She was alone. She stretched the stiffness out of her body. She padded to the kitchen as Sam came through the front door.

"I made espresso," he offered. "You only have instant."

She wanted to joke, to tease. All she could do was sit at the table and hold the hot cup in her hand. She was raw. He'd been there for her. Had held her through the night, brought her coffee. She should feel better, healed. She should appreciate that she had someone like Sam who was here now. Instead her anger sat heavy in her stomach, flared as the espresso met the heat of it within her.

"Thank you." She tried to keep her voice calm. Her tone mild. "For last night and for this."

"You're not alone," Sam said.

She nodded. What he didn't understand was that it wasn't about the now. It was about the past, the one she'd chosen to revisit because of Neha and her notes, her manipulations. The woman had shoved Meena into the truth in the cruelest of ways.

"You also have the aunties," Sam added. "Tell them all of it."

Meena shook her head. She couldn't focus on anyone except Neha. Too bad the woman was dead; Meena would have loved to unleash it all on her. "I need to think. I'll shower and then deal with it."

Sam stood. "I'm right across the hall. Wally too."

She cupped his face as he leaned over to kiss her. She barely stayed in control until she heard the snick of the door closing with Sam on the other side.

She paced around her living room, searched for stasis. Then she stood in the middle of the floor, her hair a wild nest—she didn't even care. She stroked the wood panels on the bookshelves. Even with the knickknacks gone, these shelves were full of Neha's books. She'd been careless with them just as she'd been with Meena.

Meena moved to the desk. The woman had sat here with her fancy fountain pen and perfect penmanship, writing her notes while Meena was out there, lost, without a home, without family. She had done nothing. Worse, she played games, toyed with Meena from beyond the grave.

Meena ran her hand over the stack of blank journals and reference books. With a swipe she swept them off, onto the floor. Her chest heaved, not from exertion. Anger thick in her veins, she moved on to the built-in shelves. Meena imagined Neha casually picking out a book to sit in a chair in front of a toasty fire and read while Meena lay curled in a bottom bunk believing there was no one in the world who was hers. Neha had flipped pages knowing that it was a lie, knowing where Meena had come from, where Meena might be.

This apartment wasn't a gift—it was a minefield, littered with hidden bombs designed to mess with Meena, to torture her. Another swipe of the hand and more books cascaded to the floor. She kept going until half the books on the shelves were heaped at her feet. She stepped over them with slight regret for the dented covers and crumpled pages. Methodically she kept going, from row to row. The books were Neha's, hopefully her most precious items.

"What is going on?"

Meena stopped and stared at the wide-open door. *Uma.* It was just as well that it was the grumpy auntie; she could go toe-to-toe with this one. "I'm doing a little cleaning."

"I see that." Uma stepped in and closed the door behind her.

"I'm not in the mood for company." Meena crossed her arms, her skin sweaty under her gray sweatshirt.

"I came down to tell you to cut out the noise," Uma said.

Meena raised her chin.

"Are you mad at something specific or the world in general?"

A tiny laugh tickled Meena's throat. If anyone knew anger, it would be Uma. Meena wondered if rage was genetic. Meena was tempted to lay it all out, ask Uma if she'd given birth to an unwanted baby thirty-four years earlier. "I've asked you this before, but I'm asking again. Did you like Neha?"

Uma picked up a pile of books and stacked them on the sofa. "Not particularly. We loved her, but Neha wore *bitch* as a badge of honor."

"You loved someone you disliked?"

Uma laughed. "People do it all the time. It's called family."

"Well, I don't have one of those."

Meena saw Uma assessing her. "Whose fault is that?"

Meena sucked her teeth. *Possibly yours. Neha's.* She needed to lash out.

"You should talk through whatever's making you so mad." Uma crossed her arms. "Clearly you've bottled up a lot, and it's showing."

"Are you volunteering?"

Uma laughed. "I don't have that kind of time."

"Right," Meena said. "Whatever you can spare is reserved for your friends."

Uma raised her brow. "Yes. It is."

"You tell each other everything, right? No secrets."

"Oh, I don't know about that," Uma said. "Fifty-plus years of friendship is bound to have some things that aren't shared."

"How philosophical."

"What's got you so mad?"

Meena ignored her. Ground her teeth.

"My advice? Go find a bartender," Uma said. "Get whatever's going on in there out."

Meena let loose a bitter laugh. "It's not that simple."

Uma snorted. "It's as hard as you want to make it, and it seems you don't want easy."

"You think you have me figured out."

Uma stacked more books from the floor on the coffee table. "You're not complicated." She looked directly at Meena. "You don't trust anyone. It's a way of protecting yourself. I'm not a therapist, so I don't claim to know why, but once you find a place to land, maybe try a little vulnerability. Your fortress is made of sand, and it looks like it's collapsing."

Hurt warred with anger at the truth. "You're full of pithy advice. What's made you so wise?"

"Age."

"And regrets?"

"I wouldn't want a life without a few mistakes."

"Even at the expense of others?"

Uma gave her a look. "If you're trying to say something, get it out."

Meena retreated. Not to protect Uma; she didn't want to be the first to speak the truth. If Uma was her biological mother, Meena didn't want the older woman to see the neediness in her face. "As you can see, I'm busy. Close the door on your way out."

"The guy across the hall," Uma said. "He's solid. And strong. If you decide to land there, it'll be the smartest thing you can do."

Meena wrapped her arms around herself. Exhausted, she was ready to collapse. "Whatever's between Sam and me is not your concern."

"Then you haven't learned a single thing about the Engineer's House." Uma opened the door.

Meena's knees gave out, and she fell into a pile of books. She curled her legs in and leaned her head on her knees. She was too tired to think or feel. Numb, she stayed in that position, surrounded by the chaos of Neha's beloved wreckage.

܀

Meena spent the rest of the day cleaning up the aftermath of her breakdown. She'd been tempted to find a bartender, but instead she'd gone to the liquor store for more boxes. She didn't want to talk or think. The monotony of stacking books, packing boxes, taping them up, stacking them in the corner, that was what would help her recover.

A fortress of sand.

The boxes closed and stacked in the corner of the dining room, Meena sat on the sofa surrounded by someone else's possessions. No matter how much she got rid of, there was still more of Neha here. She'd been trying to make this place her own, yet she'd been taking her time, getting distracted. She'd chosen to stay but hadn't made this her home. Reading magazines, getting rid of things, it was all so haphazard.

She didn't want tragedy to be the end place on the map of her life. She wanted to redraw it. A Buddhist monk had once told her that all that exists is impermanent. Meena realized that she'd approached her adult life as if it were fixed, even as change happened all around her.

The anger had been let out. A sense of control seeped in. She could breathe again. Focus.

Meena made one more trip outside. The early sunset meant it looked like midnight even though it was barely seven. With a pizza box in hand, she knocked on Sam's door. She was going to put things back together, focus on what she had instead of what she didn't.

He opened it.

"It didn't feel right to walk in." She locked her knees to stop her feet from shuffling.

"Are you coming in?" He stepped back, waited for her to decide.

"Are you busy or in the middle of something?" Meena let herself in.

"Wally and I were in the backyard," he said. "How are you doing?"

She held up the box. "New York Pizza."

"On Mass Ave.?"

She nodded. "It doesn't taste anything like a Manhattan slice, but it's not bad."

He grabbed two plates from the kitchen and brought them to the small table in the nook between the living room and hallway. "Want something to drink?"

"Water is fine." She needed something to calm the butterflies in her stomach. She sat and opened the box. The tangy smell of sauce infused the air. "Did Wally have his dinner?" The dog was snoozing in his crate with the door open.

"Yup." Sam sat across from her. "He's had a lot of playtime today."

They ate in silence for a minute. "I was, I don't know . . . I was a mess yesterday. Thank you for being there."

He wiped his mouth with a paper towel and leaned back in his chair. "That's what a relationship is, to support one another."

Her heart expanded. "Is that what this is?"

"Are we on different pages?"

She shook her head. "It's just that the label is a first for me. I'm not sure I can live up to it."

"We can figure it out as we go along."

She gave him a lopsided smile. "I've passed up so many opportunities to have friends, have relationships." She chewed on a bite. "I want people in my life." There. She'd said it out loud. "I want that continuity, where every conversation isn't the first conversation. Inside jokes, memories that you revisit years, decades from now." She shrugged. "If there's a handbook on how to do that, I'd read it cover to cover."

"Why now?"

"This place, this building. You," Meena said.

He reached out his hand, put it over hers, and squeezed.

Instead of blinking back the emotion in her eyes, she let the tears fall. "You deserve someone better."

He smiled. "So do you."

She nodded. Accepting that it was within her control. She only had to reach for it, not let fear of loss drive her actions. The butterflies fled, and her stomach reminded her that she hadn't eaten anything all day. With her hand clasped in his, she picked up a slice with her other hand. "Even not-great pizza is good."

"It's the perfect food." Sam grinned. "*But* when you have a great slice, it's heaven."

"The third Friday of each month was pizza night," Meena said. "My dad would pick it up from this place on Main Street on his way home, and I'd set the table. My mom would divide one can of Coke into three glasses and dilute it with ice because an entire can was too much sugar for one person."

"Smart woman." Sam tapped the side of his head. "Though she was probably never hungover."

Meena laughed. "No. They weren't big drinkers. Not that I saw, anyway."

"Tell me you've had an entire can of Coke in one sitting," Sam said. "It's very important that you've defied your parents in at least this one thing."

She shook her head. "Not yet, but I'm willing to try."

"I'm willing to deal with the aftermath of your sugar rush. It's the best hangover cure on the planet."

"Despite what happened the day after Thanksgiving, I'm not a big drinker."

"Ah, when you tried to kiss me."

"When I invited *you* to kiss *me*."

"Hmm," Sam said. "I remember it differently."

She finished off her slice and reached for another. "You would."

"You're smiling."

"Being here, with you, it's a good feeling."

He released her hand and patted his belly. "I'm stuffed."

Between them, they'd eaten half the pie. She didn't want to ruin the contentment but needed to tell him the rest of it. "I've decided I don't want to know who my birth mother is. It's better to keep things as they are."

He leaned forward, his hand on her knee. "Are you sure?"

She nodded. "I spent a lot of time wrestling with Neha's motives, whether she'd done this intentionally to toy with me or if it was a way to pit the aunties against each other. I won't know Neha's true intention. Regardless, I have a home now. I'd be a fool to turn it away, turn the people here against me."

"Perspective," Sam said. "Maybe now is when you need it."

She nodded. "I like being here, living across the hall. And the aunties, they're not my enemies. They've been kind to me, and I projected motive onto them. Whoever it was made a choice to give me up. A choice to not want me in their life. I can live with that. I have lived with it. I had a great mother. I was loved by her and my father. Even though they're gone, it's enough to have had them for as long as I did."

"You don't think whoever it is knows about you?"

Meena shrugged. "Maybe. Very likely based on the little carrots I've dangled in front of them. But I started it and I'm ending it. I'll leave it be and hopefully get back to some semblance of friendship with the three of them."

"It might not be that easy," Sam said. "You will still wonder. You're innately curious. You're a journalist."

"Maybe." Meena considered. "But I'm also great at avoidance. It's my superpower."

He tugged her hand and pulled her up, wrapped his arms around her. She clung to him, breathed in his scent, soap and wet dog. This was enough. She leaned back and he let her go.

"Do you know the aunties have a bet about our relationship?" Meena asked.

He grinned. "They bet on the temperature on the first day of spring. I don't recommend getting in on it—they'll fleece you."

She laughed. Together they cleared their plates and put away the pizza. Not ready to leave, she asked if they could watch his favorite James Bond movie. She curled into his body, and he played with a thick strand of her hair. When the movie ended, she decided to leave. She wanted to sleep in her own bed, in her own home, by herself tonight. To accept it as hers. To view it as both her history and her future.

She gave Wally a few rubs, then gave Sam a kiss before heading back to her apartment. Without the books, the living room was even more open, less oppressive. Tomorrow she would figure out how she wanted to decorate. It was time for Neha to be laid to rest.

CHAPTER
FORTY-THREE

The apartment was clear of most everything. Meena kept only the dining table and chairs. It was where she'd started her journey from that first meal with the aunties to now, where she could see the steady view of the garden and the street. She looked forward to the familiarity of it as seasons changed.

In the last two weeks, she and Sam had hauled out, binned, boxed up, and donated all Neha's things. Last week she'd bought a brand-new bed, one with a headboard—which was a sign that you've crossed into your thirties, according to the internet. She'd decided her bedroom would be neutral, in grays and whites, throw pillows adding a little bit of color. Sam didn't understand why beds needed throw pillows, so she'd texted him links to half a dozen design articles. She'd gone with bright purples from deep to lavender. Instead of the vanity, she'd added two armchairs in gray, one on either side of the fireplace.

For the living room, she wanted something that complemented the bones of the apartment with a modern flair. She would slowly add to the bookshelves. For now there were colorful candle jars to give them a less empty feeling. The sofa would be the centerpiece in deep navy, and there would be a Dutch-style oblong coffee table in light wood and a gray armchair on either side of the fireplace as a nod to symmetry. She'd splurged on a worktable, switching out the antique desk for one with a clean, flat design and an ergonomic chair. The gray rug was replaced by a thick white one that covered the whole of the room. Wally would likely get it dirty, but she wanted the room to feel bright and open. All of it had taken a toll on her savings, but it was worth it. She had a home. Not just a base.

She even had a local assignment, a feature on kundalini yoga in the Berkshires in western Massachusetts. Meena looked out into the backyard from her seat at her new desk. It was too soon to tell, but the patch of grass where she'd sown the wildflower seeds was beginning to regain color after winter hibernation. She looked forward to seeing what would grow.

Plans. Future. Not the "wait and see if I'm still here" type. She was committed to tending to the patch of flowers. Just as she'd joined Sam's pub trivia league with his friends. She had more than ten personal, nonwork, nonnetwork contacts in her phone, including Ava and Dinus.

She watched as Wally ran around the yard. Sam was giving him a little more freedom by leaving him in the yard on his own. She waited for Sabina to charge down and stop the dog from digging against the back fence.

There was a soft knock on her door.

"Come in," Meena said.

Sabina came in, a folder in her hands. "I'm hoping we could talk."

Meena moved to greet her. "Of course. Would you like chai? Or something to drink?" Now that she'd put it all behind her, she was fine with being casual and friendly with the aunties. She might still wonder . . . she might still look for a sense of familiarity . . . but she planned to focus on what she had and let the rest of it go.

Sabina stayed still in the living room. "It looks different."

Meena nodded. "It's more me now. Though I didn't know what 'me' was. I'm just glad there are a lot of home decor blogs with advice. You won't believe how many quizzes I took to figure out what I wanted. I like it." She chewed her lip. She didn't want Sabina's approval, exactly, but a compliment would be meaningful. "Sam likes it, but then again, he's not really a style maven. He's happy that he can stretch his legs out and rest his feet on the coffee table. He also wants me to get a TV, a giant flat-screen, but he has his own. I'm fine using my computer." She forced herself to stop talking.

"You've been very busy." There was weight in Sabina's voice, an uncertainty.

"I know it's different, but it was time. I've been here for a little over six months."

"Yes," Sabina said. "And Neha died a year ago this week."

She hadn't realized the time. She would need to call the lawyers and figure out what needed to be done in order for her to take full ownership. "I'm sorry. It must be hard for you," Meena said. "All of you. If my clearing this out causes you more pain, it wasn't my intention."

Sabina cleared her throat. "In our culture, we have a little ceremony and a meal to mark the death anniversary. There is a sraddha puja, at the mandir. It's to clear the path for the deceased and link their souls to their forefathers. The family schedules and performs it. We have a slot at the mandir for tomorrow morning. Thursday is an auspicious day."

"I see. Sam didn't mention it."

Sabina shook her head. "None of the men are coming. It will be only Uma, Tanvi, and me there. It's our duty to fulfill, as Neha doesn't have family here. I talked to her parents, and they're not planning on doing anything."

Meena nodded.

Sabina straightened her spine and walked up to Meena. "I know that you are trying to make a go of it here, that you want to stay. I'm here to ask you to reconsider."

Meena sat down. "Why?"

"You told me time and again that your career is important, that you enjoy traveling from place to place. I think you might have gotten caught up in this building, the story of it. We are happy to know you, but you should think about what you're giving up."

"I can work from here," Meena explained. "I have an assignment coming up."

"This building, it requires permanence from its residents," Sabina argued. "The apartments need caretaking. It's not a place to store your things. It needs life. People."

"I'm people," Meena assured her. "I am taking care of what's mine."

"For how long?" Sabina sat next to her. "You have said you often travel eleven months of the year. What happens when you miss it? When the excitement of a mundane life wears off and you want to go back out into the world?"

"I am thinking through it," Meena said. "Reconsidering the type of jobs I take."

"Or there is another option." Sabina held out a folder. "Here. Take a look."

Meena took the manila envelope from Sabina. "What's this?"

"It's an offer to buy the apartment."

"I don't understand."

"This is a big responsibility, to live in this building, to do what upholding tradition requires," Sabina said. "This is my way of giving you the option to not have the burden."

The word burrowed into Meena. *A woman's burden.* "This apartment is entailed to me."

"With an out clause." Sabina tapped the document. "At the one-year mark, you can sell it. I'm sure the attorneys gave you the information."

"Yes. But how do you know about it?"

"About a decade ago, I had a clause added in for situations where there were no heirs," Sabina said. "Neha did not have children or siblings. Her cousin, the only child of her mother's only sister, died in a motorcycle accident, and he was younger than Neha. I spoke to her about it. She did not want to sell to me after her death. I told her she could do whatever she wanted with it but to have something in the will in case the apartment stays empty. It's not just walls and rooms, it is living history and needs to be cared for as such."

"I see." Meena clutched the envelope. Neha's only heir was a male cousin. Dead.

"You don't really want to live here. This, the redecorating, it's temporary," Sabina said. "You're happy moving from place to place. Look at the offer. This is Back Bay, Boston. This apartment has been appraised for two point seven million dollars. You can go anywhere for that, do anything. Leave this all behind and get back to the life you left."

Meena understood what was left unspoken. She wasn't welcome here. She was an outsider. This time not by choice. Her eyes burned. She cleared her throat. "I see."

"Do you?"

Meena looked closely at Sabina and knew. She was staring into familiar eyes. Her own. Meena was adept at letting someone see or not see through her eyes. Sabina was letting her see. *A woman's burden.* Neha's aunt's son. It all fell into place.

Bile choked her. "That's not the real reason, is it?"

Sabina crossed her arms. "It is the only reason I can give."

Meena shook her head. "You won't even speak the words."

Sabina's hands clamped together.

"Are you that skilled that you can forget the first time you gave birth?" Meena asked. "Pretend I don't exist?"

"Aren't you the one who claims to not live in the past?" Sabina said.

Meena stopped herself from fidgeting on the sofa. The cushion was still stiff from being so new, but it supported her when her legs couldn't. "I guess avoidance is genetic."

Sabina snapped her eyes to Meena.

"How long have you known?" Meena wanted it all laid bare. She waited. Let silence do the work.

"I suspected." Sabina clasped her hands together. "I knew Neha. In my background check I found the write-up of your parents' death. I still could not be sure until you said you were adopted. The final confirmation was when you told me your birthday."

"Some dates are unforgettable," Meena said. "It's March eighth for me. The day I lost my family. Did you know my name?"

Sabina shook her head. "I never knew it. I . . . never considered you mine. Not even when I was pregnant. I pushed you out and others took you away."

"You didn't want to hold me?"

"Or see your face. I only knew you were a girl because the doctor who delivered you said it aloud in the room."

All adoptions start with a loss.

"I made a choice to carry the pregnancy to term." Sabina rolled back her shoulders. "That was all. I never let you be real to me. You were someone else's, my body was only an incubator, my punishment for breaking the rules. Something I regret to this day."

Meena closed her eyes as she absorbed each word. This was a different ache from the pain and loss she'd suffered in the past. This was personal and impersonal. They sat side by side. One had been born from the other, but they had no connection beyond a casual acquaintance. Two spoons of sugar in her tea. The one time Sabina had braided Meena's hair. Small acts that could have been meaningful had they known who they were to each other.

Sabina spelled it out. "You can understand now why it is better if you go."

The anger chafed. "I guess you don't want me to give you a card on Mother's Day?"

"I built my life in the shape it was meant to have. I have children, a husband."

"Yes," Meena whispered. "A legacy. You also have friends."

"They don't know."

"You want me gone to protect you. Your life."

"And you," Sabina added. "I don't want to face my past every time I see you. And you shouldn't want to see me knowing I never want to be a mother to you."

Meena turned her back, hated that she'd stood down first, but to face this rejection in real time threatened to sink her.

"It is a very fair offer." Sabina waited a beat before she let herself out of the apartment. Meena refused to cry. Refused to curl up in a fetal position. She stayed upright and focused on the buds beginning to form on the trees in the back garden.

⁂

The envelope still in hand, Meena went through the double doors of her bedroom and down the steps to the yard. She needed air. It was cold but not brutal. The wind breezed through her thin sweatshirt. It didn't matter. She let the cold dull the ache in her heart.

Bitterness rose in her throat. She'd never searched for her birth mother, never wanted to until the damn notes and the mystery of it all. Now it was all here, in cruel indifference.

"Hey." Sam sat next to her on the bench. "What's wrong?"

Her voice was neutral. "Two point seven million dollars. That's the price for Sabina's peace of mind." She handed him the envelope.

"What?"

Meena rubbed her eyes, wiped the wetness from her cheeks. "At first, when I thought I wanted to know, I had hoped for Tanvi. She's so sweet and warm. Then I thought it was better to not know because I didn't want to face the truth that she wouldn't want me. I settled on Uma. Both of us can do indifference in a very comfortable way. Instead

I get Sabina. The perfect caretaker of the Engineer's House, the person who always puts this place and herself first."

Sam put his arm around her. She chewed the inside of her cheek as they sat in silence.

"The thing is there is no win here," Meena said. "If I leave, I give up the first place I've wanted to make mine. I would be a mercenary, someone who ran off for two point seven million dollars. If I stay, she'll think it's out of spite. That I want to force myself on her day in and day out. Her biggest regret. Have you ever been someone's mistake, Sam? It's a really shitty thing to hear."

"I can't believe she told you that."

Meena tilted her head and glanced at him. "That's because you see the good in people."

"I'm not a fucking saint, Meena," Sam said. "She shouldn't have said this to you or done it like this." He threw the envelope to the ground.

"I don't know what to do." Meena stared at the fence where she'd planted the seeds. "I want to see the wildflowers bloom. I also want to feel welcome in my own home. I can't have both."

He took her hand, entwined his fingers with hers. She clung to him.

"Tell me what to do, Sam."

He cleared his throat. "You know I can't do that."

She let go and stood up. Paced. "I'm so fucking sick of having to do everything on my own. I was so scared. I didn't know anything. I had some money from insurance, I don't know if it was life or house, I couldn't process it, but it was twenty-five thousand dollars. At sixteen, it seemed like a lot, but then I had to figure out college. Which cost so much more than that. I had to find a way to survive, choose between working and college. Learn about scholarships. I've been hoarding money; I know I have a safety net, but I don't trust that it's enough."

She stood in front of him. "I am so tired of being on my own. I can do it, I'm good at it. But . . ."

He stood up and wrapped his arms around her.

"I can turn it off; I've done it before." She moved out of his arms and picked up the envelope. "I can sign this, pack up my stuff, and leave. Forget all of this."

He watched her. "Including me."

Her heart finally accepted what she hadn't allowed herself to admit. "I will never forget you. You're not . . . you're not a guy across the hall that I enjoy spending time with. You're more. I don't—" She rubbed her chest with her thumb. Things were fracturing inside, and she couldn't control it.

"You can go, but the past will still be there. Inescapable." He ran his hand through his hair. "I still take my parents' call every year, even though it cuts me up inside, even though I know I'll be useless for a month after the call. When we're tied to people, we think about them, miss them. Need them. You can run, or you can stay," Sam said. "You have to make the call as to which life you want to live."

She sat back down. The envelope in her hand.

"For what it's worth," Sam added, "I'm sorry that you had to be an adult at sixteen. That wasn't your call. The rest of it, doing it on your own, that's a choice. You make it every day."

She put her face in her hands.

He knelt in front of her. "A shitty thing happened to you. I'm sorry for that."

When he was on his knees, they were at eye level with each other.

"You're more to me too. You're not the only one that's careful with their heart. I won't risk being the only one who commits. If this is a relationship, you can't just cut and run when things get hard. I won't sign up for that."

He touched his lips to her forehead, then walked away. She let the cold wrap around her. The envelope in her lap. She stayed until the streetlights behind her flickered on. With freezing hands and feet, she walked back to her apartment, closed the doors behind her, and curled up on the bed.

Her bed. The first one she'd ever bought. The bedding she loved so much with its little yellow daisies embroidered on white linen. It was warm and cozy, the perfect cocoon for her chilled body. She closed her eyes and hoped for sleep to take her for a few hours so her brain and heart could get a little rest.

CHAPTER FORTY-FOUR

Her eyes were red and sticky, and Meena struggled to open them. The morning sun was bright enough to wake her. She could lie here forever if not for her bladder. Once she washed her face and cleaned the gunk from her eyes, she wandered to the kitchen. She had instant coffee and milk in the fridge. One thing, then another. That was the plan for the day.

She spotted a large cup and a bag from a bakery on Boylston Street with a sticky note.

If you need anything, I'm across the hall. So is Wally.

Her heart burst. She'd never been in love. It was foreign, but somewhere in her being, she knew this was what she felt for Sam. Joy. Bliss. And even as a part of her heart was hurting, the space where he existed was lush and alive.

She sat at the dining table and took a big sip of coffee. It was perfect, as was the bag with three pastries—a croissant, an apple tart, and a chocolate doughnut. She munched on the doughnut. Waited for the sugar to wake her foggy brain.

"Knock, knock." Tanvi popped her head in. "There you are. Good morning."

"Hi."

"It looks so lovely in here." Tanvi closed the door behind her. "You have a good eye, but I can tell you're afraid of color with all this white and blue. You need some prints, some fun in here. Let's wander down Newbury today, look for some art or a vase, something to add pop. It's beautiful outside, sunny and high fifties. We can have lunch, make a day of it."

Meena didn't want to think about motive or whether Tanvi knew about yesterday. She wanted to sit and enjoy her coffee. "Maybe another time. I have a few things to work on today."

"Like what?"

"I have a few pitches to put together, story ideas."

Tanvi sat in her designated chair next to Meena. "Is that how it works? You come up with an idea and see if someone will want it?"

"Sometimes," Meena said. "In the beginning, yeah. I've worked consistently for a long time, so I have editors who call me for assignments too. Freelancing is a little bit of everything. I've been off the road for a bit, so I need to generate something for myself."

"It seems risky."

"I suppose. There are good months and lean months. You make money to ride out the periods when there isn't a lot that comes through."

"And you never wanted a steady job?"

Meena shook her head. The idea of staying in one place had never been a consideration. Until now. "Apple tart?" Meena held out the bag.

"Maybe a small piece." Tanvi glanced around the living room. "It looks so different. You can see the history when it's not overwhelmed with everything Neha had stuffed in here."

"What do you think it was like? For your grandfather."

Tanvi brushed her hand over the wood flooring. "I've heard stories from my parents. They were all men, so I imagine there was a lot of ego, testosterone, and fumbling around."

Meena laughed.

"They brought spices with them," Tanvi said. "A suitcase of clothes and another with dal, marchu, turmeric, coriander, and other things they would need to sustain themselves. They were all vegetarian, and in the 1930s, I don't imagine Newbury Street was full of vegan restaurants like it is now. They had to learn to cook—my grandfather excelled in that. He was the one who fed everyone. I'm sure there was a lot of chatting, a lot of planning, bragging."

"Do you think they liked being here?"

Tanvi smiled. "I'd like to believe that. They were ambitious, and wanted to study in America, build something here, a home for those who came and went and a legacy of their own for us. My father often spoke about living under the British rule. He posited that one advantage was that they learned how to navigate white culture, they assimilated with clothing, language, and social norms. That made it better for them, I think."

Meena listened to Tanvi recount stories she'd heard. Almost a hundred years wasn't a long time when it came to the origin of the earth, yet it made a huge difference in terms of the way life was now. The people who'd lived here were who she'd come from. She stroked the floor with her bare feet and wondered if her great-grandfather had ever stood in this space. If he hadn't been here, she wouldn't exist.

She'd lived her life leaving the past behind, never considering the value of knowing where she'd come from, which people had had to come together with others to make it possible for her to exist. That her roots were not just a birth mother and father, but went beyond that for generations, centuries. She'd believed she'd been untethered, yet the invisible strands of genetics would always be here, and she had the opportunity to learn about them, to live in a place they'd built. Doubly so between Sabina and Neha. Meena belonged here.

"It's nice that you have this," Meena said.

"Yeah." Tanvi gave her a soft smile. "I'm sure they weren't all great. Uma could likely tell you about the problematic parts, but the very fact that they came here, left what they knew for the unknown in a time when they were likely the only Asian Indian people here, there is something to be proud of, not just for those of us in this house, but for our immigrant story."

Meena handed Tanvi the rest of the apple tart. "Thank you for sharing with me."

Tanvi took it. "I guess sometimes a second breakfast is a good thing. But I will let you get on with your day. I'm going to shop. I might even pick up a housewarming present for you."

Meena finished off the croissant. "If you give me an hour, I'll go with you. I can work on my pitches later."

Tanvi rose to her feet. "Excellent, we can talk color."

"Just keep in mind, I'm on a budget," Meena said. "Like nothing-over-fifty-dollars budget."

"Well, we can always window-shop." Tanvi headed for the door. "Text me when you're ready."

With Tanvi gone, Meena headed for the shower. A little roaming was what was next, and that was what she would do. As she grabbed clothes out of the built-in dresser, she spied the yellow envelope on the bed. It was crumpled, but the contents were still secure. It could wait. She left it where it was. A long, hot shower, a walk on a sunny day, a little window-shopping. That was all she wanted for now.

CHAPTER
FORTY-FIVE

Meena waited for Sam to take Wally for a walk before she sneaked into his apartment and dropped off her gift. During her walk with Tanvi, she'd found a street artist, an engraver. She'd gone back later in the day to commission a little piece for Sam. She'd picked it up from her this morning and couldn't wait to leave it for him.

She placed it on his coffee table, in the center, and stacked his clutter in one corner so he didn't miss it. It was a large clear glass mug with *Fucking Saint* etched on it in a handwritten script. She'd stuffed the mug with homemade dog biscuits, which were apparently a thing. She scurried out of there before he came back.

Meena had spent the last two days doing whatever came next. She'd reveled in just being, living. Yesterday she'd wandered around the other side of the Charles River in Cambridge and then into Somerville. The weather was holding up, though Meena knew that it wasn't uncommon for Boston to have an April blizzard. She hoped there wouldn't be one. She welcomed the renewal, not just in the season, but in herself.

Even though she hadn't touched the offer, she'd refused to let it weigh her down. Maybe she was avoiding it, pretending it didn't exist, but it was hard to miss, the manila envelope on the nightstand. When she'd gone through therapy in high school, her therapist, Cindy, would tell her to respond, not to react. Ignoring the envelope wasn't avoiding; she was taking time to figure out her response. It had been three days since she'd seen Sabina. They hadn't encountered each other in passing, Sabina had not spent time in the backyard, and the hallway was in its undecorated form, with a fresh bouquet of flowers and a bowl of pot-pourri. The Engineer's House was atypically quiet.

She heard Sam and Wally come into the building, then heard his door close. Meena couldn't wipe the grin off her face as she imagined him laughing when he saw the mug. Her heart was completely full with a mix of a schoolgirl crush and a layer of grown-up self-assurance. She hugged the feeling close to her.

Her phone buzzed with a text from Zoe. Instead of texting back, she called.

"The apartment is huge," Zoe yelled into the phone. "Now that it's got a lot less in it."

Meena laughed. She'd sent Zoe pictures before the furniture arrived. "I'm not overdoing it, right now just a few things to sit on, somewhere to eat."

"It's a fantastic place," Zoe said.

"You'll have to come visit," Meena offered. "In the summer."

Meena grinned. It was all clear in this moment. Just like that, the anxiety and uncertainty faded. This was hers, by birth and by right. Doubly so.

"I'd love to." Zoe hesitated. "But what if you get an assignment in Tibet or something? You'll pop off, and I'm not one for solo holidays."

"We can sort it out."

"Then it sounds like a plan."

"You know that planner you gave me?"

"Tell me you've been using it."

"In a way," Meena said. "I flirted with Sam, and now we're dating, seeing where this could go."

"Oh my God."

Meena laughed. "I know. It's . . . I don't know how to describe it."

"Teenage-girl crush?"

"It feels bigger than that. More. I don't want to get ahead of myself. It just feels nice."

"Enjoy every second of it," Zoe said. "One day he'll make you watch him play video games, and you'll want to remember that you do really like him."

"I will. OK, I'll write down the dates once you figure out when you want to visit and block out my calendar," Meena said.

"Who are you?"

Meena Dave. Meena laughed. "I'm happy."

"I like it," Zoe said. "All right, let's do it. A holiday in Boston. If you don't make me do any historical tours, it'll be a blast."

"Don't worry. I'm going to take you to all the parts of Boston where we fought the British and won. There's an entire Freedom Trail dedicated to the markers of our independence from you lot."

"In that case"—Zoe smirked—"I'll be sure to carry the Union Jack and wave it around."

They chatted for a bit longer. Once off the phone, Meena wandered around the apartment. She ran her fingers along the wall by the front door. Took a deep breath and exhaled. Then she went to her bedroom and grabbed the envelope. She dug out a pen and notebook. After a few minutes of thought, she wrote out a note, petty maybe, but it felt good. She pressed the metal clip together to open the envelope, slid in the note, then pressed it back in place. Then Meena ran up two flights of stairs and slid the envelope under Sabina's door.

She'd responded to Sabina's offer.

Because she didn't want to ruin her good mood, Meena slipped out the front door and walked over Storrow Drive to the esplanade. Half the city was running, walking, biking, or sitting along the river. It was what the locals did on a warm day after a cold winter.

She smiled and waved at an older couple who walked past her from the other direction. She was going to be a local. She didn't need Sabina to make her feel welcome. The city would; the other aunties and Sam would. Sabina might not have wanted her then or want her now, but Sabina's wants, and wishes, would not define Meena's life, would not prevent Meena from making her apartment a home.

She walked along the footpath with the earth firm beneath her sneakers.

CHAPTER
FORTY-SIX

Meena played tug-of-war with Wally on the cold grass while Sam sat on the bench. Over the past week, they'd traded little items back and forth. He left her mostly food, while she left him a few gags, like a tuxedo T-shirt. On the back she'd written in block letters, *Vora. Sam Vora.* She'd drawn a tiny martini glass next to it for laughs. Last night they'd gone to pub trivia and come in fourth, which Ava had not been happy about. They had strict instructions to get it together for next week.

"He's getting so big." Meena lay on the ground, and Wally changed the game to climbing over her.

"Off." Sam pointed to the floor.

Wally obeyed and sauntered away to sniff something by the fence.

Meena brushed off her jeans and sat on the bench. "He's learning."

"Finally."

They watched him go from bush to bush, sniffing. He found a twig and played as if it were the best thing that had happened in his dog life. The sun warm on her face, Meena leaned back and curled her legs under her. It was a peaceful Sunday afternoon. Until Sabina came through Sam's porch and into the yard.

"Hi, Sabina," Sam greeted her. "Welcome back."

Meena tilted her head. "Were you away?"

"I was visiting a cousin in New Jersey," Sabina said. "Meena, I'd like to speak with you."

"OK."

"In private."

Meena sat up. "It's fine. Sam knows everything."

The look of surprise on Sabina's face was a small pleasure.

"I guess you didn't want to keep it between us," Sabina said.

"Auntie, I knew before," Sam clarified. "Neha told me. A part of it."

"You chose to fill her in. Chose Neha's side." Sabina turned to Sam, betrayal and hurt visible on her face.

For the first time, Meena could see age on Sabina's face. Her usually flawless skin was pale, and there were more lines around her lips.

"It wasn't Sam," Meena said. "Neha left me notes." She gave Sabina a short summary of Neha's bread crumb trail. "We didn't know about you until last week, when you admitted it."

"We?"

"I trust Sam," Meena said. "As I wrote declining the offer, I won't ever speak of this again. I will keep your secret, but I'm not selling. I'm not leaving."

Sabina visibly stiffened. "It doesn't matter that I don't want you here?"

That hurt. Meena had softened her heart to make room for others: Sam, Zoe, Tanvi, Wally . . . that made her vulnerable too. Hannah had taught her how to hold her own, and Meena could handle it. And whatever else came her way.

"Sam, tell her how it is," Sabina pleaded. "If this is revealed, it will ruin me, this place, everything we've built here."

"How so?" Meena asked. "I did write in my note that while I'm biologically your eldest, I'm not going to make claims on anything. I want to keep what I have, build on it. That's enough."

"Then what?" Sabina asked. "You'll pass it down to your children? Continue the legacy?"

Meena stood. "If I have any, yes. Because whether you want me or not, I have the same birthright as you. More, considering both my biological parents have claim. You don't have to like it, but it's true."

"It was a mistake," Sabina said. "You were never supposed to find me, come back."

Sam stood and put his hand on Meena's back.

"I didn't choose this." Anger rose in Meena. "I wasn't looking. I never wanted to find you. I didn't think about you. Even when I lost my parents, I never thought, *Hey, I still have a birth mother out there somewhere.* Never. You didn't exist to me. This was all Neha's doing."

"So then go," Sabina said. "I am nothing to you, and you are no one to me. You can walk away with almost three million dollars and get on with your life."

Meena hunched her shoulders and crossed her arms to protect herself. "You made a choice. When you were seventeen. I'm making one now. I will live with yours, and you can live with mine. We can be enemies or acquaintances, it's up to you. I'm not going anywhere."

Sabina looked up, lowered her arms, and made herself tall. "I see." She turned to leave.

Meena knew she should let her go; she owed Sabina nothing, should want nothing from her. "The thing is," Meena said, "I was sixteen years old for a very long time."

Sabina stopped.

"Even in my twenties," Meena continued, "I was older, I knew more about the world, how to navigate, move through, make a living. Inside I was still this young girl, frozen in time, by one event. I learned how to cope, to fake maturity, but the fear I carried with me, that was the fear of a little girl who'd lost everything. This place, not just the people in it but the history of this place, the one you are the curator for, gave me something, a past that hadn't disintegrated into ashes. By coming here, by choosing to stay here, I finally let that sixteen-year-old girl grow. I hope you find a way to do the same."

Sabina turned. There were tears in her eyes. The eyes she shared with Meena.

"You chose," Meena said. "I did not. Still, we both lost something. I'm not staying here to make you face it, relive it. I'm staying for me. All I can hope is that you find a way to come to terms with your choice and this circumstance."

There was nothing left to say. Grief made her tired. With head high and chin up, Meena walked back to her apartment, happy when Wally followed her in. She looked back to see Sam talk to Sabina, put his arm around her, give her comfort.

Meena marveled at his empathy and didn't resent him for it. There was no hatred or anger left in Meena's heart for Sabina. The woman had been forced to face her past just as Meena had. There was no blame. Sabina had made the best decision for herself at seventeen, as it had been her right to do, and there was nothing wrong with not wanting to rescind that decision because Meena had shown up on her doorstep. None of this was fair to either of them, but if they could find a way to coexist, to have an occasional cup of chai, that would be enough.

She poured water in a short bowl for Wally and stroked his fur as he lapped it up. He turned his wet face and nuzzled her neck, then jumped on her. She lay on the floor in the kitchen and played with the fur ball who'd grown from a puppy into forty-five pounds of dog. Laughter echoed in her home and Meena reveled in it.

CHAPTER
FORTY-SEVEN

Meena checked her face in the small mirror she'd hung next to the door before heading out. Her hair was loosely tied back, and she'd added a cropped faux leather jacket she'd found on the sale rack at Anthropologie to her long dress. The tiny red flowers on the black silk were as playful as the handkerchief hem. She'd also added her usual black boots. Nerves danced in her stomach, but she wanted to do this.

Sam met her in the hall. "Ready."

She took a deep breath and nodded.

He took her hand as they headed to the alley where he parked his car. As they drove west, away from the city and suburbs, the landscape changed. It was sparser, greener as the weather warmed.

"Thanks for coming with me," Meena said.

"I'm glad you asked me." Sam took his eyes off the road for a second to give her a smile.

"You *are* a badass, going ten above the speed limit."

"That's how we fucking saints roll."

Some of the tension eased with laughter, only to return as she saw the sign for Northampton. She'd programmed her childhood home's address into the GPS, and the phone noted they were ten minutes away.

As they passed the center of town, she recognized some storefronts and streets, and the large historical building of the music academy. Within minutes they were away from downtown, and the GPS called out for Sam to make a left. They crossed over the Mill River via a one-lane bridge and made their way to Meadow Road. They pulled up in front of a place that used to be her home.

Meena stepped out of the car and stared at the white house with a wraparound porch. "Our house was blue. The windows had these little white shutters. We didn't have a porch, but there was a small deck in the back, off the kitchen."

Sam stood next to her as they leaned against the car.

Meena pointed down the street. "The school bus stop was all the way down there, and I remember walking home from it after school. In the winter sometimes it would already be dark by the time I got off the bus. We knew all the neighbors. It's so strange. This could be any street, anywhere. I recognize some of the neighboring houses, but with my house not here, it's not my street. I know that doesn't make sense."

"It does," Sam agreed. "There's no anchor for your memory."

"Exactly."

"Do you know where they're buried?"

"Saint Mary Cemetery," Meena said. "There weren't that many remains, but what they found, they put in a joint box. I had to figure all of that out. I had some help, but . . ."

"You did it."

She nodded.

"Do you want to visit them?"

Meena opened the car door. "I do."

It took a few questions to the office staff to find her parents' plot. It was the first time she'd been back since the funeral. There was a pink stone with white writing. **JAMESON AND HANNAH DAVE.** Meena ran her hands over the rough and smooth stone. "I remember it being so big.

Imposing." She sat on the ground next to it, the cool grass crunching beneath her. "I should have brought flowers."

"Next time." Sam sat on the other side of the stone. His jeans stretched at the knees.

Meena's eyes welled up. "I should have come back, visited them. I should have thought about them instead of trying to forget." Her voice broke. "They must be so disappointed in me."

"From what you've told me, you did what you believed they would have wanted," Sam said.

"*Get on with it*—my mother's favorite saying." Meena smiled.

"That's what you did," Sam said. "You didn't get over it or them; you kept going. They would be proud of you."

Her throat tight, she stopped fighting the feelings, released them. Meena rested her head on the stone. In a soft whisper she told them about her life, that she'd struggled but was happy, that she'd found home again. Then she stood and stroked the stone one more time. "Next time I'll bring flowers."

On an impulse she leaned down and touched her lips to the top of the headstone. She hoped her parents would feel her love for them the way she had when her dad gave her head a peck with a side of hot chocolate and cookies.

She reached out and took Sam's hand. "Thank you. That's all. Just thank you."

He squeezed her hand. "I think you should treat me to a late lunch."

She laughed. "Always trying to get me to ask you out."

"And yet you haven't asked."

"Come on." Meena tugged him back to the car. "There's a brewery in Brattleboro, across the state border, I read about."

Over lunch Meena told him about her next assignment, her first for the *Boston Globe*. She was looking forward to it, a local piece, one for which she didn't have to travel any farther than the T would take her. She would be back in time for dinner.

"I have a surprise for you," Meena said.

"Did you sneak in and leave something in my apartment?"

Meena fished out her phone. "Nope." She opened the gallery and pulled up a picture. "Meet Huckleberry."

Sam took the phone from her.

"He's four months old, a husky-shepherd mix. I met him at the MSPCA a few days ago."

"He's cute."

"Do you think Wally will like his new best friend?"

Sam put his pint down. "What did you do?"

"I filled out an application and gave them a check," Meena said. "They're going to call you for a reference. And if it all works out, he'll be mine."

"What about"—Sam cleared his throat—"when you have to leave?"

"I'm staying, Sam. I'm committing to being here. For me, but also for you. For us." Meena moved from the chair across from him to the one next to him. "I've fallen for you, Sam. I like what we're doing, building between us." Her heart thumped faster as she put her hand on his forearm. "You are kind, intelligent, and steady. And have you looked in a mirror? You're also attractive in an obvious way. I feel . . . um . . . I care about you."

He put his hand over hers. She could see the gold flecks in his dark-brown eyes as he leaned in.

"You forgot to mention that I'm a fucking saint," he said.

She leaned in and kissed him. His soft lips took over as he wrapped one arm around her and pulled her closer. She cupped his face and poured everything she felt for him into the kiss. He broke it and touched his forehead to hers. "We need to go home."

She brushed his lips once more. Ten minutes later they were back in the car.

"Home. I like that." She held his hand as he drove them back east to Boston.

She didn't have to look back. She wasn't leaving Northampton in the rearview mirror as she'd done the last time. She would come back, visit the cemetery, and remember that before the pain, there had been joy.

~❦~

By the first week of May, the apartment was mostly finished. There were throw pillows and fresh flowers. It was far from full, but that suited Meena's minimalism. She put the final frame on the fireplace mantel. Over the past few days, she had printed out the photos she'd taken from the beginning, from Halloween to chai making. Wally in different stages of growth, Sam in his James Bond tux. The frames peppered the living room, dining area, and bedroom. The mantel held the bulk of her collection.

The aunties were there in all their glory, from raking the backyard to Diwali dinner. She'd included Sabina, because she was a part of Meena's home, even if they no longer spoke to each other. She sat on her new couch. It needed to be broken in. The cushions were still stiff, but it would get there. Her home was beginning to seem lived in. She'd put a crate for Huckleberry next to her worktable by the window and a dog bed by the fireplace, along with a basket of toys for both Wally and Huck.

Sam had insisted she change the name of the pup to something fierce, something that resembled his stern face. At first she'd told him she was keeping it just to irritate him. Now, though, she referred to the dog as Huck and couldn't wait to pick him up next week. In the meantime, in between bouts of work, she watched a lot of dog-training videos. Sam had given her a book on it that Meena kept by her bedside.

Meena heard a quick knock on the door, and then Sabina came in. Meena stood and braced herself.

Sabina glanced around the apartment. Today she was in a long red silk kurta that was like a dress that hit at the knees, black leggings underneath. Her hair was in its usual thick braid down her back.

"Is there something you needed to say?"

Sabina nodded.

Meena sat but kept her back straight, her legs taut.

Sabina joined her on the sofa. "What you said, about growing up. I spent time thinking about it. When I found out I was pregnant, I was . . . I have never known fear like that. It was this one time. I was tired of being the good girl that did what everyone expected. Neha's cousin was here for a few weeks to look at colleges. He was the first boy to flirt with me. What a cliché, right?"

Meena stayed quiet.

"When I missed my period, and then another one, I didn't know what to do." Sabina hugged a throw pillow. "It wasn't what Indian girls did. Sex was for after marriage. I thought my parents would disown me. Put me out on the street. I couldn't leave. Not this legacy. I wanted to be a caretaker of this house more than anything else. I went to Neha. She was older. When I started to show, Neha set up a fake internship where I would study landscaping at Smith College for six months. A live-in opportunity to strengthen my college application. I stayed by myself in a studio apartment near the college campus, the one and only time I lived alone. She'd arranged it all. She even found a family a month before my due date. After you were born, Neha took care of all the paperwork and the exchange. Two days after I gave birth, I was home. I went on as if those nine months never happened."

"Did you manage to forget?"

"Not the fear," Sabina clarified. "I will never forget how scared I was to be disowned, to be kicked out of this house, the only home I ever knew, have ever wanted."

"I *was* thrown out," Meena offered. "Not because of something I did, but because of circumstances beyond my control. I survived."

"It doesn't escape me," Sabina said. "You're stronger than me. Even now. To stay here, to do what you want knowing I'm not welcoming you."

Meena rolled her shoulders back. *Damn right.* She was strong. "I learned how to be strong."

"I have accepted that you aren't leaving." Sabina sighed. "I want to come to an agreement."

"I'm not obligated to meet any of your conditions."

"You said you weren't interested in exposing me. Yet you told Sam."

"He and I are close," Meena said. "I won't keep things from him."

"I can never tell my husband or children about you."

It shouldn't have hurt. Yet it did. "Fine with me."

Sabina stood. "We're agreed. We will be neighbors and nothing more. I hope you can keep your word."

"I will. *If* you tell Uma and Tanvi all of it." Meena wanted to have meaningful relationships with the other aunties. She couldn't do that with a secret like this.

"I can't," Sabina said. "They will never forgive me."

"I am not going to close myself off to them. I also don't want this hanging over my head. It's your secret, not mine."

Sabina gritted her teeth.

"Your choice." Meena gave her an ultimatum. "This is the only thing I'm asking of you."

"Can we come in?" Tanvi poked her head in. "Sabina, I didn't know you were here. I sent you a text that we were coming down here."

Meena looked up as Uma and Tanvi rushed in.

"We brought chai." Uma waved the thermos.

"I have cookies." Tanvi held up a plate. "What's going on?"

Meena shrugged and picked up a cookie. "What are you guys doing here?"

"We need you to settle a bet," Tanvi said.

Meena smiled. "Whoever had March twelfth for Sam and me to become boyfriend and girlfriend wins your bet."

Uma whooped. "I had March tenth. I win."

Meena laughed as Uma did a small victory dance. They chatted. Sabina and Meena with the other two but not with each other. If Tanvi and Uma noticed, they didn't let on. Before the aunties left, they complimented her apartment and then themselves in the photos.

Meena closed the door behind them and left it unlocked as she went to her worktable. She had photos to edit, emails to respond to, and a schedule to make for upcoming assignments. Later she would go over to Sam's and they'd order takeout and watch a movie while Wally snoozed on the rug. Next week Huck would join them. They would go to pub trivia. She was settling in, and it felt good. Right.

CHAPTER FORTY-EIGHT

Four days later Meena was in downward dog when Uma and Tanvi barged into her apartment. A thermos and a Tupperware in their hands. There was concern on their faces. She came out of the pose, and before she could fully stand, she was enveloped in a hug by Tanvi. Uma stroked her arm.

"What's going on?"

"We're so sorry," Tanvi said. "We should have tried harder to figure it all out."

Meena pulled out of their grasp. "What are you talking about?"

"Sabina told us everything."

Meena exhaled, relieved. She didn't know what she would have done if Sabina hadn't.

"Come sit." Tanvi pulled her to the table. "Are you hungry? Have you eaten?"

"She's a grown person." Uma opened the plastic container. "Let her be."

"I just want to take care of you," Tanvi brought mugs from the kitchen and poured chai.

"I'm fine," Meena assured them. "We've reached a truce of sorts."

Uma snorted as she shoved the container of parathas toward Meena.

Tanvi patted Meena's arm. "I'm not fine. I'm angry and upset. We missed so many months with you."

"You didn't," Meena said. "You've been taking care of me. And I don't need much."

"I'm angry that she's being a bitch," Uma grunted. "She should have dealt with all of this better. You deserve more."

"It was her choice," Meena offered.

"Not about her choice." Uma took a paratha, folded it in half, and shoved it in Meena's hand. "For her secrets and for trying to get rid of you."

"I can't do anything about that." Meena took a bite, if only to please Tanvi.

"It's not you." Uma went to the kitchen and rummaged around in the pantry. She brought over a plate of cookies. "Did you make these?"

"I've been practicing."

Uma bit into one. "Too much baking soda."

"Thanks for the tip."

Tanvi sipped her chai. "We're mad, and it's going to take time. She should have come to us. Instead she relied on Neha, trusted someone so . . . so, well, you know."

"At least she helped Sabina through it all," Uma said.

"And held it over her head," Tanvi added. "Made Sabina her personal servant."

"She wrote me notes." Meena wanted them to know the whole of it. The aunties looked confused. Meena went to the drawer of her worktable and pulled out the envelope of notes. One of the few things she'd kept. She didn't consider them Neha's, but her own. The three women scanned them.

"What a mind fuck." Uma shook her head.

"Tell me about it," Meena said.

"I didn't know this was happening to you."

"That's on me. I wasn't exactly an open book."

"You weren't even a closed book," Uma said. "Just a series of Post-it Notes."

"Did Sabina tell you about the father?" asked Tanvi.

"Neha did." Meena took another sip. It needed sugar, but then she remembered that it was always Sabina who added sugar, so she drank it plain. "And Sabina filled in parts."

"She told us he was Neha's cousin," Uma said. "His name was Akash."

"He was very attractive." Tanvi took a paratha, rolled it up, and dipped it in her chai before taking a bite. "I remember. You come from good genetic stock. At least on your father's side."

"I had wanted it to be you." Meena put her hand on Tanvi's arm. "When I learned that one of you could be my birth mother."

"Oh." Tanvi's eyes welled up.

"What am I?" Uma jabbed her thumb into her chest. "Chopped liver?"

"She's the nicest one." Meena shrugged.

"I really am."

"So what does all of this mean? With Sabina. I don't want you to stop being friends," Meena said. "I also want to join in, be a part of the events here. I might even attend another post-Thanksgiving day of fun."

"You do know that we're all family," Uma explained. "In our culture there is no cousin; we don't even have a word for it in Gujarati. It's brother, sister, niece, nephew. That's how it is in the building. Sabina is our sister. We're angry, but we will work it out."

"How long is that going to take?"

"We have a process for this," Uma said. "If one of us does wrong, they get put in friendship jail. The time is arbitrary, based on the offense. Sabina is going to be in there for a long time."

"What about you?" Tanvi asked. "How are you and Sabina?"

Meena shrugged. "She doesn't want me here, and I'm not going anywhere. Which is fine. Honestly, I had the best mom I could have asked for. I don't want or need another one."

"But you need your aunties, right?" Tanvi asked.

"Now that I have them, I don't know how I managed before."

Tanvi and Uma laughed, and Meena joined in. This was enough. More than. With Sam across the hall and these two in her life, she had built herself a home.

EPILOGUE

From her bedroom veranda, Meena looked down at the lush garden. The heat of June bore down on them, but the aunties were not deterred as they tended to the trees, plants, and flowers.

"I don't understand why this is growing here." Sabina pulled up a weed from the grass near the footpath.

It was from the wildflower patch Meena had planted. It seemed the seeds had been carried, either by birds or wind, and spread throughout the grass. And some of what she'd planted was invasive and beginning to take over a chunk of the backyard. Meena felt slightly guilty. But only slightly.

"It's from my wildflower bed," Meena called down.

"You need to replant it where it belongs," Sabina ordered.

Meena nodded. The two of them weren't friendly, but they were getting to be more civil. The other aunties and Sam were good buffers.

"I think it looks nice like this," Tanvi observed. "Like little accents on the lawn, a little purple here, some yellow there."

Meena took the steps down. "What if we turn the whole thing into a wild garden?"

"No," Uma and Sabina said in unison.

"Yes," Tanvi said at the same time.

"I vote yes too." Sam, Wally, and Huck came down from his apartment.

"No digging." Sabina knelt and grabbed Huck by the face, scratched behind his ears.

Where Sabina refused to show even an impersonal fondness for Meena, she had the opposite relationship with Huck. Whenever Meena's dog wasn't with Wally, he would run up the steps to find Sabina. Meena suspected that Sabina kept a jar of treats for him, but she never asked.

Satisfied with getting love from everyone, Huck ran to her and leaned against her leg. She reached down and gave him a few pats. She breathed in the summer air laced with honeysuckle and roses. It was a scent she would forever know as the scent of home.

ACKNOWLEDGMENTS

I am so grateful and blessed to be surrounded by so much love and support. It hasn't been easy to get here, and I wouldn't have kept going without all who helped in small and large ways.

To my parents, Arvind Ambalal Patel and Pushpa Arvind Patel, who instilled a love of reading and learning in me from an early age and taught me to never give up. To my sister, Amy, who pushes me to do better, be better, and climb higher.

To my friends who have been on this journey with me for decades, read early drafts of bad writing, and still believed I would get here one day: Kathleen Conlon, Stephanie Crane, Laura Holton (who is also real-life Wally's human), Sean Rudd, Colleen Skeuse, Elizabeth McDonough, Patrick Gallagher, and Sonal Patel.

To Cindy Lynch, who told me to not get in my own way and believed I would be an author one day. I did it, Cindy!

To my writing friends, for being in the trenches, celebrating success, commiserating, gossiping, and all the things in between: Jennifer Hallock, Jen Doyle, Caroline Linden, Farah Heron, Nisha Sharma, Falguni Kothari, Sonali Dev, Annika Sharma, Alisha Rai, Suleena Bibra, Kishan Paul, Sophia Singh Sasson, Sona Charaipotra, Sulekha Snyder, and Sarah Cassell (who gets credit for this title).

To my extended family of aunts, uncles, and cousins as well as my friends in Boston, Spokane, London, New York, and New Jersey.

You've heard me talking about this at one point or another, and well, here we are.

To Christa Desir for seeing the potential in my raw manuscripts and helping me become a better writer.

To my editors, Megha Parekh and Jenna Free, who push me to keep growing as a writer.

To my agent, Sarah Younger, who has this unique ability to offer unyielding support while always speaking the truth. I can't imagine being here without you.

To the team at Lake Union Publishing: S. B. Kleinman, Haley Swan, Jim Poling, Nicole Burns-Ascue, and Kellie Osborne.

Finally, Holly Pickett, whose photojournalism and bravery taught me perseverance and a deep belief in telling the stories that need to be told. This is for everyone who is fighting for their dreams: don't stop practicing, be patient (to a degree), and keep going, especially when traveling against the current.

ABOUT THE AUTHOR

Photo © 2021 Andy Dean

Namrata Patel is an Indian American writer who resides in Boston. Her writing examines diaspora and dual-cultural identity among Indian Americans and explores this dynamic while also touching on the families we're born with and those we choose. Namrata has lived in India, New Jersey, Spokane, London, and New York City and has been writing most of her adult life. For more information visit www.nampatel.com.